W9-CAD-907

# THE UNDERGROUND MAN

# THE UNDER- GROUND MAN

## A NOVEL BY
## J. P. HAILEY

**DONALD I. FINE, INC.**
*New York*

Library of Congress Cataloging-in-Publication Data

Hailey, J. P.
The underground man : a novel / by J. P. Hailey.
p.     cm.
ISBN 1-55611-215-7
I. Title.
PS3558.A3275U64   1990
89-45145
CIP

813′.54—dc20

Manufactured in the United States of America

10 9 8 7 6 5 4 3 2 1

Designed by Irving Perkins Associates

For Lynn,
Justin and Toby

# 1

TRACY GARVIN PUSHED THE long blonde hair out of her face and said, "There are two men in the outer office."

Steve Winslow looked up from his desk. "Two?"

"Yes."

"Together?"

"No."

"I have two potential clients?"

"That's right."

Steve grinned. "A new world record. Who are they?"

"One is a Mr. Walsh. The other is a Mr. Thorngood."

"What do they want to see me about?"

"They wouldn't say."

Steve raised his eyebrows. "Neither of them?"

"No."

"Better and better. Describe them. What are they like?"

Tracy frowned. "Well, they're quite different. Thorngood's about fifty. Walsh is older, say about seventy-five. But that's the least of it. Mr. Walsh is . . . how shall I say it . . . well, he looks like a street person."

"Oh?"

"Yeah. His clothes are dirty. His hair's uncombed. And he's unshaved. Not that he has a beard—he's just unshaved, if you know what I mean."

Steve nodded. "Aha," he said. "And he won't tell you what he wants?"

"No. And the impression he gives is not that he has anything to hide, but that it's none of my damn business. He'll discuss it with the lawyer. He's a cantankerous old cuss. He doesn't have an appointment, but he wants to see you, and he's prepared to sit there until doomsday until he does."

"I see," Steve said. "And Mr. Thorngood?"

"Just the opposite in every way. Impeccably dressed. Tailor-made three-piece suit. Looks like he just stepped out of a barber chair, and probably did."

"And he won't tell you his business either?"

1

"No, but in his case it's not just stubbornness. He says it's a delicate matter, and he'll discuss it only with the attorney. He's nervous and impatient, which seems out of character for him. He strikes me as someone who's used to getting his own way."

Steve frowned, considered a moment. "All right," he said. "Show Mr. Thorngood in."

Tracy hesitated a moment. "Mr. Walsh was here first."

"That's all right," Steve said. "You said he's prepared to wait. Show Mr. Thorngood in."

Tracy took off her glasses and folded them up.

Steve recognized the gesture. It was a habit she had when she was annoyed about something.

Steve held up his hand. "Tracy. Mr. Thorngood is a businessman. His time is valuable. Let's not waste any of it for him. You wanna argue this with me, argue it later. Meanwhile, show the gentleman in."

Tracy gave him a look, opened the door, and flounced out. She returned a minute later, ushering in Mr. Thorngood.

He was, Steve felt, exactly as she'd described. An aggressive executive type, confident and sure of himself. When he saw Steve, however, a look of doubt crossed his face. Steve wasn't surprised. Though in his mid-thirties, Steve looked younger. He was dressed as usual in corduroy jacket, jeans and T-shirt. This attire, combined with his shoulder-length hair, wasn't exactly a businessman's image of a lawyer.

Steve rose, extended his hand. "Mr. Thorngood."

After a moment's hesitation, Thorngood shook it. "Mr. Winslow."

"Please be seated," Steve said. "Tracy, stay and take notes."

Thorngood shot a look at Tracy Garvin. In sweater and blue jeans, she wasn't his image of a legal secretary either. More like a college student.

Thorngood frowned. "My business is strictly confidential."

Steve smiled. "Of course." He sat and gestured to Tracy to do the same.

Thorngood frowned again. "Perhaps I didn't make myself clear. I prefer to speak to you alone."

"I understand perfectly," Steve said. "Miss Garvin is my secretary. Anything you tell me, she's gonna know. So if you don't want her to know it, don't tell me."

Thorngood hesitated a moment, then seated himself in the clients' chair.

Tracy pulled up a chair, sat down, and opened her notebook.

"All right," Steve said. "What's this all about?"

Thorngood rubbed his hand across his brow. "My son was arrested last night."

"For what?"

"Murder."

"Murder!" Steve said. "But with a man of your prominence— I mean, there was nothing in the paper."

"So far my lawyers have kept it out of the papers. They can't for long. By tonight it will be public knowledge."

"Lawyers?"

"Yes. Cunningham, Randolph, and Bloom."

"If you have your own lawyers—"

"I know, I know," Thorngood said. "They're a conservative firm. Handle mostly corporation work. They themselves suggested outside counsel."

"Why me?"

"Because you're the one. The one they told me about. You defended in the Harding case."

"I was co-counsel."

"Right. With Fitzpatrick, Blackburn, and Weed, a conservative law firm, slightly out of its depth."

"Establishing the precedent," Steve said. "I see. That doesn't necessarily mean it would work again. What's the case?"

Thorngood took a breath. "My son is accused of killing his girlfriend."

"Did he?"

Thorngood frowned. "That's not the point."

"Maybe not, but it's relevant."

Thorngood frowned again. "I prefer to tell it my way."

"Go ahead."

"The girl is Kathy Wade. David had been seeing her for a couple of months. David is my son. My only son. And he'd been seeing this girl. This Kathy Wade. Or so I'm told. David is not particularly communicative about his affairs. So I didn't know about this Kathy Wade. I mean, the first I heard about her she was dead."

"Go on."

Thorngood took a breath. "This is hard. I'm piecing this together from what I learned after the fact. What David told me. And the police. But he'd been seeing her off and on for a couple of months. But nothing serious. And there wouldn't be. Not the type of girl I'd have approved of, really. Part-time actress, full-time waitress. Nothing serious. Just a casual fling."

Steve took a breath. "Go on."

"Well, it was last night. They'd been on a date. David had her up to his apartment. He has his own Manhattan apartment. Upper East Side."

"Yes?"

"Well, they'd been drinking. Among other things. Police found marijuana in her purse."

"Yeah. So?"

Thorngood gulped. "This is very hard."

"I understand."

"Her neck was broken."

"How?"

"How? What do you mean, how? Twisted. Broken."

"Yeah? What else?"

"And . . ."

"Yes?"

"She was naked and her clothes were torn."

"I see."

Thorngood looked up sharply. "What's that mean?"

"Nothing. Just the sort of thing people say. So, what's David's story?"

"You'll have to get that from David."

"You talked to him. What did he tell you?"

"What do you mean?"

"Did he kill her?"

Thorngood frowned. "That's not the point."

"Oh?"

"That's not the issue here. That's for a jury to decide."

"Of course. But a lawyer has to have the facts. What are the facts? Did he kill her?"

Thorngood rubbed his head. "These are the facts. David didn't *say* he killed her. He was with her when she died."

Thorngood pulled a checkbook out of his jacket pocket. "I'm prepared to offer a retainer of a hundred thousand dollars."

Steve held up his hand. "Hang on to that for a minute. We're still talking here."

"I've told you all I know. There rest you'll have to get from David."

"That remains to be seen. Tell me, what defense does your son have?"

Thorngood looked at him in surprise. "Surely that's your department."

"Yeah, but I'd like your input. Suppose I took this case. What possible defense would I have?"

"Surely there are several. Accidental death is one. Self-defense is another. Also the body was nude. That brings up the possibility of rough sex."

"As the defense tried in the Chambers case."

"Exactly."

"That didn't work."

"Yes and no. He pled guilty to a lesser charge."

"Is that what you're looking for here?"

"Of course not. I want my son freed. But if worst came to worst, you have to consider every possibility."

Steve looked at him for a moment. Then he shook his head. "No, I don't."

"I beg your pardon?"

"I'm sorry. I'm not taking the case."

Thorngood looked at him in disbelief. "Didn't you hear me? I'm offering you a hundred-thousand-dollar cash retainer."

"I'm turning it down."

"You can't turn it down. Not an attorney in your position. It's too big a case. My attorneys controlled publicity this morning, but that's all they can do. By tonight it will be all over the media. By tomorrow it will be front-page news. You mentioned the Chambers case. You remember what the publicity was like? Well, this is the same thing. I'm a prominent person. The press will eat it up. It's a chance for you to make a name for yourself. A young attorney in your position, you can't turn it down."

"I just did."

Thorngood drew himself up. "Why?"

Steve looked him right in the eye. "Because I think your son's guilty."

Thorngood's face hardened. "That's not your decision to make. You're not a judge and jury. You're an attorney. My son is innocent until proven guilty, that's the law. He has the right to a trial by jury. He has the right to an attorney."

"Yes he does," Steve said. "He just doesn't have the right to insist that that attorney be me." Steve stood up. "I'm very sorry."

Thorngood sat there, not quite believing it. Then he stood, shot Steve a look of contempt, and walked out of the room, slamming the door behind him.

Steve turned to Tracy Garvin.

She was staring at him. "Why did you do that?"

"I told you. He's an important businessman and I didn't want to waste his time."

"No, I mean why did you turn him down?"

"You have to ask me that? A guy kills his girlfriend. Rough sex. Can you see me defending that?" Steve clapped his hands together. "All right, Tracy. Now that that's out of the way, let's give Mr. Walsh our full attention."

# 2

STEVE HAD A CHANCE TO SIZE up Mr. Walsh while Tracy ushered him into the room and sat him in the clients' chair. The description, he figured, had been accurate. Only it hadn't gone far enough. Mr. Walsh was indeed unshaven and dressed in the clothes of a street person. But there are street people and street people. Some of them are sniveling and pitiful and helpless. Some of them are loud, truculent and obnoxious. Some of them are nauseatingly polite, thanking and god-blessing each and every person who ignores their entreaties.

Mr. Walsh didn't fall into any category except the one regarding his appearance. He had a fright wig of snow-white hair framing his unshaven face. The hairs of his stubbly beard were considerably darker, perhaps naturally, or, Steve reflected, perhaps colored by dirt. The latter was certainly possible, as there were dirt smudges on the cheeks and nose.

He wore a flannel shirt, slightly askew and not tucked into his gabardine pants, a sweater-vest fastened by a single button, and a heavy tweed overcoat that had obviously seen better days. The coat looked as if someone had slept in it, which someone obviously had. The overall effect was to give Mr. Walsh the appearance of the most pitiful of street people—the lunatic, the mental incompetent.

Except for the eyes. The eyes belied the whole image. They were sharp and focused and clear.

They took in Steve Winslow at a glance. If Mr. Walsh was surprised by Steve's appearance, he didn't show it. If he was impressed, he didn't show it either. His mouth was set in a straight line. His head was up and his jaw was out, quarrelsomely, as if expecting a fight.

"So," he said. "You're Winslow."

Steve smiled. "That's right. I'm Steve Winslow. This is my secretary, Tracy Garvin. And you're Mr. Walsh?"

"That's right. Jack Walsh."

"What can I do for you, Mr. Walsh?"

Walsh jerked his thumb. "You can tell her to leave."

Steve smiled again. "I'm afraid not, Mr. Walsh. Miss Garvin is my secretary, takes notes on everything I do. If you don't want to talk to her, you can't talk to me. It's as simple as that."

Walsh looked at Steve. Then at Tracy. Then back at Steve. With a snort, he flopped himself down in the clients' chair. "All right. She stays."

"Fine," Steve said. He shot Tracy a look, then settled himself behind his desk. "Go ahead, Mr. Walsh. What is it you want?"

"I want to see you about a will."

Despite himself, Steve couldn't keep the surprise off his face. He'd expected a personal injury, a grievance against the city, harassment by some police officer or other.

But not this.

"A will?" Steve said.

"Yes, a will," Walsh said irritably. "What's the matter? You're a lawyer, you never heard of a will before?"

"I've heard of wills, Mr. Walsh. But I've never actually drawn one."

"Who asked you?"

"No one asked me, but if that's what you're after, perhaps you're in the wrong law office."

"No, I'm in the right law office, all right."

"How is that?"

"Because I'm talking to the lawyer. The other office I went, I didn't get past the damn receptionist."

"Is that so?" Steve said. "Tell me, how did you find me?"

"Saw your picture in the paper once. Looked like someone might be willing to talk to me."

"Oh, really? And what paper was that?"

Walsh frowned. "What the hell difference does that make?"

"It doesn't," Steve said. "Just making conversation. All right. You want to see me about a will. Whose will?"

"Mine."

"You want me to draw you a will?"

"I already told you I didn't."

"What *do* you want?"

"Information. Legal advice."

"About a will?"

"Yes."

Steve frowned. "That's not my field of expertise. I do mostly criminal work."

"You passed the bar, didn't you? You went to law school?"

"Yes."

"Then you know enough to answer my questions. At least you should. If you can't, just say so."

"All right, Mr. Walsh, why don't you tell me what this is about?"

"Fine. Here's the thing. A while back, I made a will. Quite a while back, actually."

"Leaving what to whom?"

Walsh shook his head. "That's not important."

"You may think it's not," Steve said. "But I'm a lawyer. If you want advice on a certain document—"

Walsh waved his hands. "No, no, no. You're getting way ahead of yourself. Just listen. I'll tell you what the problem is. Then you'll know if these things are important or not."

"Fine," Steve said. "Tell it your way."

"I will, if you'll stop interrupting."

Steve shot Tracy an amused look. "Sorry. Go ahead."

"All right. I made this will. Drawn up by lawyers. Signed in their presence. Signed by witnesses. All nice and fancy and legal."

"So?"

"Suppose I were to make a new will?"

"What about it?"

"Suppose I change my will, but I don't want anyone to know it? Can I do that?"

Steve frowned. "I'm not sure I know what you mean."

"Exactly what I said. Suppose I change my will and no one knows it—is it legal?"

"When you say no one, you mean the heirs?"

"I mean no one. When I say no one, I mean no one. No lawyers. No witnesses. No one. Suppose I change my will myself, and nobody knows I've done it. Is it legal?"

Steve smiled. "That's kind of like the tree falling in the forest and there's no one there to hear it."

"No, it isn't," Walsh said, impatiently. "I don't mean like I dig a hole and bury it and no one ever finds it. Suppose I change my will and no one knows I've done it, but I make arrangements that after my death the new will would be discovered. My question is, would it invalidate the prior will and stand in its place?"

"If it was legally binding, it would. That's what the phrase, 'Last Will and Testament,'" means. The last will drawn by the decedent is the one that takes precedence."

"I know that. I know that. It's the first thing you said. If it's legally binding. That's the whole point. How can I make sure it's legally binding?"

"The safest way is to have it drawn by an attorney."

"I know that. But if I don't. If I draw the will myself. Can the will I draw myself take precedence over the will prepared by lawyers and signed in the presence of witnesses?"

"Yes, provided it's legally binding."

Walsh threw up his hands. "We're talking in circles here. If I draw the will myself, how can I make it legally binding?"

Steve sighed. "All right. First of all, you don't type it. You make it entirely in your own handwriting. And when I say entirely, I mean entirely. That is to say, you can't use letterhead. You start with an entirely blank sheet of paper."

"Fine. What else?"

"You use a pen, of course, for the entire document. You date it. You state your full name. You state that you are of sound mind and body. You state specifically that you revoke all prior wills. You state that this is your last will and testament. Then you state specifically how you wish to dispose of your property. This is where it gets tricky, and this is where you need a lawyer."

"Why?"

"Because in most wills there are specific bequests and a residuary clause. Do you know what that means?"

"Of course I do. Why is that tricky?"

"Because the value of a person's property may fluctuate. Which puts the beneficiary of the residuary clause at risk."

"How is that?"

"Because the specific bequests are fixed, whereas the residuary clause isn't. For example, suppose you had a hundred thousand dollars to leave. You make five bequests of ten thousand dollars each. Those people are going to get ten thousand dollars no matter what. Your beneficiary is going to get fifty thousand dollars by the residuary clause. Say before you die you suffer business losses and your property sinks to fifty thousand. Since the ten thousand dollars bequests are fixed, those five people get ten grand each, and your principal beneficiary gets nothing."

Walsh shook his head. "No, no. That's not a problem. I understand all that, anyway. I don't need a lawyer to help me with it. I make all my specific bequests, and then I say, all the rest, remainder and residue of my property I leave to blah, blah, blah. Right?"

"That's essentially right."

"Fine. What else do I have to do?"

"If there's anyone you wish to disinherit, don't just omit them. Mention them by name and state that you are disinheriting them. 'To Cousin Fred I leave nothing because he's a schmuck,' or words to that effect."

Walsh never cracked a smile. "What else?"

"When you've finished all that, you sign your will. That's the last thing you do. And sign it at the very bottom."

Walsh looked at him. "Why *wouldn't* I sign it at the very bottom?"

"You would and you should. That's the place to do it."

"Then why do you even mention it?"

"To make sure there's no confusion. See, you already started the document, 'I, so and so, being of sound mind and body,' etc., etc. Since you are writing in longhand, some people might argue writing your name at the top in that manner constitutes a signature. Whether it does or not is a moot point if you simply sign it at the bottom. Also, signing it at the bottom verifies the fact that the will is indeed over, that there isn't an additional page kicking around someplace that somehow got lost."

"Fine. Fine. So if I do all that, I'm set?"

"You should be."

"And this will take precedence over the prior will, even though that will was prepared by lawyers and signed in the presence of witnesses?"

"It should."

Walsh frowned. "Why do you say 'should?' "

Steve smiled. "Because anyone can hire a lawyer to argue anything. If the heirs named in the prior will want to contest the new one, they can. It doesn't mean they can win, and if you follow the instructions I've given you exactly, they shouldn't win. But if you want a hundred percent, dead certain, money-back guarantee, you must understand that there's nothing in life that's a sure thing."

"Yeah, yeah, sure," Walsh said. "Protect your backside. But practically speaking, the handwritten will would be good?"

"That's right."

"I see," Walsh said. He thought for a moment.

"Was there something else?" Steve asked.

"Yeah," Walsh said. "Suppose there's some delay?"

"What do you mean?"

"Well, suppose the handwritten will isn't found for a while?"

"Why wouldn't it be?"

Walsh waved it away. "That's not important. I'm saying what if. Suppose for some reason this handwritten will is misplaced. The lawyers produce the will they've drawn. It's probated. People inherit. Then the new will is found."

Steve frowned. He looked at Walsh narrowly. "What's your question?"

"What would happen then? Would the new will take precedence? Would the old will be upset? Would the heirs have to give the money back?"

Steve pursed his lips. "They *might.*"

Now it was Walsh's turn to frown. "Why do you say 'might?' It's my understanding they would."

"Your understanding's correct. And ordinarily they would. But . . ."

"But what?"

"You'd have a situation then. Be one hell of a legal dogfight."

"I know that. But who would win?"

"The beneficiaries named in the handwritten will. Except for one thing. Collusion." Steve shook his head. "Big problem, Mr. Walsh. If the beneficiaries named in the prior will are in a position to prove that the handwritten will was *deliberately* withheld, that it was *planned* that way, that they had been tricked into thinking they had inherited when they had in fact not, then they *would* have legal recourse. They would have a cause of action against you."

"I'd be dead."

"Against your estate. And if they were able to successfully sue your estate, reducing the amount that you have left to leave, they would be able to divert the money away from your beneficiary and into their own pockets just as effectively as if they had inherited under the old will."

"I see, I see," Walsh said. "That's all right. That's not the case."

"Oh, isn't it?" Steve said. "You come in here and ask me that specific question, I have to assume that that's *exactly* the case."

Walsh grinned. "Yes, but you're a lawyer. You don't go blabbing everything you know. There's a law of privileged communications, right? Everything I tell you is confidential. So, no problem. Collusion? What collusion? We're talking hypothetically here.

"So that's it. If the will is entirely in my own handwriting and signed and dated and revokes all prior wills, I'm home free." Walsh stood up. "Fine. What do I owe you?"

Steve shook his head. "No charge. I didn't do anything."

"I mean for the consultation."

Steve smiled. "No charge."

Walsh frowned irritably. "Of course there's a charge. There's no such thing as free advice. Free advice ain't worth taking. If you give me free advice, then you're a fool, and I'd be a fool to follow it. Here, let me see."

He pulled his overcoat aside and rummaged in his pants pocket. He pulled out a dirty, crumpled bill and laid it on the desk. "There," he said. He rummaged in his pocket again, pulled out another crumpled bill, set that on the desk. "And there. Now we're square. You get what you pay for. Now if you gave me bum advice and it don't work out, you'll feel bad. Of course, I'll be dead, so I won't know. But you'll have to live with it."

Walsh nodded shortly. "Thanks for your time."

"Now wait a minute," Steve said. "You can't just ask for advice and then go running off and try applying it—"

Walsh was already halfway to the door. Over his shoulder he said, "That's what you think."

A few more steps and he was gone, slamming the door behind him.

Steve looked after him, shook his head, and grinned at Tracy Garvin. "Son of a bitch," he said. "What do you make of that?"

Tracy shook her head. "What do *I* make of it? What do *you* make of it. Here's a guy off the street, and you sit here talking to him about specific bequests and residuary beneficiaries as if he were just some normal client. I mean, what can he possibly have that he wants to leave?"

"I have no idea," Steve said. "Whatever it is, I just hope he doesn't get into trouble. A person who wants to get his law from a lawyer and then apply it to the facts himself is usually a fool. I just hope in his case it doesn't make any difference."

Steve sighed and ran his hand over his head. "Well, Tracy, I'm afraid our two clients didn't amount to much. The first case was a total washout, and the second earned us a whopping two bucks."

Tracy got up from her chair. "You want this written up?"

"Oh, absolutely," Steve said. "And duly reported to the IRS. I can't wait till they see that one. 'Consultation fee: two dollars.'"

Tracy walked over to the desk, picked up the bills and smoothed them out. "Oh shit," she said.

Steve looked up. "What's the matter?"

"Your two-dollar fee."

"What about it?"

Tracy smoothed the bills out and handed them over.

They were hundred dollar bills.

# 3

STEVE WINSLOW LEANED BACK in his chair, put his feet up on his desk, and opened the New York *Times*. A former actor, Steve read the paper inside out, starting with the drama section. It was skimpy this morning—no articles, no reviews, mostly only movie ads. Steve moved on to the sports. The Knicks had won again. Not surprising—their first good season in years and they were on a roll. The Yankees were rumored to be about to make a managerial change. That was news? Hell, you could run the same column every six months.

Steve sighed. Shit. Another day with nothing to do but read the paper. And just when he'd thought he had it made.

For a while, Steve Winslow had been the most obscure lawyer in New York City. A lawyer with only one client who'd handled only one case. And handled it in such a way as to make himself look like an incompetent clown. Then the Marilyn Harding case had come along and changed all that. He'd made a splash in that one all right, right on the front page of the *Daily News*. It was sensational.

Too sensational. He'd made a name for himself all right, and he had a law practice now. But it wasn't a normal law practice. Because the type of publicity he got wasn't the type that attracted your standard brand of client. It was the type that attracted mainly the undesirables and the kooks.

And not in great numbers, either. Most days there were none. Some days there was one. Today there'd been two. Mr. Thorngood and Mr. Walsh.

One undesirable and one kook.

Steve sighed again, put the section of the paper down. So much for drama and sports. Time for the hard news. Pro-life protests, terrorists, and the budget deficit. Steve picked up the first section, opened the front page.

Tracy Garvin came in the door. "Someone else to see you."

Steve folded the paper, kicked his feet off the desk and sat up. "You're kidding."

Tracy smiled. "I know. It's a deluge. Three in one day."

"Who is it?"

"A Mr. Carl Jenson."

"What does he want?"

"He wouldn't say."

Steve grinned. "Again? You must be getting a complex."

"Not as long as you keep reading them the riot act when they try to throw me out."

"Never fear," Steve said. "So what's he like?"

"He's about thirty, medium height and build, brown hair, blue eyes."

"That's a police description. How does he strike you?"

"I don't like him. And not just 'cause he wouldn't talk to me. He's got a pleasant enough face—not ugly, not handsome—just ordinary. It's just his manner. I mean, he's well dressed. Presentable. There's nothing I can put my finger on. I just don't like him."

Steve grinned. "You're advising me against taking him on as a client?"

"Of course not. It's just a feeling, and he may be a nice guy, but you asked me so I told you."

"All right," Steve said. "Show the gentleman in."

Tracy went out and returned moments later ushering in Carl Jenson. She made a show of closing the door behind her, indicating that she intended to stay, before saying, "Mr. Jenson to see you, Mr. Winslow."

The gesture was wasted. Jenson strode up to the desk. Steve rose to meet him.

"Mr. Winslow?"

"Yes."

"I'm Carl Jenson."

"Pleased to meet you."

They shook hands.

"Sit down, Mr. Jenson," Steve said. "What can I do for you?"

Jenson sat in the clients' chair. Steve sat at his desk. Tracy pulled up a chair, opened her notebook. Jenson gave her a look, but said nothing. Tracy frowned slightly. Steve's eyes twinkled. She'd been hoping Jenson would object to her being there so Steve would dress him down.

"I was hoping we could exchange some information," Jenson said.

"I beg your pardon?"

Jenson put up his hands. "I know, I know. You're an attorney. You don't want to tell me anything. But I think once you understand the situation—" Jenson smiled. "Well, I'm sure we can work something out."

"I'm not so sure we can," Steve said. "But what did you have in mind?"

"It's about Uncle Jack, of course."

"Uncle Jack?"

"Yes. Perhaps you didn't catch the name. I'm Carl Jenson."

"Your name I caught. Your drift is what I'm having problems with."

"But surely he mentioned me."

"Who?"

"Uncle Jack."

"And who is Uncle Jack?"

"Then he didn't mention me. That's strange. No wonder you're confused. I'm sorry. I keep saying Uncle Jack. I mean Jack Walsh, of course."

Steve's face was absolutely neutral. "Jack Walsh?"

Jenson smiled and put up his hands. "Sure, sure. Play it safe and conservative. Like you never heard the name. All right. I'll tell you. I'm referring to Jack Walsh. My uncle. The man who came to your office this morning to consult you."

Jenson stopped, looked at him. Steve said nothing. Jenson frowned. "Or perhaps he used another name. That would be just like him." Jenson smiled. "But you couldn't miss him. I mean the bum."

"The bum?"

"Yeah, the bum. The street person. The man who looked like he rolled in the gutter before he came up here."

Steve said nothing. His face remained positively neutral.

"Surely you remember him," Jenson said dryly.

Steve sighed. "Mr. Jenson. I think I made my position clear. I have no intention of discussing any of my clients with you in any way. If you came for information, you're in the wrong place. Now, if you want to talk, I will let you talk. If you want to keep making statements that are really questions, and trying to get a rise out of me, I suggest that you leave."

Jenson nodded. "Sure, sure. You say that now. But once you understand the situation . . . All right. All right. You listen, I'll tell you."

Jenson stopped and leaned in confidentially. "The first thing you have to understand is that the man is sick. I don't mean physically sick. Physically he's strong as a horse. No, I mean mentally sick. The man has lost it. Gone off the deep end. So whatever he told you, you shouldn't take it at face value."

Steve closed his eyes for a moment, then opened them. "Mr. Jenson," he said. "We don't seem to be getting anywhere. And I doubt if there is anywhere to get. In the interests of expediency, I am going to discuss this with you as if I knew what you were talking about. Which quite frankly I don't. But setting that aside, and without admitting for a moment that I even know the man you're talking about, let's discuss him. This man —your uncle—Jack Walsh—what makes you think he's not mentally competent?"

"Are you kidding?" Jenson said. "Just look at him. He sleeps in the subways. He lives like a bum."

"Mr. Jenson, there are thousands of homeless people in New York City. Granted, some of them are mentally incompetent. But a large number of them are merely poor."

"But he *isn't* poor," Jenson said. "That's the whole point. The man's worth millions."

"Millions?"

"Yes, of course. Didn't he tell you that?"

Steve frowned. "Again with the questions." Steve rubbed his head. "Mr. Jenson, what makes you think your uncle consulted me?"

"I don't think, I know."

"How do you know?"

"I followed him here."

"You followed him?"

"Yes."

"Why were you following him?"

"To see where he went, of course. But, oh, you don't mean that. You have to understand. None of us had seen him in weeks."

"Us?"

"Yes. The family. His family."

"And who might that be?"

Jenson frowned. "But surely you know that. If you don't there's no point. But you won't let on, because you won't tell me what he told you."

"Who's the family?" Steve rephrased his question.

"I don't know why I should answer your questions when you won't answer mine."

"Any reason why you don't want me to know who his family is?"

"None at all."

"So what's the problem?"

"I was just pointing out that it wasn't fair."

"I never claimed to be fair. You sought this interview. I told you it was going to be one-sided."

Jenson glared at him for a moment. Then he shook his head. "All right, have it your way. The family. Let's see. There's me. My sister Rose—that's Rose Tindel. Her husband, Jason Tindel. My cousin Pat, Pat Grayson. Her husband, Fred Grayson. My Aunt Claire, Claire Chesterton. She's Uncle Jack's niece."

"Wait a minute. Your aunt is your uncle's niece?"

"No, no. That does sound strange, doesn't it. Jack Walsh is really my great-uncle, but I call him Uncle Jack. My mother was his brother's daughter. They're both dead now. So's my father. I always think of him as Uncle Jack."

"I see. So that's the family?"

"Yes. Except for Jeremy. He's eighteen. He's Jack's sister's grandson. His parents were killed in a car accident when he was three. Aunt Rose brought him up."

"All right," Steve said. "And you say none of you had seen him for weeks?"

"That's right."

"And then today?"

"I saw him on the street."

"Speak to him?"

"No."

"Why not?"

Jenson waved his hand. "You don't understand."

"I'm trying to understand. You're not giving me much help. Why wouldn't you speak to your uncle? Why would you just follow him?"

"Because he wouldn't speak to me."

"Why not?"

"I told you. He's strange."

"So what was the point of following him?"

Jenson's eyes flicked momentarily. "To see where he goes. What he's up to. Which is why I'm here."

Steve sighed. He thought for a moment. He turned to Tracy Garvin. "Miss Garvin. This man is not consulting me as a client. I don't need notes of this interview. Besides, I think your presence is inhibiting him."

Tracy's face fell. She looked at Steve as if she couldn't quite believe he'd said that.

"So," Steve said, "why don't you go call Mark Taylor. See if he's turned up anything on the Halsburg case. If he has, coordinate with him and set everything up."

Tracy stared at him. There *was* no Halsburg case. She blinked. Then nodded. "Yes, Mr. Winslow," she said. She folded her notebook, got up, and went out the door.

Steve Winslow turned back to Jenson. "All right," he said. "It's just you and me here. We can stop beating around the bush. If you won't quote me, I won't quote you. What the hell's going on?"

Jenson smiled. "You now admit Uncle Jack called on you?"

"I'll admit anything you like. I can always deny it later. But say Uncle Jack was here. Why shouldn't I listen to him, and what's it to you?"

"That's more like it," Jenson said. "All right, let's talk turkey. My uncle's worth a lot of money. It's his. All his. Made it himself. A self-made man. It's a classic success story. Who was it—Horatio Alger, right? Anyway, that's him. Made it in the stock market. Started with a hundred bucks, parlayed it into a small fortune. In his day, the man was a genius. Sharp as a tack. Now . . ." Jenson shrugged.

"What happened?"

"He got old. Senile. Lost it."

"Just like that?"

Jenson's eyes shifted. "No. It was gradual."

"Nothing happened to trigger it?"

"Why do you ask?"

"Just curious."

"No, his mind just started getting muddled."

"When?"

"Within the last year."

"Before that he was fine?"

"Yes."

"And he had a home?"

Jenson nodded. "Now you've got it. That's the whole point. He had a home. A life. A family."

"Where was home?"

"He had a house in Long Island. Great Neck. Gorgeous house. Lived there thirty years. One day he up and sells it, goes and lives on the subway." Jenson smiled and shrugged. "What more do I have to say?"

"How does that affect you?"

Jenson looked at him. "Are you kidding? I was living there. In the house. We all were. Suddenly he sells it out from under us. No word, no warning, we're out on the street. You know what it's like trying to get an apartment in the city these days? Forget it. Right now we got a bungalow in Teaneck, New Jersey. We're all jammed into it and lucky to get it. Meanwhile he's running around the subway system begging quarters with the winos. All the time, the man's worth millions."

"So," Steve said, "what is it you want?"

"I told you what I want. Let's swap some information. Maybe we can help each other."

"How so?"

"Look. The man's insane. You can't accept employment from a man who's mentally incompetent. The way I understand it, he's not responsible for his actions, so anything he does wouldn't be legally binding. So you start working for him, you could find yourself out on a limb."

"Whereas?" Steve said.

"Whereas, if you cooperate with me, I could make it worth your while."

"Oh?"

"Yes. You have to understand. I'm his heir. We all are. We're blood relations. When he dies, his money goes to us."

"It does?"

"Yes, it does. In equal portions, share and share alike. I've seen the will."

"I see," Steve said.

"I'm sure you do," Jenson said. "But that's just the thing. Uncle Jack's lost his marbles. He's not responsible for his actions and he might do anything. You see the situation. Now he's consulted a lawyer, and of course that worries me. What if he should try to change his will? He can't, of course, because he's not legally competent, but what if he tries? What if he decides to disinherit all of us, and leave the whole shooting match to some wino he met on the subway?"

"What if he did?"

"Well, I don't think you'd want to be in the position of helping a man who didn't know what he was doing throw away his money by doing something idiotic."

"I see."

"So I'm asking you point blank. Did Uncle Jack consult you about his will?"

Steve shook his head. "You're inquiring into matters which I'm not at liberty to discuss."

Jenson's jaw dropped open. "Are you kidding me?"

"No, I'm not."

Jenson got to his feet. "I don't believe this," he said. "After all I told you. I mean, you sent your secretary out of the room so we could talk man to man. I thought you understood the situation, then you make me an answer like that." Jenson shook his head. His face was flushed. "Some attorney," he said. "What did he promise you? A hundred grand? Two hundred? It doesn't matter, 'cause you aren't going to see a penny." Jenson drew himself up and glared at Winslow. "What a fucking disgrace," he said. "A man's trying to defraud his family out of millions, but you can't discuss it. Probably even think you're gonna help him do it. Well, fat chance. I'd like to see you try to collect your fee."

Jenson turned and stalked out, slamming the door behind him.

# 4

in the door.

"Well?" Steve said.

"That man is definitely pissed off."

"No, no," Steve said. "I mean—"

Tracy held up her hands. "Relax. Mark Taylor's men picked him up. They'll follow him until further notice."

Steve exhaled and his features relaxed. He smiled. "Nice work."

"Just routine."

"Yeah, as if we *had* a routine. How'd you work it out?"

"Nothing to it," Tracy said. "We have no Halsburg case. No surprise there. We have no cases at all. Any name you picked would do. So you had to be trying to tell me to get a message to Mark Taylor without tipping off Jenson. The only thing I could think of was you wanted to have him followed, or you wanted him thrown out of your office. I couldn't really see you calling in detectives to give the guy the bum's rush—not at that point, anyway—so I figured you must want him tailed."

"You figured right."

"Why?"

"Cause I think I made a bad mistake, and I want to try to make up for it."

Tracy frowned. "What do you mean, a bad mistake?"

Steve rubbed his head. "Tell you what. There's no point my going through this whole thing twice. Why don't you give Mark Taylor a ring, tell him to drop down here. I need to fill him in anyway."

"Sure," Tracy said. She went in the outer office to make the call.

Steve Winslow leaned back in his chair and rubbed his head again. Jesus Christ. Once, just once, it would be nice to have a client come in, tell him the facts and retain him in the case. Just once it would be nice to approach a case from the point of view of knowing what the hell was going on.

23

Steve chuckled. No, it probably wouldn't. A case like that would probably be boring as hell.

The door opened and Tracy Garvin ushered Mark Taylor into the room.

Taylor said, "Hi, Steve," and flopped his two hundred and twenty pounds into the clients' chair. Taylor was Steve's age, in fact had been his roommate at college. He had been an exceptional linebacker with pro aspirations, before an injury had ended the dream. Instead he ran the Taylor Detective Agency, and had offices in Steve's building. Or rather, Steve had offices in his building. The Taylor Detective Agency had been there for years. When Steve had finally scraped up enough money to set up a practice, Mark Taylor had put in a word with the super to get Steve in.

"Hi, Mark. You pick him up?"

"Oh, yeah. He's covered. I got a man on him, and he'll stick like glue, if that's what you want."

"That's what I want."

"That's what I figured. Of course, I couldn't be sure." Taylor grinned, jerked his finger at Tracy Garvin. "Tracy here calls me up, says, 'I think Steve wants someone followed.'"

"That's not what I said," Tracy protested.

"Maybe not in those words," Taylor said, "but that's the gist of it. Anyway, she gives me a rundown of what happened, says she figures that means you want this guy tailed. The way she tells it, I figure you do too. But I'm a nice guy, and I don't want Tracy out on a limb taking the responsibility on herself, so I gave her the chance of a lifetime, Taylor special, money-back guaranteed surveillance."

Steve grinned. "What the hell is that?"

"I told her I'd follow the guy, and if it turned out that wasn't what you wanted, there's no charge."

"It's what I wanted."

"Good. Then I'll bill you. So what's the scoop? Why am I tailing this guy?"

"I don't know."

"Well, that's helpful. Glad you called me down here. Otherwise, I'd be working in the dark."

"Yeah, well that's the problem," Steve said. "In this case, we're working in the dark."

"You got a client?"

"In a way."

"Oh, great. I can't wait to find out what way that is." Taylor turned to Tracy. "Is he putting me on?"

"No."

"All right, Steve, what's the pitch? What do you mean, in a way? You got a client or not?"

Steve shrugged. "That's open to interpretation. More to the point, no client asked me to tail Jenson. I did that on my own initiative."

"Is Jenson the client?"

"No."

"Then who is?"

Steve rubbed his head. "O.K. Let me give you a brief rundown. This morning an old ragged man off the street comes into my office and asks me a whole bunch of questions about probate law."

Mark Taylor started at him. "What?"

"That's right."

"A street bum?"

"One of the homeless. And he doesn't tell me his problems, like you'd expect a guy like that to do. No names, no specifics. No, the guy just wants to discuss abstract points of law."

"A homeless guy?"

"Yeah. He asks me a whole bunch of questions and I answer them. He still doesn't say why he wants to know. Then he gets up, throws two hundred bucks on my desk, and walks out."

Taylor's jaw dropped open. "A homeless guy paid you two hundred bucks?"

Steve grinned, put up his hands. "Hang on. You ain't heard nothing yet. This afternoon another man comes into my office. Carl Jenson. The person your men are tailing. Tells me the street guy's his uncle—his great uncle actually. And get this— he tells me this uncle's an eccentric multimillionaire who's lost his marbles, sold his house out from under him, and went to live with the homeless on the subway."

Taylor blinked. "You're kidding."

"Not at all. Jenson's argument is his uncle's mentally incompetent, so anything I do for him won't be legally binding. His pitch is, if I throw in with him against his uncle and help him get his hands on the money, he'll pay me a whopping big fee."

"Jesus Christ. So that's why you decided to have him tailed?"

"Actually, I decided the moment he told me his uncle was worth money."

"Why was that?"

"Because that's when I realized I'd made a big mistake."

"How?"

"By giving his uncle advice."

"Why? Because he's not mentally competent?"

Steve shook his head. "No. Besides, we've only got Jenson's word for that. For all we know, the guy may be perfectly sane."

"A millionaire living on the subway?"

"That doesn't necessarily mean he's insane. But that's not the point. The point is, I shouldn't have given him advice at all."

"Why?"

"Because he didn't tell me what his problem was. He just discussed abstract points of law."

"What's wrong with that?"

"Everything. A lawyer's not a reference book. A lawyer's job is to take the facts of the case, and apply the law to them. If the lawyer doesn't get the facts, if the lawyer just tells the client the law and lets the client go off and apply the law himself, that's the worst thing a lawyer can do."

"Why?"

"Because every case is different. And the law may or may not apply. And even if it does, the law is constantly changing. That's what legal precedents are all about. You take the facts of the case and you say, 'Ah, that's similar to this previous case. The same laws should apply.' Or, if you don't want it to apply, you say, 'Ah, the reason it's different from Coosbaine vs. Markowitz is this,' and then you argue that point, and if you win, *your* case becomes a legal precedent.

"But, you see, it all depends on the facts of the individual case. So for a lawyer to tell a client the law without knowing the facts of the case is totally irresponsible. The results could be disastrous."

"Then why'd you do it?" Taylor asked.

Steve shook his head. "I told you. I made a mistake. This morning I had two men waiting to see me. A businessman and a homeless man. I asked Tracy to show in the businessman, and she needled me about it—the homeless man was here first."

Tracy opened her mouth to protest.

Steve held up his had. "No, no. You were absolutely right. I'm just explaining what happened. Anyway, I saw the businessman first. For a number of reasons: the businessman would be impatient, he wouldn't want to wait; the street guy would be more interesting, I saved him for last. Perfectly reasonable. But for all that, Tracy was basically right. All liberal protestations notwithstanding, I'm a snob and a bigot and I saw the rich man first."

Steve chuckled and shook his head. "So what do I do? I take the rich man with his hundred-thousand-dollar retainer and throw him out of my office."

Mark's eyes widened. "Hundred-thousand-dollar retainer?"

"Yeah."

"You turned down a hundred thousand dollars?"

"Believe me, we didn't want it."

Taylor rubbed his head. "Jesus Christ."

"So I throw him out of my office, then I bring the street guy in, sit him down, treat him like a king, and sit there talking probate law with him like it was the most natural thing in the world."

Steve frowned and shook his head. "Only it wasn't. And if he'd been a normal client and not a street person, I wouldn't have been talking abstract law with him. I'd have made him tell me the facts of the case. If he wouldn't, I'd have sent him on his way. Only I didn't. I was too busy bending over backwards playing Mr. Liberal. But hey, what's the harm? None of it matters anyway, the guy's only a street person. What the hell difference does it make how he changes his will? Then Carl Jenson tells me the guy's a multimillionaire and suddenly it makes all the difference in the world. The guy asked me for advice. I gave it to him. If he goes out and tries to apply it himself, the results could be disastrous.

"And that's just for starters. Add to that the fact the man may or may not be a lunatic. Throw in the fact he's got a half a dozen greedy relatives trying to prove he is. Add in the fact they're the people in the will he's talking about. And top it off with the fact some of the things he's asking me about smacked of collusion and fraud."

Taylor whistled. "Jesus Christ."

"Right," Steve said. "The bottom line is, I am in one hell of a mess. And the worst thing about it is, it's my own damn fault. I put myself there. I got no one to blame but myself.

"So, you ask me why I want to follow Jenson. I guess the answer is, because it's too late to follow the bum.

"So, stick with Jenson and find out anything you can. If by any chance he should lead you to Jack Walsh—that's the bum by the way—drop Jenson and tail him. Frankly, I don't think he will. But tell your men to be alert."

"Right," Taylor said. "But how will they know?"

"Know what?"

"The street guy. Suppose Jenson goes looking for this guy on the subway? Suppose he talks to the homeless down there. There's a million of 'em. How are they gonna spot this Jack Walsh?"

"I never said it was gonna be easy, Mark. But if it's our man, I think you'll know it. The way I see it, if Jenson finds him, he'll stick to him like glue."

"If that happens, then what?"

Steve shrugged. "Damned if I know. Anyway, that's our best-case-scenario. Frankly, I doubt if Jenson will see him again."

"So what's the point?"

"Damned if I know. All I know is, I'm in a mess and I want all the information I can get."

Taylor thought that over. He shook his head. "Jesus, what a mess."

"Yeah," Steve said. He thought a moment. Then he chuckled. "The way I see it, there's only one saving grace."

"Oh yeah? What's that?"

Steve jerked his thumb over his shoulder. "I'm off the hook with Tracy."

Tracy looked at him. "What?"

Steve smiled. "Yeah. About the homeless man and the businessman. Seeing the rich man first." Steve shrugged. "The way things turned out, I actually saw the rich man last."

# 5

MARK TAYLOR TOOK A SIP OF coffee from the paper cup on his desk, ran his hand through his curly red hair, and flipped open his notebook. "All right, Steve, here's the rundown. If yesterday is any indication, Carl Jenson is a lily of the field—he toils not, neither does he spin. After leaving your office, he walked down Broadway to the local OTB and hung out all afternoon placing bets."

Mark grinned. "Now, in a case like that, my operatives have a certain amount of leeway. If he feels he must in order to maintain his cover, a man may place a reasonable amount of small bets and write 'em off on his expense account. On the other hand, if the guy should happen to win, it's another story entirely—the guy was playing with his own money all along, and he pockets the winnings. In this case, my man happened to hit the daily double at forty-eight to one, and even on a two-dollar bet that's a pretty nice bonus."

Taylor took another sip of coffee. "Your buddy Jenson is another story. He bet every race, never got a nibble. Not that it would have done him much good. He was betting two bucks a pop, usually at very short odds. Once he bought a dollar box on the trifecta—that ran him six bucks. And once he put ten bucks on the nose of a heavy favorite that went off at even odds. The nag finished fourth."

"How'd he take losing?"

"About how you'd expect. It pissed him off, and he'd bitch and moan and tear up his tickets and gripe about his luck to anyone willing to listen." Mark shrugged. "But what the hell. A guy bets like that, he's not desperate and he's not plunging. He's not gambling for the money, he's gambling for recreation."

"Some recreation," Steve said.

"Hey," Taylor said. "He may have had a fine day. A guy like that probably enjoys pissing and moaning about his luck more than he enjoys winning."

Taylor referred to his notebook. "At any rate, he hung out there until seven o'clock. Then he had dinner at a Sabrett stand on the corner, and walked uptown to 57th Street. There's a bridge club there, apparently has a penny-ante poker game in the back room for some of its more select clientele. How Carl Jenson falls into that category is beyond me, but apparently he did, 'cause he went in there and stayed until eleven o'clock. My man had to hang out in the main room and play rubber bridge for four hours. At two cents a point, that's a heavy game, and he wound up throwing back twenty bucks of his horse race winnings."

Taylor grinned again. "The guy tried to tell me he was playing the ponies on his own money and playing bridge on mine, but I wouldn't go for it. I told him give me a break, gambling's gambling. As it is, the guy made a tidy profit.

"Anyway, with my man in the other room, I can't tell you how well Jenson did at the poker table, except when he came out he didn't look happy. Of course, the way my man tells it, griping is Jenson's middle name.

"Anyway, Jenson left at eleven o'clock, took the subway down to 14th Street, caught a PATH train to New Jersey, and took a taxi home. At least, I'd assume it was home. It was an address in Teaneck, New Jersey, which is where the guy told you he lived."

Taylor took another sip of coffee. "Now, that's the whole story, and it ain't much. I know it's not what you wanted, but I had a good man on him, and I'm sure he didn't miss a thing. He phoned in from OTB and I talked to him myself, after I'd talked to you, so he knew exactly what we were after. So he was on guard, particulary when Jenson took the subway. And the one thing he's sure of, is Jenson never made a move toward any street person. Never paid any of them the least attention. As far as he could tell, Jenson had only one interest in life, and that was Carl Jenson."

Taylor shrugged. "And that's it."

"Well," Steve said. "That's about what I expected. But I had to try. At least we got the guy's address. We can peg him if we want."

"Right," Taylor said. "You asked me to tail him yesterday and I did. I got no one on him today. But a guy of his type, he's probably still sleeping now. If you want me to slap a man on the house in Jersey, I can. But it's gonna cost you money, and you're probably just gonna get more of the same. But of course that's up to you. So how do you want to play it?"

Steve thought a moment. "Tell me, how much is yesterday's surveillance gonna run me?"

Taylor smiled. "Is two hundred bucks the figure you were looking for?"

Steve grinned. "Damned if it isn't. All right, Mark. You called the turn. We've given our men a run for his money. I don't see there's much else we can do. Wrap it up and send me the bill." Steve shook his head. "Unless he turns up dead in some alley, clutching a particularly strangely worded handwritten will, I would say we can close the books on our homeless millionaire."

# 6

IT WAS NEARLY TWO WEEKS later. Steve Winslow was seated at his desk reading the morning paper. Since the homeless millionaire incident, Steve had varied his reading routine. Now he scanned the obituaries before turning to the drama section. So far, the name Jack Walsh had not appeared. Steve didn't really expect that it would. On the other hand, he wasn't that sure that it wouldn't.

He'd already done the obituaries and the drama and moved on to the sports, when Tracy Garvin came in closing the door behind her.

"Someone here to see you," she said.

"Oh? A man or a woman?"

Tracy hesitated.

Steve grinned. "Don't tell me our visitor is of indeterminate sex."

"No. He's male."

"So what's the problem?"

"Well, you said a man or a woman. I was afraid the answer to that would be misleading."

"Oh really? This is almost fun. Don't spoil it by explaining. Just show the visitor in."

Tracy nodded, went out and came back moments later ushering in a young man.

At first glance the mystery was solved. Steve had to suppress a grin. Tracy was absolutely right. "There's a gentleman here to see you," would have been slightly misleading.

The visitor was a teenager—of that much Steve was certain. Beyond that he couldn't really tell. Steve was far enough removed from his own teens not to be able to judge the age that accurately. He put his visitor's age somewhere between twelve and twenty.

Of course, the young man's appearance didn't help him any. His head had been shaved into a bristly mohawk that had been dyed a shocking green, and he had a gold earring in one ear. The effect, Steve supposed, was to make him look tough, or

33

bad, or cool, whatever it was teenagers aspired to these days. In Steve's mind it merely made him look young.

Tracy Garvin couldn't help giving Steve an I-told-you-so look as she said, "Mr. Winslow, Jeremy Dawson."

Steve Winslow stood up. "How do you do, Mr. Dawson?"

Jeremy Dawson looked at him. Then at Tracy Garvin. Then back at Steve. He snuffled his nose and wrinkled up his brow. He squinted at Steve. "You the lawyer?"

"That's right. I'm Steve Winslow. Why?"

Jeremy didn't look convinced. He smiled, but the smile was somewhat forced. "I dunno." He shook his head. Shrugged. "You just don't look like a lawyer."

Steve shot Tracy a look. "Well," Steve said, "appearances can be misleading."

If Jeremy caught the irony, he didn't show it. He nodded. "Yeah. That's true. So you're the lawyer?"

"Yes."

"The one Uncle Jack came to see."

"Uncle Jack?"

"Yeah. Jack Walsh."

Steve took a breath. "Oh dear."

Jeremy looked at him. "What?"

"I'm sorry," Steve said, "but we may have a little trouble here. Sit down, Mr. Dawson, I'll try to explain it to you."

Jeremy looked at Steve for a minute. He appeared to be unwilling to sit because he'd been asked to do so, as if part of his attitude was to defy any suggestion on principle. After a moment, however, he turned and seated himself in the chair.

Steve sat at his desk. Tracy, looking terribly amused, pulled up a chair and flipped open her shorthand notebook.

"All right," Steve said. "Look. If you want to come in here and ask me questions about a client, I can't answer them. The relationship between an attorney and client is privileged. I can't violate that confidence. So before you say anything, you should know I have no intention of answering any questions—"

Jeremy held up his hands. "Hey, man. No problem. You can skip the sermon. I heard it already from Uncle Carl. That's Carl Jenson. The guy who was in here a couple of weeks ago trying to pump you for information. He didn't get it. I know all about it. I overheard him talking to Fred and Jason. So you can skip the spiel. I'm not here for information. I'm here 'cause I need help."

Steve frowned. "That might present a problem."

"Why?"

"I don't know till I hear the facts. It's conceivable there could be a conflict of interest here. I might not be free to act in your behalf."

Jeremy shook his head. "I don't want you to act in my behalf."

"No?"

"No. I don't want you to help me. I want you to help Uncle Jack."

Steve frowned again. "Perhaps you'd better explain."

"Yeah, right. Well, Uncle Jack's in trouble."

"What kind of trouble?"

"They locked him up."

"Locked him up?"

"Yeah."

"Whaddya mean?"

"In Bellevue. They locked him up in Bellevue."

"You mean they had him committed?"

"That's right."

"Who?"

"Jason and Fred."

"When did this happen?"

"Last night."

"You wanna tell me about it?"

Jeremy shrugged. "Not much to tell. They'd been planning it for months. I'd overhear them sometimes. They had it all set. Had this doctor at Bellevue lined up to commit him. Doctor, hell. Damn headshrinker. These guys got some nerve callin' themselves doctors, you know? But Jason and Fred found this guy, sold him a story. Probably promised him a wad of cash too. Had him draw up the papers."

"The papers?"

"Yeah. They were all set to commit Uncle Jack. The only problem was, they couldn't find him. Two weeks ago, when uncle Carl was up here—that's the first time they'd seen him in months." Jeremy shrugged. "Of course, Uncle Carl's such a douchebag lamebrain. He couldn't stick with him. Uncle Jack just ditched him. That's why Carl was in here giving you such a hard time. 'Cause he knew he'd blown it and he felt like a total asshole." Jeremy grinned and shook his head. "I tell you, Jason and Fred really gave it to him good. For losing him, I mean."

"Why'd he tell 'em?"

"What?"

"If he knew they'd be mad, why'd he tell 'em he saw the guy at all?"

"He had to. He saw Uncle Jack in the street. He called Fred right away, told him he'd spotted Uncle Jack and to rush right down with the commitment papers. By the time Fred got there, Uncle Jack had given Carl the slip. That's why Carl was so hot to get the information out of you. He knew he'd fucked up royally and was in the dog house, and he wanted to do something to get out from under."

"And yesterday?"

"Same thing. Only this time it was Fred spotted Uncle Jack. He called Jason, they rushed the papers over, and this time they served him."

"Who did?"

"Two hospital orderlies. Found him in a subway station. Put a straight jacket on him and carted him away."

"And he's in Bellevue now?"

"That's right."

"So whaddya want me to do?"

"Get him out."

"Why?"

Jeremy scrunched up his face. "Hey, man. What kind of question is that?"

"I want to know how you come into all this. Why do you want your uncle out?"

"He isn't crazy."

"No?"

"No. Why should he be locked up if he isn't crazy? If you ask me, if anybody's crazy it's Jason and Fred."

"Oh?"

"Oh, not *crazy* crazy. I don't mean like they're nuts. I just mean like they're weird."

"You still haven't answered my question."

"What question?"

"What's your interest in this?"

"To get Uncle Jack out. Oh, you mean why." Jeremy shrugged. "I dunno. I like him. I guess that's it. I like him. Like, you gotta understand. My family's kind of weird. The whole setup, I mean. Like I never had a mother or a father. I was brought up by Aunt Rose—there's a winner. And Jason and Fred. And Carl, for Christ's sake." Jeremy rolled his eyes. "You have no idea what it's like. And all of 'em living in the big house in Great Neck, livin' there and sponging off Uncle Jack. If you ask me, he's the only straight one in the bunch. Sure, he's weird. Sure, he's old. But crazy? No. He never treated me like—I don't know—like some stupid kid got no business being there.

"So it's not right. Them locking him up, I mean. It's not because he's crazy. It's just 'cause they want to get their hands on the money.

"So you got to get him out. Can you do it?"

Steve sighed and rubbed his head. "It's a little complicated."

"Complicated? What's complicated? They put him in Bellevue, he isn't crazy, he shouldn't be there, he should get out."

"It's not that simple."

"Why not?"

"Well, let me ask you some questions. Where you living now?"

"Jersey, why?"

"When'd you move there?"

"Six months ago."

"Why?"

"You know why. Carl told you. Uncle Jack sold the house and we all had to move. Why are you asking that?"

"I told you. I'm not really free to discuss this or give you any information. So it simplifies things if I ask you for the information we need to discuss."

Jeremy thought that over. "I gotcha. O.K. Shoot."

"You say Uncle Jack sold the house. So where's he living?"

"Like nowhere."

"Nowhere? You mean he has no home?"

"Right."

"So where's he sleep?"

"On the subway."

"I take it Uncle Jack has some money?"

"You kidding? He's worth millions."

"And yet he has no home and sleeps on the subway with the bums and winos." Steve spread his hands wide. "I rest my case, Your Honor, the man is nutty as a fruitcake."

Jeremy shook his head. "You can't go by that."

"Oh yeah? Well, a judge can."

"That's not fair. Sleeping on the subway doesn't prove a man's nuts."

"Well, it doesn't prove he's sane, either. I gotta convince a judge a man who sleeps on the subway's sane, I gotta come up with a pretty good reason. So you tell me. Why's he doing it?"

"To spite them."

"To spite who?"

"Jason, Fred, Carl. All of us, really."

"Again we come back to why. Just 'cause they're after his money?"

"Yeah, well partly. But that's not really it."

"Well, what is?"

"Well, I guess it's about Julie."

"Julie?"

"Yeah. You don't know about Julie?"

"Assume I don't. Who's Julie?"

Jeremy snuffled. "This is stupid."

Steve nodded. "Yeah."

Jeremy looked at him. shrugged. "O.K. Have it your way. Julie's this woman Uncle Jack met about a year ago. When the family found out they went nuts."

"What do you mean, when the family found out?"

"Oh, like Uncle Jack had been acting different for awhile, you know? Like not talking. Which wasn't like him. So Jason and Fred were concerned about it. I heard 'em talkin'. They were wondering what's up. They asked Uncle Jack questions, trying to worm it out of him. He wasn't talking.

"Then one day he brings her to the house."

"Julie?"

"Yeah, Julie. I tell you, Jason nearly hit the roof."

"How come?"

"Well, for one thing, she's young. Well, not *young* young. She's like forty. But compared to Uncle Jack."

"So what happened?"

"I told you. Jason went bananas. Fred and Carl too. I mean, this is the worst thing that could happen. Like they're all expecting one day Uncle Jack's gonna kick the bucket and they're gonna come into the money. And now this. You should have heard 'em. I mean, it's twenty-five years since his wife died. He's never been serious about another woman since. Suddenly, at age seventy-five he's got a girlfriend. Well, Jason and Fred take one look and see their inheritance going out the window. What if Uncle Jack should marry?"

Steve looked at Jeremy narrowly. "How would you feel about that?"

Jeremy shrugged. "Hey, it's his life and his money. At seventy-five it's hard to figure, but if the guy wants to have fun, that's his business."

"What about you? Don't you stand to inherit?"

"Oh, sure. A nice trust fund with Aunt Rose in charge. Whoopdedo."

"Still, something to lose."

Jeremy shrugged. "Uncle Jack wouldn't screw me. Even if he got married, so what? There's enough to go around. Jason and Fred, they want it all."

"And Carl?"

"Carl too, but he's a numbnuts, you know? Well, they all are, but Carl in particular, you know what I mean?"

"Yeah. So what happened with Julie?"

"About what you'd expect. Jason and Fred start working on Uncle Jack, trying to poison him against her. I tell you, it didn't work. He just got pissed off. Clammed up more than ever. Told them to fuck off.

"That's when they got smart. Instead of working on him, they started working on her. Not directly, you know. They hired a private dick to dig into her background. The guy nosed around, and it turned out there was something to find.

"This woman—Julie Creston—she was an actress. Turns out Creston was her stage name. Her real name was Harwell. She was from Minnesota. Came out here when she was young, tried to make it as an actress. Evidently had a rough time getting started. Anyway, about twenty years ago she's busted twice for prostitution."

Steve nodded. "I see."

"Yeah," Jeremy said. "So did Fred and Jason. When they found out, they figured they hit the pot of gold at the end of the rainbow. They took the report and gave it to Uncle Jack."

"What happened?"

"He hit the ceiling. Went bananas. Screaming. Cursing. I was upstairs in my room, I still heard him. He laid it on the line. If they ever mentioned it again, if he ever heard one word of this, he'd kill them."

"So what happened then?"

"Then they did what they should have done in the first place. From their point of view, I mean—really they shouldn't have done nothing, it was none of their business. Anyway, instead of going to him they went to her." Jeremy shrugged. "At least that's what I figure they did."

"Why do you say that?"

"Because I didn't actually hear them talking about it. All I know is what happened."

"What was that?"

"Julie disappeared."

"What?"

"Yeah. Uncle Jack went to see her, she was gone. Packed up. Moved out. No forwarding address.

"So the way I see it, Jason and Fred went to her, dangled that report in front of her face. Told her they'd smear her with it."

"How could they do that if Uncle Jack didn't care?"

"Yeah, but she didn't know that. And she was working now. As an actress, I mean. She'd done an *Equalizer*, a *Kate and Allie*. Probably told her they'd sell her story to the *National Enquirer*."

Steve frowned. "That's pretty thin."

"Well, it worked. When Uncle Jack went to look for her, she was gone.

"Well, that's when the shit hit the fan. Uncle Jack came back, gave us all hell. Never seen a man so mad. Screaming. Cursing. His face was bright red, his veins popping out of his forehead. I thought he'd have a stroke.

"And he's ordering everybody out of the house. 'Get out of my house!' that's what he said. Over and over. 'I want you out!'"

"Did they go?"

"Are you kidding? They told him he was an old man, he didn't know what he was talking about.

"Well, *they* knew what he was talking about, all right. They just didn't believe him. Didn't think he was serious. I didn't either, frankly. I mean, he was just upset. He couldn't really mean it.

"But the next day it was the same thing. He'd calmed down, but he hadn't changed his mind. It was his house, we could damn well get the hell out.

"Of course, nobody listened to him. Nobody took him seriously.

"After a while he gave up. Stopped talking about it. Everybody figured it had blown over.

"Next thing you know, a moving van's pulling up outside. The guys are packing up Uncle Jack's stuff, putting it on the truck. That's how we found out he's sold the house.

"Well, naturally Jason and Fred are hysterical. What's happening? Where's he moving to?

"Found out he's not moving anywhere. His stuff's just going into storage.

"Jason says, 'You're crazy. Where you gonna live?' Uncle Jack say he don't give a shit, he'd rather live on the subways than with him.

"So that's it. The moving van packs up and goes. Uncle Jack leaves with 'em. Two days later the new owner shows up with the papers, tells us we got till the end of the month to pack up and get out."

Jeremy stopped and looked at Steve. "So you see, he's not crazy. Not like they said. He had a reason for what he did.

"So, whaddya think? Can you get him out?"

Steve frowned. "I don't know. The way you tell it, it's a sympathetic story, makes a good case. Will you testify to all that?"

Jeremy looked horrified. "Christ no. Are you kidding? These guys may be creeps, but they're family. I gotta live with them. Shit no, they can't even know I talked to you. I played hooky to come here. I should be in school now. It's no big deal—I done it before—so even if the school calls home, they won't figure I'm here. They won't know.

"And they don't have to know, do they? 'Cause I'm not asking you to do anything for me. It's all for Uncle Jack.

"So will you do it? Will you get him out?"

Steve frowned. He looked at Jeremy, who was gazing up at him like an expectant puppy asking to be walked.

An expectant puppy with green hair and an earring.

Steve shook his head. "I'm not sure I can," he said.

"All right. But will you try?"

Steve sighed. "Yeah. I'll try."

# 7

MARK TAYLOR FLOPPED HIS bulk into the clients' chair, pulled out his notebook and said, "Shoot."

"I've got two jobs for you," Steve said. "One's easy, one's hard."

"I like the sound of the hard one."

"Why's that?"

"More money in it. You got a big retainer?"

"No."

"Then I like it less. What's up?"

"Remember the homeless millionaire?"

"Him again?"

"Yeah."

"What about him?"

"He's in Bellevue."

"I'm not surprised. So?"

"So I gotta get him out."

Taylor nodded. "That figures. I'm surprised the shrinks let him call you."

"They didn't."

"No? Then how'd you hear about it?"

"From a kid with green hair."

"What?"

Steve gave Mark Taylor a rundown on his meeting with Jeremy Dawson. Taylor listened without interrupting, adding an occasional grunt or writing an occasional note.

When Steve was finished, Taylor said, "O.K., what's my end of this?"

"Julie Creston."

"What about her?"

"Find her."

"How?"

"You're the detective. I'm just a lawyer. You got her stage name, her real name, some shows she was in, and a couple of hooker busts. You even know where she came from. She might have just gone home."

"Yeah, and she might not," Taylor said. "And this was months ago. By now in all probability she's in another state doing another job under another name."

"I thought you liked the hard ones, Mark. More money and all that."

"Yeah. But I like to get results. O.K. I'll put some men on it. So what's the easy job?"

"That *is* the easy job, Mark."

"You're kidding."

Steve grinned. "Yes, I am. That's the hard job. The easy job is a piece of cake." Steve jerked his thumb over his shoulder. "Tracy's typing up a writ of *habeas corpus* for Jack Walsh. When she's finished, I need to have it served."

Taylor nodded. "Can do. What happens then?"

"Then we got a dogfight. The hospital will resist it and we'll wind up with a competency hearing."

"How does that work?"

"I don't know. I never had one."

"So how you gonna handle it?"

"Smoothly, effortlessly, and with a great casual flair."

"Fuck you. I mean really."

Steve shook his head. "Beats the hell out of me." He grinned. "Frankly, all I know about 'em comes from reading Perry Mason murder mysteries."

"You're kidding."

"Not at all. Of course, Erle Stanley Gardner was a lawyer, so they should be fairly accurate."

"Steve—"

"I know, I know. I'm only half kidding, Mark. The way I understand it, here's the way it's gonna go. We'll serve the *habeas corpus*. A judge will schedule a competency hearing and order Bellevue to produce Jack Walsh in court. Bellevue won't do it."

"Why not?"

"You see, that's the whole point. Walsh has been committed. That means a psychiatrist at Bellevue has certified him insane. Declared him incompetent. Well, if Bellevue takes the position Jack Walsh is incompetent to handle his affairs, they also have to take the position he's incompetent to testify in court.

"So they won't produce him. Instead they'll produce the admitting psychiatrist to testify that he's in no condition to be there.

"That's fine. I'll immediately raise a big stink, demanding that they produce Jack Walsh. At the same time, I'll be hoping like hell they don't do it."

"Why is that?"

"You never saw Jack Walsh, did you?"

"No."

"Right. If you had, you wouldn't ask. Anyway, I don't want to give the judge and the attorney a chance to go after him. I want to go after the psychiatrist."

"The psychiatrist?"

"Yeah. Him and the relatives. First I'll attack the psychiatrist on the grounds he had no basis for making his judgment. Then I'll attack the relatives to show that they were motivated by personal interest."

"Can you do that?"

"Probably. The relatives are a greedy bunch. I don't expect them to come off well.

"The psychiatrist is another matter. If I could show he had a financial stake in this, I'd be home free. But that's probably out of the question. Most likely he'll be some highly respected shrink just doin' what he thinks is right."

"So there's nothing you can do?"

"No, there's plenty I can do. What I'll have going for me is the fact the shrink only saw the guy once, and has to be basing his diagnosis on things the relatives told him."

"So, say you can do all that. Then what?"

"Then," Steve said, "the judge isn't going to be swayed by the doctor's assurance of the patient's incompetence. He'll issue a court order, and Bellevue will have to produce Jack Walsh in court."

"Yeah. And what happens then?"

Steve shrugged. "Then we're fucked."

# 8

JUDGE WASHBURN ADJUSTED his glasses, picked up a paper from his bench, and squinted at it. "This is a hearing in the case of one Jack Walsh. Application has been made to declare Jack Walsh incompetent and have Rose Tindel and Jason Tindel named conservators. The Tindels are represented by Robert Franklyn. Mr. Franklyn, are your parties in court?"

Franklyn, slim, tall, carefully groomed and impeccably dressed in a three-piece suit, smiled, bowed and said, "Yes, Your Honor." He turned and gestured to Jason and Rose Tindel.

Franklyn's clients had been well coached. The Tindels oozed respectability. The were dressed neatly, conservatively. Their expressions radiated a mixture of frank sincerity and benevolent concern.

"And who are the parties with them?" Judge Washburn asked.

Franklyn indicated a couple sitting next to the Tindels, similarly dressed but slightly younger. "That would be their cousins, Fred and Pat Grayson." He indicated a somewhat severe looking older woman. "Claire Chesterton." Moving down the row. "And Carl Jenson."

Judge Washburn nodded. "And on the other side we have . . ." He referred to his paper, ". . . a Mr. Steve Winslow appearing as attorney for Jack Walsh."

Steve rose and bowed to the judge.

Judge Washburn hesitated a moment before proceeding. Steve smiled. With long hair, blue jeans, corduroy jacket and bright red tie, he was the only one in the courtroom who looked slightly out of place.

Judge Washburn said, "Mr. Winslow has filed a writ of *habeas corpus* ordering that Jack Walsh be produced in court." Washburn turned to Franklyn. "Is Mr. Walsh here?"

"He is not, Your Honor," Franklyn said. "Mr. Walsh is in Bellevue hospital. He suffered a nervous breakdown, and is presently in no condition to appear in court. I have the admitting psychiatrist from Bellevue here to testify to that effect."

Judge Washburn nodded again. "I see. Mr. Winslow's petition states that Mr. Walsh is being held at Bellevue against his will. He asks that that commitment be set aside and the petitioner released."

"That is utter nonsense," Franklyn said. "He is not being held against his will. He is a sick man, entrusted to the care of competent physicians. He has been placed there by caring family members, attempting to see that his best interests are protected."

"This complaint alleges that Jack Walsh was hauled off the subway, incarcerated at Bellevue, and denied access to his attorney. Furthermore, the complaint alleges that Jack Walsh is medically and emotionally sound, and that there is no reason whatsoever for his commitment."

Franklyn's smile was frosty. "May I ask if Mr. Winslow's contention is borne out by the opinion of a reputable psychiatrist?"

Winslow's smile was equally cold. "May I ask how one is expected to obtain such an opinion when one is denied access to one's client?"

Judge Washburn held up his hand. "Gentlemen, this is not a debate. Let's try to move things along. Now, I note the commitment papers were signed by one Jason Tindel. Let's hear from him first. Jason Tindel take the stand."

Jason Tindel got up, looked at the other relatives who nodded encouragement. He walked to the witness stand, and sat.

"Does Your Honor wish me to question the witness?" Franklyn said.

"I'll ask the questions," Judge Washburn said. He turned to the witness. "Mr. Tindel, what is your relationship to the petitioner, Jack Walsh?"

"My wife is his great-niece. She is the granddaughter of his sister."

Judge Washburn frowned. "Has he no closer living relatives?"

"No, Your Honor."

"I see. And you have signed the commitment papers, placing

Jack Walsh in Bellevue, and are seeking to have him declared incompetent and you and Rose Tindel named conservators. Is that correct?"

"That's right."

"What grounds do you have for feeling that Jack Walsh is not competent to carry on his own affairs?"

Jason Tindel chuckled, shook his head. "I have so many, Your Honor, I don't know where to begin. Jack Walsh was once a very sharp man. But he's seventy-five, and I'm sorry to say, recently his mind is going."

"Could you give me examples?"

"I certainly could." Jason Tindel ticked the points off on his fingers. "Within the last year he's estranged himself from all his relatives. He's sold his house out from under him and gone to live on the subway with the bums and bag ladies."

Judge Washburn frowned. "On the subway, Mr. Tindel?"

"That's right, Your Honor."

"And how do you know this?"

"For one thing, he told us. When he left, I mean. He told us that was what he was going to do. For another thing, I saw him myself."

"And when was that?"

"Shortly after he moved out. I saw him on the street. I must say, it was quite a shock. He was dressed in rags like a bum. Naturally, I followed him to see what he was up to. And he went down in the subway and hung out with the bums on the platform."

"I see," Judge Washburn said. "Was there anything else?"

"Yes, Your Honor. He's also withdrawn over two hundred thousand dollars in cash from his bank account."

Judge Washburn raised his eyebrows. "Two hundred *thousand?*"

"That's right."

"And what did he do with this money?"

Jason Tindel shrugged. "As far as I know, he's been carrying it on him."

"Two hundred thousand *in cash?*"

"That's right. The man is a millionaire, Your Honor. Yet he dresses like a bum, lives on the subway, and is carrying large sums of money in cash around with him. Under the circumstances, much as we hated to do it, we felt we had to take what steps we could in order to conserve his estate."

"I see," Judge Washburn said. He looked at Franklyn. "Do you have anything further to add?"

Mr. Franklyn smiled. "No, Your Honor. I think the witness has stated the case quite admirably."

Washburn nodded. "Mr. Winslow?"

Judge Washburn watched with some interest when Steve Winslow arose. The witness had certainly left the young attorney enough openings. Jason Tindel's testimony, while devastating, was certainly a mass of opinions and conclusions. Tindel didn't *know* that Jack Walsh carried large sums of money on him. Tindel didn't *know* Jack Walsh lived on the subway—he'd only seen him there once. Judge Washburn expected Steve Winslow to rip into him on those points.

Steve didn't. He merely smiled and said, "And what do you do, Mr. Tindel?"

The witness was clearly unprepared for that question. He frowned. "I beg your pardon?"

"What's your job? Your occupation? What do you do?"

Jason Tindel cleared his throat. "At the moment I'm between jobs."

"You mean you're unemployed?"

"I don't mean I'm unemployed. I'm between jobs."

"Are you employed?"

"No."

"Then you're unemployed, aren't you?"

Tindel frowned again. "I'm not employed at the moment."

"I understand. Are you collecting unemployment insurance?"

"No."

"Have you *applied* for unemployment insurance?"

"No."

"Do you *intend* to apply for unemployment insurance?"

Franklyn arose. "Your Honor, I fail to see the point of this."

"Surely the interest of the parties is relevant," Steve said.

"It is," Judge Washburn said. "As you well know," he added with a glance at Franklyn. "Proceed, Mr. Winslow."

"Do you *intend* to apply for unemployment insurance?"

"No, I do not."

"Are you *eligible* for unemployment insurance?"

Tindel took a breath. "No."

"I see," Steve said. "As I understand it, in order to be eligible for unemployment insurance, you must have worked twenty-six weeks out of the last year. Am I correct in assuming you haven't done that?"

Franklyn was on his feet again. "I point out, Your Honor, to qualify you must work twenty-six weeks for an employer who is paying FICA wages and withholding unemployment insurance. Many people are self-employed or work other jobs which don't qualify."

"Exactly," Jason Tindel snapped. "I happen to be self-employed, so the questions really don't apply."

"Oh, you're self-employed, Mr. Tindel?"

"Yes, I am."

Steve Winslow smiled. "So we come back to my original question. What do you do?"

"I'm a consultant."

"A rather broad field, Mr. Tindel. With whom do you consult?"

"I am employed by various firms."

"Name one."

"What?"

"Name one firm you've worked for in the past year."

"In the past year?"

"Yes."

Jason Tindel frowned. "Well, now . . ."

"And what is your field, Mr. Tindel?" Steve put in. "What do you consult on?"

"The stock market."

"Ah," Steve said. "The stock market. And are you a stock broker, Mr. Tindel?"

"No, I'm not."

"No, I didn't think so," Steve said. "So, you give people advice on the stock market. If that advice pans out, you've got a nice tip coming. Is that right?"

"No, it isn't," Tindel said hotly.

"Oh? In what way is it wrong?"

"Well, it's . . . Well, damn it. You just make me sound like a race track tout."

"I certainly beg your pardon, Mr. Tindel," Steve said. "I don't know how anyone could have possibly have gotten that impression.

"Let me ask you something. You stated that Jack Walsh's estate is worth several million dollars?"

"That's right."

"You're attempting to have Jack Walsh declared incompetent?"

"That's right."

"And yourself and your wife named conservators?"

"Yes."

"And in the event that that happens, you and your wife will suddenly find yourself in control of several million dollars?"

Jason Tindel said nothing. He merely glared at him.

"Well," Steve said. "That's certainly a nice position for someone who's unemployed to find himself in." Steve shrugged. "No further questions."

Judge Washburn looked at the witness. Then at Franklyn. "Have you anything further with this witness?"

"No, Your Honor," Franklyn said.

"Very well," Judge Washburn said. He referred to the paper. "Now, at the time of his incarceration, Mr. Walsh was observed in the subway station by Mr. Fred Grayson. I think we'll hear from him next."

Fred Grayson seated himself on the stand. Once again, Judge Washburn took up the questioning.

"Mr. Grayson, what is your relationship with the petitioner, Jack Walsh?"

"My wife is also his great-niece. She is the granddaughter of his brother."

"I see. Now on the afternoon in question you observed the petitioner, Jack Walsh on the subway?"

"Actually, first I saw him on the street."

"Where?"

"On 34th Street, between Madison and Fifth Avenue."

"What was he doing?"

"Ah, walking along."

"What did you do?"

"I followed him."

"Where did he go?"

"He walked east to Park Avenue, down a block to 33rd Street, and went into the subway."

"What did he do there?"

"Well, there were some bums with blankets camped out at the far end of the station. He walked down there and began talking with them."

"What did you do?"

"There was a pay phone in the station. I called Jason Tindel, told him to rush the papers over."

"The commitment papers?"

"That's right."

"How is it you had commitment papers ready?"

"Jason and I had previously approached a doctor at Bellevue Hospital and apprised him of the situation. He drew up the papers, and told us if we could locate Jack Walsh, he would have him brought in for observation."

"So you called Jason Tindel and told him to bring the papers?"

"That's right."

"What happened then?"

"I stayed in the station, keeping my eye on Jack Walsh. About forty-five minutes later Jason showed up with two hospital orderlies. They served the papers on Jack and took him off to Bellevue."

"Did he object?"

"Yes, he did."

"How?"

"Screaming, kicking. He was like a wild man."

"How did the orderlies subdue him?"

"With a straight jacket."

"Jack Walsh was taken to Bellevue in a straight jacket?"

"That's right."

"Did you accompany him to Bellevue?"

"Yes, I did."

"Along with Jason Tindel?"

"That's right."

"What happened there?"

"A psychiatrist examined him and ordered him committed."

"Was the examination done in your presence?"

"No, it wasn't."

Judge Washburn frowned. "I think that's all. Do you have anything else, Mr. Franklyn?"

"No, Your Honor."

"Mr. Winslow?"

"Yes. Mr. Grayson, are you employed?"

"Yes, I am."

"What do you do?"

"I'm a diamond broker."

"Is that right? Where is your place of business?"

"I operate out of my own home."

"And where is that?"

"Teaneck, New Jersey."

"Teaneck, New Jersey? Is that also the home of Jason Tindel?"

"Yes, it is."

"Now, when you say a diamond broker—that means you sell diamonds?"

"That's right."

"But a diamond broker's different than a diamond merchant, isn't it?"

"Yes, it is."

"In what way?"

"A diamond merchant sells gems. A diamond broker arranges sales."

"I see. In other words, you don't sell your own gems?"

"No."

"You have no stock or inventory? No diamonds of your own?"

"That's right."

"You find a person who wants to buy diamonds, and another person who wants to sell diamonds, and you act as a middleman?"

"Yes."

"Now you say you conduct your business out of your own home?"

"That's right."

"Which is Teaneck, New Jersey?"

"That's right."

"Is that the same place you were conducting your business from a year ago?"

"No, it is not."

"And where were you conducting your business from then?"

"Great Neck."

"That's also where you were living?"

"That's right."

"Is that also where Jason Tindel was living?"

"That's right."

"The place in Great Neck, where you and Jason Tindel were living and where you were conducting business—was that also the house of the petitioner Jack Walsh?"

"That's right."

"How long had you been living there?"

"For twelve years."

"I see. So when Jack Walsh sold the house out from under himself, he also sold it out from under you and Jason Tindel, is that right?"

"Yes."

"Tell me, had you ever paid any rent on the house in Great Neck?"

"No."

"You'd been living there for twelve years, and never paid any rent?"

"Uncle Jack wouldn't charge his relatives rent."

"I see. But you *are* paying rent on the house in Teaneck?"

"Yes, I am."

"Gee," Steve said. "After twelve years of not paying any rent at all, that must be a considerable shock. Tell me something— if Jason and Rose Tindel are declared conservators of Jack Walsh's estate—would you stop paying rent then?"

"I don't know."

"You never discussed that matter with them?"

"No, I did not."

"The matter ever cross your mind?"

After a pause, the witness said, "No."

"Then you have no interest whatsoever in the outcome of this hearing?" Steve said.

"I want to see that Uncle Jack's interests are protected."

"By protected you mean placed in the hands of Jason and Rose Tindel? The people with whom you have not discussed whether this action would enable you to stop paying rent?" Steve smiled. "Thank you. I have no further questions, Your Honor."

"That's all Mr. Grayson," Judge Washburn said. He glanced at his notes. "It is at this point that I would like to question the petitioner. Unfortunately, he's unavailable. Now, Mr. Franklyn, you say you have a psychiatrist here to testify to that effect?"

"That's right. A Dr. Gerald Feldspar. He is on the staff at Bellevue Hospital, and is the doctor who admitted Jack Walsh."

"Very well. Dr. Feldspar take the stand."

Dr. Feldspar turned out to be a plump little man, some sixty years old. He wore thick-lensed glasses, and had a rather pompous manner. He bustled up to the witness stand, sat down, pushed his glasses back on his nose, and peered up at the judge in a manner that bordered on insolence.

"You name is Dr. Gerald Feldspar?"

"That's right."

"What is you occupation?"

"I am a psychiatrist at Bellevue Hospital."

"Are you acquainted with Jack Walsh, the petitioner in this action?"

"I am. He is a patient in my care."

"At Bellevue Hospital?"

"That is correct."

"How long has he been there?"

"He was brought in two days ago."

"And you were the doctor who admitted him?"

"That's right."

"Could you describe the circumstances under which you committed the petitioner?"

"Certainly. It was about three in the afternoon. I was summoned to my office with the news that a patient had been brought in. I arrived to find that two hospital orderlies had brought in the subject. He was a white male, some seventy-five years of age. He was unshaved, uncombed, unwashed, dressed in close to rags. He was disoriented, irrational, incoherent. He was also violent and had been subdued by a straight jacket."

"What did you do?"

"I attempted to calm him down and reason with him. Which was, I'm afraid, next to impossible. Upon examination I discovered the subject to be a paranoid schizophrenic with psychopathic tendencies. In, I might add, a very advanced state."

"You ordered him committed at that time?"

"I did."

Judge Washburn picked up a paper from his bench. "Doctor, are you aware that his attorney has filed a writ of *habeas corpus*, asking that the petitioner, Jack Walsh, be released, and that the court has issued a ruling to the effect that he be produced at this hearing?"

"Yes, I am."

"Then why is he not here?"

"He is not competent to be here, Your Honor."

"I understand your contention. Could you elaborate?"

"Yes, Your Honor. Certainly, Your Honor. As I said, the patient is confused and disoriented. He also suffers from delusions of persecution. His advanced state of paranoia makes the patient very hard to reach. It also makes him violent. I have no doubt that given time we will be able to help him to some degree, but at the present time he is a danger to himself and to others. At any rate, his presence here in court would serve no purpose. He is not competent to understand these proceedings, let alone take part in them. To bring him into court now would only confuse and frighten him, and deepen his neurosis, and make our job of reaching him that much harder."

"I see," Judge Washburn said. "Mr. Franklyn. Have you anything to add?"

Franklyn rose. "Just a couple of questions, Your Honor. I'd like to make one point clear. Dr. Feldspar, did I notify you of the court order to produce the petitioner at this hearing?"

"Yes, you did."

"As well as the *habeas corpus* served on Jason Tindel?"

"Yes, you did."

"Did Jason Tindel also inform you of that fact?"

"Yes, he did."

"Then the fact that Jack Walsh is not here in court has nothing to do with any failure on my part or on Jason Tindel's part to comply with the *habeas corpus*, is that right?"

"Absolutely. Mr. Walsh is not here for medical reasons, as I have testified."

"Thank you, Doctor. That's all."

Judge Washburn said, "Mr. Winslow?"

Steve Winslow took his time. He rose slowly, walked around the table, stopped, and looked around the courtroom. First at the judge, then at Franklyn, then at Mark Taylor and Tracy Garvin, who were seated just behind his table, then at the relatives, and finally at Dr. Feldspar.

"Medical reasons?" he asked.

"Yes."

"By that you mean psychiatric reasons?"

"That's correct."

Steve chuckled softly and shook his head. "Well now, Dr. Feldspar, I must say I have some trouble following this." Steve gestured around the courtroom. "This is a competency hearing. The purpose of this hearing, as I understand it, is to determine whether or not Jack Walsh is competent. And yet, here you are, testifying that he's not competent to take part in it."

"That happens to be the case."

"I understand your contention. It just seems like something out of Joseph Heller, doesn't it?"

"I beg your pardon?"

"Referring to the novel, *Catch 22*. You say Jack Walsh isn't competent. I say he is. I say, O.K., bring him here and we'll prove it. You say, no I can't do that. I say, why? You say, because he isn't competent." Steve shrugged. "Little bit of a problem there, Doctor. I understand you're a psychiatrist, but it seems to me you've also made yourself judge and jury."

Dr. Feldspar drew himself up indignantly. "I've done nothing of the sort. I'm giving you an expert medical opinion based on the existing facts. Now you may not happen to like it, but it happens to be the case."

Steve smiled. "Ah, Doctor, interesting word. *Opinion.* That's just it. It is your opinion that Jack Walsh is incompetent. It is my opinion that he's not. So it seems we have a difference of opinion. On the very matter we want the court to decide. Fine. Then let's discuss it. What is the basis for your opinion, Doctor?"

"I'm afraid as a layman, you couldn't possibly understand."

"Well, I'm willing to try. Go ahead, Doctor. Let's talk diagnosis, prognosis, and the care and feeding of the paranoid schizophrenic."

"Oh, Your Honor," Franklyn protested.

"Yes, yes," Judge Washburn said. "Mr. Winslow, if you could try to avoid such flippancy."

"Sorry, Your Honor," Steve said. "All right, Doctor, you ordered Jack Walsh committed. Let's talk about that. You say you were summoned to your office, you found two orderlies had brought in a man in a straight jacket?"

"That's right."

"And was this the petitioner, Jack Walsh?"

"Yes."

"You examined him and ordered him committed?"

"That's correct."

"Tell me about the examination."

"I beg your pardon?"

"What did you do? What tests did you administer that allowed you to conclude that Jack Walsh was insane?"

"I've already stated. I attempted to reason with him."

"Which you could not do?"

"That's right. The man was violent and abusive. He could not be reached."

"If you couldn't reach him, how could you examine him?"

Dr. Feldspar smiled frostily. "Now *you're* the one invoking Joseph Heller, Counselor. If the patient is too insane to be examined, he can't be certified insane?"

Steve smiled. "Touché, Doctor. Are you stating that such was the case?"

"Not at all. I examined him thoroughly before I committed him."

"So we come back to my original question. How did you examine him?"

"As I said, I tried to reason with him. Unfortunately, he was irrational."

"So what did you do?"

"I administered certain tests."

"What sort of tests?"

"I doubt if the specifics are of any relevance."

"We'll be the judge of that, Doctor. If we can't have Jack Walsh here, we'll have the reason why. Go on. What sort of tests?"

"I tested him for rational thought. Coherence."

"In what way?"

"Nothing complicated, I assure you," Dr. Feldspar said. "I administered the type of test that could be understood by a ten-year-old."

"Such as?"

"Simple word association. I asked him to complete a sentence for me. Again, nothing complicated. I'm talking about simple proverbs, something any ten-year-old child would know."

"Such as?"

"Well, for instance, a rolling stone gathers no moss."

"A rolling stone gathers no moss?"

"Yes."

"You said to Jack Walsh, 'A rolling stone gathers no moss?' "

Doctor Feldspar shook his head. "No."

"Oh? I thought you said you did?"

"No, no. You don't understand. I asked him to complete the phrase. I said to him, 'A rolling stone.' His task was to complete the phrase by saying, 'gathers no moss.' "

"Did he do so?"

"He did not. Despite several opportunities."

"Jack Walsh never said, 'gathers no moss?' "

"No."

"What *did* he say?"

"I beg your pardon?"

"Well, did he refuse to answer, or did he say something else?"

"He replied with *non sequiturs*. Irrational and illogical."

"And abusive?"

"Yes."

"Generally abusive, or abusive toward you?"

"Both."

"Ah," Steve said. "That's interesting. Let's talk about the abuse directed toward you. I take it Mr. Walsh made several unflattering remarks?"

"That's putting it mildly."

"Perhaps reflecting upon your person?"

"That's right."

Steve smiled. "And perhaps a few suggestions, which if taken literally, could have imperiled your physical well-being?"

Dr. Feldspar shifted in his chair. "That is correct," he snapped.

"I see," Steve said. "Now, tell me. What other tests did you administer?"

"No other tests."

"That was all?"

"That was quite sufficient in my opinion."

"You certified Mr. Walsh insane on the basis of that one test?"

Dr. Feldspar drew himself up indignantly. "I did not. I most certainly did not. You are putting words in my mouth. That was the only *test* I administered, but that was *not* the only basis for my certification."

"Oh? What other basis was there?"

"There were dozens."

"Such as?"

Dr. Feldspar smiled. "Come, come, Counselor. When a wealthy man chooses to dress in rags and live on the subways with the bums and bag ladies—"

Steve held up his hand. "Whoa. One minute, Doctor. Hold it right there. You don't *know* Jack Walsh lived on the subway, do you?"

"Yes, I do."

"You ever *see* Jack Walsh on the subway?"

"No."

"Ever observe him hanging out with bums and bag ladies?"

"No."

"No, I didn't think so, Doctor. You only know that from what Jason Tindel and Fred Grayson told you, don't you?"

"Naturally."

"But that's hearsay, Doctor. That's not admissible in a court of law."

"I'm not a court of law. I'm a qualified psychiatrist."

"I understand. But we're in a court of law now, Doctor. And these things must be proven.

"Let's go back to the commitment of Jack Walsh. Are you saying now you based your commitment of Jack Walsh on things people told you?"

"Certainly not. I based it on my own examination."

"But you just brought up his living on the subway, something you only learned from Fred Grayson and Jason Tindel."

"That is a factor. It may not be admissible in a court of law, but it is certainly a factor. I have to weigh all aspects of the situation."

"I understand. And one of those aspects is the fact that Jason Tindel and Fred Grayson told you Jack Walsh was living on the subway, isn't it?"

"It's a factor to be considered."

"But let me ask you this, Doctor. Suppose I were to offer evidence that Jason Tindel and Fred Grayson were irrational, insane, and not competent to manage *their* affairs. Would that in any way change your opinion of the sanity of Jack Walsh?"

"That's absurd."

"Why is it absurd?"

"Because it isn't true."

"Oh? How do you know?"

"Because I've talked to both Jason Tindel and Fred Grayson." Dr. Feldspar pointed. "They're here in court now. They're both rational and quite sane."

"How do you know, Doctor? Did you ever test them? Did you ever go up to them and say, 'A rolling stone?' "

Dr. Feldspar took a breath. He looked up at the judge. "Your Honor, do I have to put up with this?"

Judge Washburn nodded. "Counsel is perhaps overzealous

and unorthodox, but he is within his rights. Continue, Mr. Winslow."

"Thank you, Your Honor. Doctor, you're stating unequivocably that Jason Tindel and Fred Grayson are sane?"

"Yes, I am."

"Based on no clinical examination, but only on your discussions with them?"

"That is enough."

"Is it, Doctor? Isn't it possible for an insane man to masquerade as a sane one?"

"It is."

"Then how do you know this isn't such a case?"

"I'm a trained psychiatrist. I could not be fooled."

"Could you be lied to?"

"I beg your pardon?"

"Could you be lied to? By a sane man, I mean. Suppose I could prove to you that Fred Grayson and Jason Tindel had every reason to lie to you—the motivation being greed and profit—could you be taken in by a lie?"

"No, I could not."

"You could not, Doctor?"

"No. If they were lying to me, I would know it."

"How?"

"As a psychiatrist, I am a trained observer. I can tell when someone is lying."

"Really, Doctor? Then I can't understand why you're here."

Dr. Feldspar frowned. "What?"

"Yes. I don't know why someone with your unique talent hasn't been snapped up by the Pentagon. You're wasting your time at Bellevue. You should be down in Washington exposing spies and counterspies. Why, the country would never have to worry again."

Franklyn was on his feet. "Oh, Your Honor."

"Exactly," Judge Washburn said. "Mr. Winslow, I have warned you before. There is no jury here, and I am not going to be taken in by such remarks. So there's no real harm done. But please, let's try to confine ourselves to the task at hand."

"Sorry, Your Honor," Steve said. "But I hope the point is well taken. With regard to the relevance of what Dr. Feldspar may have been told. Would you sustain me on that point?"

"I'll go further than that," Judge Washburn said. "Mr. Winslow's questions may seem facetious, but the central point is not. Doctor, you were ordered to produce the petitioner in court. You declined to do so. Now, in making that decision, you had better have relied on what you personally observed as a trained psychiatrist, and not on what someone told you. Is that clear?"

"Yes, Your Honor."

"Fine. Then try to be responsive to Mr. Winslow's questions by answering them with what you personally observed.

"Proceed, Mr. Winslow."

"Thank you, Your Honor. Now, Dr. Feldspar, let's talk about what you personally observed. So far, you seem to have committed Jack Walsh on the basis of one test. Was there anything else?"

"Of course," Dr. Feldspar said, irritably. "I started to explain when you went off on a tangent."

"I beg your pardon. You'll have every opportunity to explain. In fact, this is just that opportunity. What else did you observe?"

"As I said, the man was irrational, incoherent, and violent."

"I see," Steve said. "Now, the irrationality and incoherence you've explained as his failure to converse with you or to respond to that particular test. Let's move on to the violence. In what manner was he violent?"

"He was struggling, kicking, screaming."

"Two male orderlies were holding him?"

"That's right."

"They had just dragged him into your office?"

"Yes."

"Against his will?"

"That's right."

"So," Steve said. "Tell me something. Does anyone want to be committed, Doctor?"

"Some people do."

"Yes, I'm sure they do. But the vast majority—do they want to be committed?"

"No."

"So your average man in the street—if someone grabbed him and dragged him into a mental institution, don't you think he would be apt to protest?"

"Perhaps."

"And struggle to free himself?"

"Possibly."

"So the fact that Jack Walsh was kicking and struggling doesn't necessarily mean that he was insane, does it, Doctor?"

"As I say, that was not the only factor."

"What were the other factors, Doctor? Talking only about what you personally observed."

"Very well," Dr. Feldspar snapped. "I observed a man some seventy-five years of age. He was dressed in rags, or close to it. He was unwashed and his hair was uncombed. It was long hair, long, messy, unkempt. His appearance, to all intents and purposes, was that of a wild man. He was kicking and screaming. He was incoherent, abusive and violent.

"Now then," Dr. Feldspar said. "I saw all that with my own eyes. And I am a trained clinical psychiatrist. But I must tell you, it would not *take* a trained clinical psychiatrist to see that the man was insane.

"Now, you can split hairs all you want, but the simple fact of the matter is, Jack Walsh is not a sane man. And nothing you can say is going to make him so."

"Is that right, Doctor?" Steve said. "Well, let me see if I have this straight. As I understand it, Jack Walsh was dragged into your office by two male orderlies. He attempted to resist this, and was violent, abusive and incoherent. In addition to that, he was wearing shabby clothes and his hair was long and unkempt. Plus he failed to respond correctly to the phrase, 'A rolling stone.' Is that right?"

"That is a gross oversimplification—"

"Perhaps it is. But let me ask you this, Doctor. You notice that I have long hair and I'm not particularly well dressed. In the event two hospital orderlies yanked me off the street, clapped me in a straight jacket, hauled me into your office, and while I was kicking and screaming and attempting to free myself, you came up to me and said, 'A rolling stone,' are you telling me that if I said 'gathers no moss,' you would decide I was sane and set me free? Whereas on the other hand, if you came up to me and said, 'A rolling stone,' and I said, 'Mick Jagger,' you'd declare me a lunatic and have me committed?"

Dr. Feldspar frowned. "Mick Jagger?"

Steve chuckled, shook his head. "A vague, obscure reference, Doctor. I'm sorry it went over your head.

"At any rate, is that essentially true? If I said, 'gathers no moss,' you would set me free, but if I said anything else— perhaps suggested what you could do with your hospital—you would have me committed?"

"That isn't fair."

"No?"

"No."

"Well, maybe not, but I think it's accurate." Steve Winslow turned to the judge. "I submit, Your Honor, that this man has shown no basis whatsoever for failing to produce Jack Walsh in court. I demand that he be produced."

Judge Washburn took a breath. "Dr. Feldspar," he said. "A court order is not to be taken lightly. I have listened to your testimony carefully. I must say I can find in it no reason to warrant your disobeying the directive of the court. I also feel that your sparring with counsel is profitless to say the least. So I'm going to make another directive. I'm going to stand in recess for half an hour. In that time I expect you to get on the phone to Bellevue Hospital. I expect you to order your staff to get Jack Walsh here by the end of the recess. If he's truly incompetent to be here, that fact will be readily evident. At any rate, that seems to be the only way to settle the matter. You have half an hour get him here. Court is now in recess."

Steve Winslow smiled at the judge, then at the doctor. He still had a big smile on his face when he turned to Mark Taylor and Tracy Garvin.

But under his breath he said, "Oh shit."

# 9

As the court officers led Jack Walsh into the courtroom, Steve Winslow realized his most fervent prayer had not been answered. Apparently Walsh had resisted all efforts on the part of the staff of Bellevue Hospital to modify his appearance. His stubble was unshaven, his face was unwashed, and his hair was uncombed. On top of that, whatever drugs they'd been giving him to damp him down had reduced his pupils to pinpoints, and given his eyes a glassy quality that made them seem to glow on their own. The end effect was not just to give him the appearance of a lunatic. Jack Walsh looked like a demon straight from hell.

His manner wasn't helping matters any either. He kept muttering and growling and trying to twist away from the court officers. The officers were smiling at each other and saying soothing things to him, which only served to further enrage him.

Fortunately, they'd come in through the side door, so the distance to the witness stand was relatively short. Nonetheless, their progress was slow.

Steve Winslow tore his eyes away from Walsh long enough to glance up at the judge's bench. Judge Washburn was a seasoned jurist, who'd undoubtedly presided over hundreds of competency hearings. As such, he naturally retained an air of judicial impartiality. He wasn't rolling his eyes to the ceiling, or glancing pointedly at either of the attorneys. Still, his eyes spoke volumes. Behind the judicial façade there was an ordinary man saying to himself, as any man would, "Why me?"

Eventually Jack Walsh was installed on the witness stand. Once that was accomplished the court officers withdrew, but remained standing and alert, ready to jump in again at a moment's notice.

Judge Washburn looked down at him from the bench. "Mr. Walsh?"

Jack Walsh gripped the arms of the witness stand. His mouth was set in a firm line. He turned to glare up at the judge with his demon eyes. "Yes?" he snapped.

"Mr. Walsh," the judge said in a fatherly tone. "I'm Judge Washburn. I have to ask you some questions. First of all, are you aware that this is a courtroom?"

Walsh exhaled noisily and shook his head. "Sheesh." He held up his hand, then pointed his finger at the judge. "First of all, Your Honor, we'll do a lot better if you stop talking to me as if I were a child of four. Yes, I am aware this is a courtroom. Now, no one will say anything to me except, 'there, there,' and 'take it easy old timer,' but I would assume this is a competency hearing. In which case, the bone of contention here is whether a bunch of greedy relatives who can't wait for me to die can find a legal way to get their hands on my money any sooner." Walsh squinted up at the judge. "Am I right so far?"

Judge Washburn smiled slightly. "That is not exactly the way I would have phrased it."

"Of course not," Walsh said. "You're a judge. You're impartial. You can't make irresponsible statements. You're not going to call my relatives greedy, and you're not going to refer to me as the nut-case, but that's what's going on here. Well, I ain't a judge, so I'm free to say what I like." Walsh shrugged. "At least to an extent."

Judge Washburn frowned. "What do you mean by that?"

"Well," Walsh said, "considering the nature of these proceedings, I understand an irresponsible statement could cost me my freedom."

"That's going a little far, Mr. Walsh," Judge Washburn said. "No one's going to judge you on a slip of the tongue. And any statement you make, you will have an opportunity to explain. Before we go any further, I just want you to understand that."

"I understand that. So now what?"

"As I said, I'm going to ask you some questions. I'd like you to answer as freely and as fully as you like."

"Fire away."

"So far I've heard the story of your incarceration in Bellevue from Jason Tindel, who signed the commitment paper, from Fred Grayson, who observed you on the subway, and from Dr. Feldspar, the psychiatrist in charge of your case."

Walsh snorted and shook his head.

"Yes," Judge Washburn said. "I'm sure you have opinions

about that. And you'll have an opportunity to express them. But first, having heard their stories, I'd now like to get it from you. So to begin with, in your own words just tell me what happened."

"Well," Walsh said, "I was in the subway station. Thirty-third and Lex. IRT line. I was talking to one of the homeless men down there. Suddenly two men approached me. Hospital orderlies in white uniforms. They called me by name, asked me to go with them."

"What did you do?"

"Told them to get lost."

"What did they do?"

"They kept hassling me. They had the papers, and I had to go with them."

"Papers? What papers?"

Walsh shrugged. "I assume they meant commitment papers. One guy waved a paper at me, but he didn't say what it was. They had the papers, and I had to go."

"So what did you do?"

"I told him what he could do with his papers."

Judge Washburn smiled slightly. "And what did they do?"

"When they saw I wasn't going to cooperate, they started circling me sort of. Then they jumped me, grabbed me, wrestled me to the ground. One guy held me while the other guy got a straight jacket on me."

"Did you protest?"

"What, are you nuts? I screamed and kicked and yelled bloody murder."

"What happened to the other man? The man you were talking to?"

"He ran." Walsh shrugged. "I can't say that I blame him. For all he knew, they were after him too."

"What happened then?"

"They dragged me out of the station, threw me in a van and ran me down to Bellevue."

"What happened there?"

"They wrestled me inside where some lunatic in a white coat with a clipboard came up and started screaming proverbs in my face. Frankly, by that time I was slightly incoherent. As I recall, I made a few choice remarks about his hospital, his proverbs, and his parentage, as well as a few suggestions involving certain choice portions of his anatomy."

"What happened then?"

"They locked me in a room, shot me full of drugs."

"What kind of drugs?"

"You think they told me? It was all 'there, there,' and 'this is for your own good.'"

"Did you object to taking the drugs?"

"Are you kidding? I wouldn't swallow nothing. When they tried to stick me, I broke the needle."

"Then how'd they get you to take them?"

"Two guys held me, one guy stuck me."

"How often did they give you drugs?"

"Whenever they damn well felt like it."

"Could you be more specific?"

"No, I couldn't. It's hard to tell time when you're doped up and locked in a room. Besides, sometimes the drugs would knock me out. All I know is, as soon as I wake up they come in and stick me again.

"Once I woke up and they were trying to shave me. They tried when I was awake and I wouldn't let 'em do it, so they tried when I was asleep."

Judge Washburn looked at him. "They don't seem to have succeeded."

"No, they didn't. I woke up, screamed, flailed my arm, broke the damn electric razor. After that they gave up trying."

"Why do you object to shaving?"

"I don't object to shaving. I object to *being shaved.* Big difference. I object on principle to anything being done to me against my will. If you can't understand that, there's no point in this hearing."

"I didn't say I can't understand that, Mr. Walsh. I just want to get your point of view."

"You got it. What else you want to know?"

Jack Walsh was so swift on the returns Judge Washburn was momentarily taken aback. He took a few seconds to gather himself. "Well now," he said. "As you understand, this is a competency hearing. Certain allegations have been made to the effect that you're not competent to handle your affairs. This hearing is for the purpose of determining whether these allegations are true. Now, as part of these allegations, I have heard testimony from certain witnesses regarding your behavior. Behavior which, if taken at face value, could be construed not to be the acts of a rational man. We have the testimony of two of your relatives . . ." Judge Washburn referred to his notes. ". . . Mr. Jason Tindel and Mr. Fred Grayson, to the effect that recently you sold your house out from under you, that you have no fixed address, and that you have taken to living on the subway in the manner of an indigent, when in fact you actually have ample funds to live anywhere you wish.

"Now, I'd like to give you an opportunity to reply to these allegations. So I ask you, are the allegations of your relatives true?"

Jack Walsh scowled. He squinted up at the judge. "You keep calling them my relatives. Jason Tindel and Fred Grayson happened to marry into the family. I don't see that that makes them kinfolk, somehow."

"Very well," Judge Washburn said. "Your in–laws, then. How's that?"

"Fine. In–law is where we are, and what this is all about. I quite approve." Jack Walsh punctuated this by nodding in agreement with himself.

Judge Washburn frowned and took a breath.

Steve Winslow stirred restlessly. Jack Walsh was making no effort to answer the question. Instead he was engaging in various evasions and deflections. In short, acting like a man with something to hide.

Judge Washburn cleared his throat. His voice took on a slightly insistent tone. "Mr. Walsh, what reason would your in-laws have for making these statements?"

"Because they're stupid."

Judge Washburn frowned. "That's hardly a complete answer."

"Also because they're greedy." Walsh nodded judiciously. "Yeah. Greedy and stupid. That about covers it."

Judge Washburn exhaled. "Mr. Walsh—"

"Yeah, I know, I know," Walsh said. "I have to prove I'm

sane. Funny, isn't it? If I were charged with a crime I'd be presumed innocent until proven guilty. Here it's the other way around. Some guy says I'm crazy, and the burden of proof is on me to prove I'm sane." Walsh squinted up at the judge. "Something a little wrong with that, isn't there?"

"Mr. Walsh, that is not exactly the case—"

"It's close enough. You'll pardon me if I don't take kindly to it. Understand, I have no contempt of court. I do have a certain amount of contempt for my in-laws."

"I understand, Mr. Walsh. Still, I am the judge, and I have to make my ruling. Now that may be unfair, but it happens to be the law. So any way you can assist me in doing it, I would appreciate. Now, with regard to the specific allegations: it has been stated that recently you sold the house in which you were living out from under yourself. Is that true?"

Walsh nodded. "Yes. And out from under my relatives. That's what really set them off." Walsh looked up at the judge. "I suppose you'd like me to tell you why?"

"That would help."

"Right. I have to justify my actions. They don't have to justify theirs."

Steve Winslow shifted in his seat, started to get up. He thought better of it. Nothing he could do at this point was going to help. Jack Walsh was going to have to sink or swim by himself.

Judge Washburn took a breath. "I think I stated my position, Mr. Walsh. At any rate, this is your opportunity to explain. If you care to do so."

Walsh nodded. "Yeah, I care to do so. O.K. Here's the story. My relatives, I'm sorry to say, are a rather shiftless lot. Particularly my in-laws. I don't want to bore you with specifics, but the fact is, there isn't a wage-earner among 'em. In a way it's my fault—they've always had me to lean on. They lived in my house, ate my food. Why the hell should they work?

"Only lately it got worse. In the last year. Suggestions started cropping up. I was getting old. I wasn't going to live forever. Inheritance taxes were astronomical. Wouldn't it be nice to get around some of them? How? By making certain gifts during my lifetime. Suggestions of that kind.

"Well, needless to say, I didn't take kindly to such suggestions. I didn't make any big deal about it, I just ignored 'em. But they got more and more persistent.

"Then they stopped talking altogether. That was somewhat strange. I wondered why.

"Then one day I overheard Jason and Fred talking. You know what they were talking about?" Walsh spread his arms wide. "Just what we're doin' here. Declaring me incompetent and grabbin' the cash.

"Well, pardon me, Your Honor, but that was the last straw. I did not need people living in my own house who were plotting against me to get my money. As far as I was concerned, that was beyond all bounds. I confronted them, and told them they could get out."

"What happened?"

"They laughed at me. Said I didn't mean it. I was an old man, I didn't know what I was doing."

Walsh shrugged. "Well, I was stuck. I didn't know what to do. If they wouldn't leave, I couldn't make 'em. I mean, I could have started legal proceedings to have 'em evicted, but I figured that would be playing right into their hands. Only a crazy man would try to get the law to throw his relatives out of his own house. If I instituted proceedings, they'd use the fact that I'd done so to try to get me certified insane.

"So I couldn't do that. But I couldn't live in the same house with them, not under those circumstances. So I thought it over and decided if they weren't going to leave, I would."

Walsh stopped and shook his head. "That was an awfully galling situation. I mean, it was my house, damn it. Why should I go and let them stay?

"So I figured there was only one thing to do. I'd sell the house out from under them. I hated to do it, but I couldn't live with them, and I was damned if I was going to let them run me out and leave them in charge."

Walsh shrugged. "So I sold the house."

Judge Washburn nodded. "And went to live on the subway?"

Walsh made a face. "What, are you nuts? Why should I live on the subway?"

Judge Washburn frowned. "Mr. Walsh, we have the testimony of Jason Tindel and Fred Grayson that you told them you were going to live on the subway. Is that true?"

"Yes, I did. And if you wanna declare me insane for making a facetious remark, I suppose you have the right to do so."

"Are you saying—"

"Yes I am. I made a wisecrack. A stupid remark. If they took it seriously, it shows how bright they are.

"When I sold the house they were hysterical. They were all over me. 'You can't do that. Are you crazy? Where are you going to live?' I said, 'I don't know, I don't care, I'd rather live on the subway with the bums than in this house with you.' It was a flippant remark and they took it for gospel. What can I tell you?"

"You're saying you don't live on the subway?"

"Of course not."

"Where do you live?"

"I got a room at the Holiday Inn on 57th Street. I had it ever since I sold the house. I didn't know how long I'd need it for, so I booked it for a year." Walsh shrugged. "Little expensive, but I got the money."

Franklyn struggled to his feet. "Your Honor, this comes as a bit of a surprise. There is no evidence in this case that this man has ever had a room anywhere, and—"

Judge Washburn held up his hand. "Sit down, Mr. Franklyn. Your surprise is noted. This will of course be checked out."

Judge Washburn turned back to the witness. "Mr. Walsh, you say you've been staying at the Holiday Inn on 57th Street?"

"That's right."

"You have a key for the room?"

"Not on me. I leave it with the desk."

"Your possessions are in that room?"

"My immediate possessions. Most of my stuff is stored in a warehouse in Brooklyn. My necessities are at the Holiday Inn."

"Yet, Mr. Walsh, we have the testimony of Jason Tindel to the fact that he ran into you in the street, and without your knowledge, he followed you to see where you would go. And on that occasion you went down in the subway and took up residence with the homeless there. What do you say to that?"

Walsh grinned. "What Jason Tindel don't know would fill a book. Without my knowledge, did you say? On that occasion, as you call it, I spotted Jason Tindel well before he spotted me. When I saw he was spying on me, I must admit I decided to yank his chain a bit. He wanted to see how I was living. Well, I told him I was living on the subway, so let him think I was. As soon as he started following me, I went down in the subway and started talking to the homeless there. I knew it would drive him nuts."

"And the time you were taken to Bellevue?"

"Same thing. Fred Grayson saw me in the street. Started tagging along. So I led him down in the subway. What I didn't know was that they'd already been in cahoots with a shrink and had commitment papers drawn. Evidently while I was down there Fred Grayson called for reinforcements, Jason Tindel rounded up the Bellevue orderlies, and you know the rest."

"I see," Judge Washburn said. "There is another allegation, Mr. Walsh, that you drew out close to two hundred thousand dollars from your bank account, and that you have been wandering around with the money on you in cash."

"Oh yeah?" Walsh said. "Funny the shrinks at Bellevue didn't mention it. Now I admit those guys are not very swift, but you'd think if I'd checked in there with two hundred grand on me, even *they* would have noticed it."

"You do not have two hundred thousand dollars in cash?"

"Of course not."

"You withdrew it from the bank."

"Yes I did. I did it so these fine gentlemen here couldn't freeze my bank account and keep me from using my own money. But carry it on me? Don't be silly. I merely switched banks. I have a new account with Chase Manhattan. You can check with them.

"You also might check with my stockbroker. Two hundred grand's chicken feed. Most of my money's in stocks and bonds. If you check with my broker you'll find I made almost that much this year playing the stock market.

"But don't tell the guy you're thinking of declaring me incompetent. Poor guy might have a stroke. I'm his biggest source of income."

"I see," Judge Washburn said. "And, uh, the manner in which you're dressed?"

"Is my own damn business. It happens to be a free country and I can dress as I like. I got this coat at Good Will. It's warm and fits me fine.

"And I like it. You know why I like it? I dress this way, and no one thinks I got any money. Nobody bothers me. If you never had money, you don't know what that's like. I'm tired of people hassling me about money, so I dress like I ain't got it and they leave me alone."

Walsh's eyes gleamed. He grinned and jerked his thumb over his shoulder. "And, I must admit, I do it to irritate them. To stick the knife in.

"But I'm sorry about all this. I'm particularly sorry I had to tell you about my room at the Holiday Inn. Now I'll have to give it up. Move. Now they know where I live, I can't live there no more." Walsh shook his head. "Bit of a shame, that."

Judge Washburn took a breath, blew it out again. Thought a moment. "Can you tell me the address of your branch bank? And the name of your broker?"

Walsh told him and the judge wrote it down.

"Very well," Judge Washburn said. "I'm going to take a brief recess. If the parties will please remain in court, this should only take a few minutes."

Judge Washburn went through the door in the back of the courtroom into his chambers. He was back ten minutes later and resumed his place on the bench.

"Let us proceed," Judge Washburn said. "During the recess I've been on the phone with the Chase Manhattan Bank, where Mr. Walsh does indeed have an account. I have also been on the phone with his broker. Also the Holiday Inn.

"These phone conversations bear out Mr. Walsh's testimony entirely. According to his broker, Mr. Walsh is not only competent to carry out his business, he's most extraordinarily adept at it.

"The court is now going to rule. The court finds no basis whatsoever for considering Mr. Walsh incompetent. The court feels that attempts to incarcerate him and have him declared incompetent have *not* been for his own good or to save him from himself, but were motivated purely out of personal gain.

"Furthermore, the court finds no valid reason for said incarceration. And finds the explanation of Dr. Feldspar inadequate at best."

Judge Washburn fixed Dr. Feldspar with a cold glare. "And you, Doctor, will have an opportunity to appear before me to show cause why I should not consider your failure to respond to the *habeas corpus* and to produce the petitioner at this hearing to be contempt of court.

"As far as these proceedings are concerned, the *habeas corpus* is granted, and the petitioner is released."

# 10

IT WAS ALL STEVE WINSLOW, Mark Taylor and Tracy Garvin could do to contain Jack Walsh during the taxi ride back to the office. It was no small feat getting him out of court, either. Fortunately, Judge Washburn had retired after announcing his decision and did not witness Jack Walsh's post-trial performance, or he might have ordered him committed all over again. Jack Walsh had jumped in the air, cackled gleefully, run over to give Steve Winslow a hearty handshake, and then raced back to goad and torment his relatives. "Fools! Idiots! Bloodsuckers!" he trumpeted, dancing up and down in front of them. Mark Taylor and Steve Winslow literally had to drag him away.

He was still bouncing off the walls when he reached Steve Winslow's office. Mark Taylor sat him firmly in the clients' chair, rolled his eyes at Steve Winslow, and then went out, closing the door behind him.

Walsh bounced right up again. "We did it," he cackled. "Did you see them? Did you see the look on their faces? No-account deadbeats. We nailed 'em good."

"Yes, we did," Steve said. "Now, if you'd just sit down a minute—"

"Don't want to sit down. Been sittin' too much. Lyin' down too. Don't want to do what nobody tells me. Don't have to, do I? That's what bein' free means. That's what it's all about."

"Yes, Mr. Walsh, but—"

"Ah, the look on their faces. Jason and Fred. And that numbnuts, Carl. Sitting there in their suits and ties as if they amounted to anything. And me in my rags and dirty face. I put it to 'em, didn't I? I nailed 'em good."

"Yes, you did, Mr. Walsh. Now—"

"Not a penny. Not one penny, that's what they'll get. They'll see. They'll have to come to me now. I'm holdin' the whip."

"Yes, you are, Mr. Walsh. Now if you'll just sit down—"

"Told you. Don't wanna sit down. In fact, I don't wanna be here at all. Got things to do."

"I'm sure you do, Mr. Walsh. But first we have a few matters to settle."

"Right, right. I owe you money. You did work and you gotta be paid. Hell of a good job, too. Let's see. A day in court, plus the preparation, filin' the papers. What's that all worth? Five grand? No problem. I'll send you a check." His eyes gleamed. "Chase Manhattan Bank. Got a bankbook back at the Holiday Inn. Stupid bastards thought I'd carry cash, never thought to check the banks." Shook his head. "Assholes."

"It's not just the money, Mr. Walsh."

"Not the money? Of course it's the money. You did the work and you gotta be paid."

"Yes, but—"

"But nothing. It was damn fine work. How'd you get on to me anyway?"

"What?"

"How'd you find me? How'd you know I was there?"

"Oh."

"I was shocked as hell. The doctors wouldn't let me talk to nobody, I figured nobody knew I was there."

"The family knew."

"Right, they put me there. But aside from them—" Walsh broke off. His eyes narrowed. "Wait a minute. Are you sayin' it was one of them?"

Steve nodded.

"Well, it sure wasn't Jason, Fred or Carl. One of the women then. Don't tell me. Aunt Claire?"

Steve shook his head. "No."

"All right. Who?"

"Jeremy."

Walsh's eyes widened and his face screwed up in disbelief. "Jeremy? The punk rocker?"

"That's right."

"You're kidding. He told you? Jeremy? That dippy little kid with green hair?"

Steve nodded. "That's right. He came in here and—"

"Son of a bitch!" Walsh cackled. "Son of a bitch! Would you believe that? I got a relative after all. Jeremy. Hot damn. How the hell'd he even know?"

"He'd overheard Carl saying you'd come here. Then when they locked you up he skipped school and came here to ask me to get you out."

Walsh threw back his head and laughed. "Unbelievable. Absolutely unbelievable. Well, that changes things, don't it? Thanks for tellin' me. Jeremy. Son of a bitch."

Walsh stopped laughing and held up his hand. "Well, thanks again. I really must be going."

Steve moved fast to get himself between Walsh and the door. "Just one moment, Mr. Walsh."

"One moment? I don't have one moment. I been penned up for days and I want out of here. I told you I'll pay you, now let me go."

"There are other matters, Mr. Walsh."

"Other matters? What other matters?"

"You consulted me about a will."

"Yeah, I asked some questions. So what?"

"But you didn't tell me why you wanted to know. When I answered those questions, I had no idea what you were getting at."

"Of course you didn't. No reason why you should."

"Well there's reason now, Mr. Walsh. If I'm acting as your attorney, I have to act in your best interests."

"And that you did, my boy, and a fine job too."

Steve Winslow took a breath. "Mr. Walsh. When I answered your questions about a will, I was discussing abstract law. But apparently you weren't. There are several million dollars involved."

"That's right," Walsh said. "And it's all mine."

"Yes it is, Mr. Walsh, and you may dispose of it any way you like. The point is—"

"The point is, the point is," Walsh mimicked. "The point is, who cares? You already made the point. I can dispose of it any way I like. It's my money and I can do what I like. That's the point. The rest of the points don't matter."

"Mr. Walsh—"

"Oh boy, that feels good." Walsh stretched his arms. "Listen, I gotta get out of here."

"One moment, Mr. Walsh. We have a problem here."

"Problem? What problem? Everything's fine."

"Mr. Walsh, the questions you asked me about a will lead me to believe you may be contemplating something that is dangerous on the one hand, and illegal on the other."

"Oh yeah? Well, don't concern yourself."

"I have to, Mr. Walsh."

"No, you don't. So I asked some questions. So I was just jokin' around. It don't mean nothin'.'"

"I don't believe that."

Walsh shrugged. "You can believe what you like. You ask me, you worry too much. Anyway, I gotta get out of here. So tell me, is five thousand all right for a fee?"

"It's fine, but—"

"Good. You'll get it. If you don't, you can sue me. A good lawyer like you, you ought to win."

"Mr. Walsh—"

"Hey, I'd love to stay and talk, but right now I got problems. I had to tell 'em about the Holiday Inn. Which means Jason and Fred will be there waiting for me. Which means I gotta get out, get away from 'em, move all my stuff, find another place to live. One they don't know about. Big pain in the ass."

"Mr. Walsh—"

"Hey, you gonna let me leave or not? I gotta get a what?—a writ of *habeas corpus* to get out of here? I'm telling you. Don't worry. You did a hell of a job. I'll recommend you to all my friends. Now I gotta get out of here before those bastards get on my trail."

Jack Walsh grinned at Steve Winslow, then at Tracy Garvin. Then he jerked the door open and was gone.

Steve Winslow dived for the phone, punched in a number. "Give me Taylor."

Seconds later, Mark Taylor's voice came on the line. "Taylor here."

"Mark, Steve. He just left."

"No sweat. My men picked him up."

"Don't lose him."

"Is it that important?"

"It sure is."

"Why the hell you wanna follow your own client?"

"Frankly, I'm afraid of what he might do."

"That's not your problem, is it?"

"Maybe not, but I feel responsible. I got him released. Also, check out the Holiday Inn. I wanna confirm his story."

"The judge already checked it."

"Yeah, but you check it too. It's not enough to know he's got a room there. I wanna know what he uses it for."

"Gotcha."

"O.K. Dig out the dirt."

Steve hung up to find Tracy Garvin looking at him. "Mark Taylor asked you why you're doing this?"

"Yeah."

"That's my question too."

Steve sighed. "Like I said. I feel responsible."

"You can handle someone's legal problems. You can't run their life."

"I know."

"So?"

"Like I said, I made an error in judgment. I gave him legal advice I shouldn't have. Now I feel I gotta make up for it."

"I know that, but—"

"Plus I got him out of Bellevue. Now I know I had a legal right to do that, but still. I mean, what if that asshole doctor's right? What if he *is* crazy?"

"What if he is?"

"And what if he *is* dangerous? What if he hurts someone? Or himself?" Steve shook his head. "It's every attorney's nightmare. You do a good job, you win a case, you put a murderer back on the street, and he kills again."

"I see that, but—"

"O.K., so he's not a murderer, but still. From everything I gather, the man intends to commit a crime. That crime being fraud. He all but told me so. And I gave him advice on how to do it. If that man mocks up a will, I'll have put myself in the position of having defrauded someone out of several million dollars."

"I understand all that. But what good is following him gonna do?"

"I don't know. Maybe if he pulls something, I can stop him.

Maybe not." Steve shrugged. "At any rate, it's something to do. I feel I have to do something."

"All right. So what do we do now?"

"Nothing we can do. Just wait and see what Mark finds out."

Taylor called back two hours later. "You're not gonna like this, Steve."

"No surprise there. So far, there's nothing about this case I like. What gives?"

"My man just called in. One of the guys tailing Walsh."

"Oh yeah? Where is he?"

"Down in the subway station."

"What!?"

"I told you you weren't going to like this."

"What's he doing down there?"

"Celebrating, it looks like."

"What?"

"Yeah. My man says Walsh left your office, walked out to Broadway and started panhandling."

"What!?"

"That's right. He started begging quarters. When he got up enough money, he bought a bottle of cheap wine, walked up to Columbus Circle, and now he's down in the subway drinking with the bums down there."

"Jesus Christ."

"Yeah, and that ain't all."

"Oh yeah? What else?"

"We checked with the Holiday Inn. Apparently all Judge Washburn asked 'em was whether Jack Walsh had a room there. Which he does. Rented for the whole year, just like he said. Only thing is, he doesn't use it."

"What?"

"That's right. His stuff's up there, and his key's at the desk, just like he said. But from what we get from the desk clerks, the guy shows up once or twice a month just to get something out of his room, but that's about it. He doesn't sleep there."

"No shit."

"None. Far as we know, he actually does live on the subway."

Steve exhaled into the phone. "Oh shit."

"You said it."

"So he really is nuts."

"Nutty as a fruitcake," Taylor said.

# 11

JACK WALSH GRUNTED HIS displeasure at the black bum with the broken tooth who was hogging the bottle. He got no response. Walsh grunted again. The bum's muddy eyes rolled to him. Walsh fixed him with a hard stare and held out his hand. The bum snuffled, took one last swig, and then slowly, reluctantly handed over the bottle. Walsh snatched it back, held it close to his body. Then slowly, deliberately, he wiped off the top. Holding the bottle to his chest, elbows out like a basketball player protecting the ball, he glanced suspiciously around him for would-be thieves. Finding his bottle in no immediate danger, he raised it to his lips and took a swig.

Looking sideways around the neck of the bottle, Walsh could see the arm and shoulder of Jason Tindel, who had ducked behind a column when Walsh glanced around. Further down the platform he could make out the topcoat of Fred Grayson. And at the far end of the platform, one of the other two men who had picked him up when he left Winslow's office. Detectives, no doubt.

Walsh lowered the bottle. The black bum held out his hand. So did the younger white bum who'd been drinking with them. Walsh gave them each a look, clutched the bottle to his chest. Then raised it, took another swig. Then, with another furtive glance around, he handed it to the white bum. The black bum's bad teeth gnashed together.

The white bum took two enormous swallows. The black bum's eyes filled with rage and despair. He growled, "Hey, hey."

The black bum reached out his hand for the bottle. It was nearly empty. The white bum handed it over. Walsh intercepted it. He gave them both a proprietary look, then wiped off the bottle and took a swig.

There was one small sip left in the bottle. Walsh looked at it longingly, then in a grand gesture, handed the bottle to the black bum, who grabbed it and wolfed it down.

Walsh turned, shuffled slowly up the platform. As he left the

84

others he picked up speed. By the end of the platform he was walking at a regular pace.

He reached the stairs marked "EXIT" and "TRANSFER TO #1" and went up. As he did he grinned to himself. Jason, Fred and the detectives would be picking up speed now. Columbus Circle station was a labyrinth of tunnels connecting the IND and the IRT lines. If they didn't close in, they'd never know where he went.

He went up the steps, hung a left and walked through the tunnel that would take him under the Broadway IRT to the downtown side. He emerged at track level and headed for the downtown exit. In that direction he could take a stairway back down to the IND he'd just left, or bear right and go out any one of a number of exits from 59th to 57th Street.

He chose the closest exit, the one with the long escalator leading directly up to the street. He emerged in Columbus Circle, walked down to 57th Street, and over to the Holiday Inn.

The desk clerk paid more attention to him than usual. Walsh understood. He was an oddity, but he was a known quantity. The desk clerk's interest was because people had been making inquiries. Probably lots of people.

Walsh got the key and went up to his room. It was, as always, exactly as he'd left it. He went to the closet, took the suitcase down from the shelf. He flopped the suitcase down on the bed, then twisted the dials on the combination lock. When he got the numbers lined up he popped the suitcase open, reached in and pulled out his checkbook and a pen. He wrote out a check to Steve Winslow for five thousand dollars. He took out an envelope, addressed it to Steve Winslow at his office, put the check in, stamped it and sealed it.

He wrote out another check, tore it out of the checkbook, folded it and stuffed it in his pocket. He took his wallet out of his suitcase, stuffed it in his pocket too.

Humming softly, he locked the suitcase, stuck it in the closet, and went out the door.

There was no one in the hallway, but when he took the elevator down he spotted Jason Tindel hanging out in the lobby. He grinned, went out the door, and headed down the street.

He stopped on the corner to drop the letter to Steve Winslow in the mailbox, then walked straight to the Chase Manhattan Bank.

He stood in line, waited his turn, and then presented his check to the teller. She was a young, Oriental woman who looked at him as if he were from another planet. He was not at all surprised when she sent him to one of the supervisors to get the check approved.

It was with obvious reluctance that the young supervisor eventually scrawled his initials on the check. Not that Jack Walsh's credentials weren't impeccable. It was just the way the man looked. That and the fact he kept grinning like a zany and even cackled gleefully once or twice. That was when Jack Walsh spotted Jason Tindel watching him through the bank window. Sitting there next to the bank supervisor who was inspecting what was obviously a large check, Walsh knew he had to be driving Jason crazy.

Finally with the check approved, Walsh returned to the teller. Even the initials on the check didn't seem to convince her, and it wasn't until she caught the eye of the young supervisor, held up the check and saw him nod his approval, that she was willing to proceed with the transaction. She stamped the check, jerked open the cash drawer and began counting out money. She counted it three times, shoved it through the slot. Jack Walsh took it, and stuffed it into his coat pockets. He walked out of the bank, straight back to his hotel and up to his room.

Inside, he locked the door, took off his coat and flung it on the bed. He rubbed his hands together, cackled gleefully again. All right. Now to business.

But first he was hungry. All he'd had today was some cheap wine. And the slop in the hospital he'd refused to eat.

He picked up the phone and started to call room service. Thought better of it. After all, Fred and Jason were watching the lobby. Might as well give them a turn.

He dialed information, got the number for Lutece. He ordered a full-course dinner complete with wine. There. Let them think about that.

Except he still had the taste of cheap wine in his mouth.

He went in the bathroom, squeezed some toothpaste out of a

tube and brushed his teeth. He did so by taking them out of his mouth—Walsh wore dentures. He opened the medicine cabinet, took out a bottle of mouthwash, and gargled. He spit out the mouthwash and replaced the dentures.

He straightened up and looked at himself in the mirror. There. Still a wild man, but with sweeter breath. He grinned at the reflection in the mirror. Here's lookin' at you, kid.

He yawned, stretched. Well now, perhaps a shower might be in order. Maybe even a change of underwear.

But later. Much later. First to business.

He went out of the bathroom, sat down on the bed, picked up the phone and began making calls.

# 12

MARK TAYLOR SETTLED BACK in the clients' chair, flipped open his notebook, looked up at Steve Winslow and Tracy Garvin, and said, "O.K. Here's the dope.

"Yesterday afternoon Jack Walsh left the subway and went straight back to his hotel, got his key from the desk, went up to his room. Two-oh-five. Two-fifteen he's back down again, walks to the corner, mails a letter, walks down to the Chase Manhattan Bank and presents a check to the teller. She directs him to the supervisor, who goes through the usual red-tape bullshit—only it being Jack Walsh, perhaps slightly more than the usual red-tape bullshit—but eventually he initials the check. Walsh takes it back to the teller, who doesn't seem too convinced but who eventually pushes the money through the window. Walsh stuffs it in his pockets and leaves."

"How much money?" Steve said.

"I don't know, and the bank won't say. I might have had a chance of finding out if it weren't for the fact Jason Tindel and Fred Grayson are after the same thing.

"When he left the bank, Fred Grayson tagged along and Jason Tindel stayed behind to hit on the bank supervisor. One of my men stayed behind to watch. From what he observed, Tindel didn't get any satisfaction. But he sure did cause a fuss. The supervisor called in reinforcements, and it took the branch manager to come out and tell Jason Tindel to get lost. After all that, there's not a prayer of them letting the information slip."

"Gotcha," Steve said. "What's next?"

"Jack Walsh went straight back to his hotel and up to his room. Fred Grayson tagged along. About twenty minutes later Jason Tindel got back there, followed of course by my other man.

"Jason and Fred confer in the lobby. Now my men can't get close enough to hear what they're saying, but apparently they're discussing shifts. Tailing Jack Walsh, I mean. Like setting up a schedule. At least that's what I figure, cause anyway they talk a bit and then Grayson leaves. So I figure Tindel's drawn the first shift, however long that's gonna be, then Grayson's gonna replace him, then probably Carl Jenson after that, and so on."

"Don't you know?" Steve said.

"No."

"You mean you lost him?"

Taylor held up his hands. "No, no, no. Nothing like that. You'll see why. Just let me tell it.

"O.K., so it's like you think. Tindel's got the first shift, I don't know how long or who's next, but I'll find out when the relief arrives.

"Only it doesn't happen that way. What does? Well, first off, around—" Mark checked the notebook, "—6:26 my man puts it, a van pulls up outside. A team of men get out, start unloading trays of food. Hot food. You know, like steam trays on wheels. The guy in charge goes up to the desk, asks for room 926. Which happens to be Jack Walsh's room. So Jason Tindel pumps one of the waiters. My man overhears. It turns out the van's from Lutece. Our homeless bum's ordered a two-hundred-and-forty-nine-dollar meal, specifying each and every item, from the Chateaubriand to the vintage wine. Moreover, the head waiter comes down grinning like a cheshire cat, so we can assume Jack Walsh was in no way stingy about the tip."

"Right, right," Steve said. "But the schedule. How come you don't know when Tindel was relieved?"

"Cause of what happened next."

"Which was?"

"Starting seven-thirty they all show up."

"They?"

"The family. The Tindels, the Graysons, Aunt Claire and the gang."

"All together."

"All of *them* together. Carl Jenson showed up about ten minutes later." Mark flipped open the notebook. "7:26, Fred Grayson, the two wives and Claire Chesterton show up together. 7:38, Carl Jenson."

"Why'd they show up?"

"Walsh sent for 'em."

"How do you know?"

"From what happened. See, with all those people milling around it got a little hairy for my men. Of course, they don't want to be spotted. With so many people there, there was a good chance someone would get wise. Particularly after Carl Jenson showed up. He's a wary son of a bitch. Suspicious nature, eyes open all the time, you know what I mean?"

"Yeah. So?"

"So anyway, the relatives are off in a corner of the lobby conferring in low tones and my men can only catch a word or two here or there. So when I say Jack Walsh sent for them, I'm inferring that from what happened."

"Which is?" Steve said somewhat impatiently.

"Yeah, yeah," Taylor said. "Sorry. Which is, they all went up to see Jack Walsh one at a time."

"Oh yeah?"

"Yeah. Like clockwork, starting at eight o'clock. It's easier if I just give it to you. Here you go. Two minutes of eight, Jason Tindel goes up in the elevator; 8:14 he's back down. They all converge on him, they're all talking at once, you can't make out a thing. Best you can tell, they're not happy. Jason Tindel, at least, does not look happy.

"8:27—Fred Grayson up in the elevator. 8:38—Grayson down. Same thing.

"8:57—Rose Tindel up in the elevator. 9:10—Rose Tindel down.

"9:26—Pat Grayson up in the elevator. 9:37—Pat Grayson down.

"9:58—Claire Chesterton up in the elevator. 10:10—Claire Chesterton down.

"And last but not least: 10:26—Carl Jenson up in the elevator. 10:36—Carl Jenson down."

Taylor flipped the notebook shut. "And that's that. When Jenson came down they all conferred one last time, apparently over shifts. Because immediately after that everybody left but Jason Tindel. He staked out the lobby and was on till three in the morning, relieved by Fred Grayson. Fred stayed on till eight, when Carl Jenson took over. Jenson's there now." Taylor shrugged. "Not that it's doing any good. So far, Walsh hasn't shown."

"By rights he should be dead," Tracy said.

Steve and Mark looked at her.

"What?" Steve said.

Tracy grinned. "I just mean it would be perfect. From a murder-mystery point of view. I mean look. Here's a millionaire. He's being visited by all his heirs one at a time. You got a detective taking notes of the exact times each one of them went in. Plus you got the Lutece van, so you know exactly when he had his dinner and what he ate. So the medical examiner would be able to determine the time of death by the stomach contents. It would be a nice, tidy little case."

Taylor shook his head. "Jesus Christ."

"Hey, don't knock it," Steve said. "You said Walsh hasn't shown yet. So take it a step further. What if he doesn't show and sooner or later a chambermaid goes in and finds him dead?"

Now Taylor stared at Steve. "Are you serious?"

Steve grinned. "No, but what the hell. It's an interesting idea, we might as well play with it. What would happen then?"

"I know what would happen then," Taylor said. "I would be sitting on top of a huge pile of evidence in a first-degree murder case, and you would be handing me oh-so plausible reasons why I should be withholding it from the police, and I would be having a nervous breakdown."

"Relax," Steve said. "You worry too much. We're only playing what-if here. Wait till the corpse turns up."

"Yeah," Taylor said. "That's the what-if I'm talking about. What if a corpse turns up?"

"In that case," Steve said. "I would instruct you to take all of your operatives' notes and make a full and complete disclosure to the police."

Taylor stared at him. "Are you serious?"

"Absolutely," Steve said. "At least within the confines of the hypothetical situation Tracy's set up.

"O.K., Tracy. It's your party. What if Jack Walsh turns up dead?"

Tracy frowned. "Now that I think about it, it's not so perfect after all."

"Oh no? Why?"

"Because the relatives all came together."

"What difference does that make?"

"Well," Tracy said. "In a book they'd all come separately. And they'd go in and out without meeting each other. In fact, none of them would even know the others had appointments. Of course, that couldn't happen in this case with them all living in the same house. Jack Walsh calls one, he gets 'em all. So they all know they all have appointments, they all come together, and they discuss everything before each one goes up and after they come down."

"Why does that make a difference?" Steve said.

"Because if they all came separately and there was no communication among 'em, no one would know who did it. Or rather, who *didn't* do it."

Taylor frowned. "You'll forgive me if I'm not following this?"

"I think I am," Steve said. "But why don't you spell it out."

"O.K.," Tracy said. "They're all together. They're all going up and coming down one at a time. There's six of 'em, right? O.K. Say the fourth person goes up and finds him dead. Well, then he knows the killer's one of the first three who already went up. And he knows the killer isn't one of the last two who haven't gone up yet."

"And he know it isn't himself," Taylor said.

"I'm serious, Mark," Tracy said. She turned to Steve. "You see what I mean?"

"Yeah, I do," Steve said. "But there's another consideration. That fourth person—you got your notes there Mark? Who *was* the fourth person? In fact, give me the order again."

"O.K.," Taylor said. "Jason Tindel, Fred Grayson, Rose Tindel, Pat Grayson—she's number four. Then there's Claire Chesterton, and Carl Jenson."

"O.K.," Steve said. "Take your example. Pat Grayson goes up and finds him dead. She knows Jason Tindel, Fred Grayson, or Rose Tindel did it. She also knows Claire Chesterton and Carl Jenson didn't."

"Seems a shame to wash out Jenson," Taylor said.

"If that were the case," Steve said. "She obviously didn't tell anyone."

"Why is that?"

"Because Claire Chesterton and Carl Jenson still went up."

"Wait a minute," Taylor said. "Why wouldn't she tell?"

"Because she's afraid they might think that she did it," Tracy said excitedly.

"Oh, come on," Taylor said.

"No, good enough," Steve said. "That's a motive for her, and that's a motive for all the others. Take that as a premise. Whoever finds him dead won't admit it. He'll lie to the others and claim they met with him and he was just fine."

"So what does that accomplish?" Taylor said. "She comes down, she doesn't tell the others he's dead. Big deal. The next person up is gonna know."

"Right," Steve said. "But only that one person. And that's what makes the whole thing so interesting. It's like one of those old logic problems. In fact it's a paradox."

"What?" Taylor said.

"I'm not following this," Tracy said. "What's the paradox?"

"It's a nobody-could-have-killed-him paradox."

"A what?"

"Look. Here's the setup. Jack Walsh is found dead. One of the six must have killed him. Now we must assume all six will operate by the same rules. That is, if a person finds him dead, they won't admit it, they'll pretend he's still alive. And we also must assume that the murderer doesn't want to be known. In other words, the murderer won't kill him if any other person would know for sure that he did it.

"O.K., that's the setup. If Jack Walsh is found dead, which one of them could have done it?"

Mark Taylor stared at him. "How the hell should I know?"

"All right, Mark. Let's make it easier. Which one of them *couldn't* have done it? Logically, I mean."

"Steve," Taylor said. "I took Math 101 for football players. I got a gentleman's C. This is out of my line."

"All right. Tracy—you know who couldn't have done it?"

"Sure."

"Who?"

"Jason Tindel, of course."

"Right. Why?"

"Because he came first. Jason Tindel called on him first. If he killed him, when Fred Grayson went up and found him dead, Fred would know Jason was the murderer."

"Right," Steve said. "And one of our rules is the murderer won't do it if anyone would know it was him. You follow that, Mark?"

"Right. If Jason did it, Fred would know. So it wasn't Jason. I'm with you there."

"Fine," Steve said. "Now consider Fred Grayson. Could he be the murderer?"

"Sure," Taylor said.

"Oh yeah," Steve said. "And how is that?"

"Cause who would know? When the third person—Rose Tindel—came up and found Jack Walsh dead, she wouldn't know whether Fred or Jason did it. Right?"

"Wrong," Steve said.

Mark Taylor and Tracy Garvin both looked at him.

"What?" Tracy said.

"Wrong," Steve said. "Rose Tindel would know."

"How the hell would she know that?" Taylor said.

"Because we have to assume that Rose Tindel is intelligent and can reason just as well as we can."

"What's that got to do with it?"

Steve shrugged. "Well, we just got through figuring out Jason Tindel couldn't have done it. Cause if he had, Fred Grayson would know it. Well, Rose Tindel can figure that way too. She can say, 'It can't be Jason, or Fred would know it, and Jason wouldn't be that stupid as to let Fred know he'd committed the crime. So it can't be him. And if it isn't him, it has to be Fred.' You follow me?"

Taylor frowned. "I think so."

"So it can't be Fred. 'Cause he can reason that way too, and he won't commit the crime if Rose Tindel would know it was him. You follow me?"

"Absolutely," Tracy said. "And the same thing with Pat Grayson, right?"

"Exactly," Steve said. "Pat Grayson knows it couldn't be Jason or Fred would know. She knows it couldn't be Fred, or Rose Tindel would know. So if she walks in and finds him dead, she'll know it's Rose Tindel. So it can't be Rose Tindel. 'Cause she wouldn't be that dumb."

"You've absolutely lost me," Taylor said.

"Oh, come on, Mark, it's simple," Tracy said. "Claire Chesterton figures the same way, right?"

"Exactly. So Pat Grayson couldn't have done it. Likewise, Carl Jenson figures out Claire Chesterton couldn't have done it." Steve grinned. "Of course, there we have a problem. Frankly, I can't see Carl Jenson figuring *anything* out. But grant him the hypothetical power, the answer is yes.

"And Carl Jenson couldn't do it, because he came last. If he did it, Claire Chesterton, who knew Walsh was alive when she left, would know it was him. So he couldn't have done it."

Steve spread his hands. "So there we are. Here the man lies dead. And none of the six of them could have killed him, because if they had someone would know it was them. And yet the man *is* dead and one of them *did* kill him, and no one has the faintest idea who it was."

"Jesus Christ," Taylor said.

"So whaddya think?" Steve said.

"Pretty neat," Tracy said. "What do you think. Mark?"

Taylor frowned. He shook his head gloomily. "I think the son of a bitch better be alive."

# 13

JACK WALSH TOOK ONE LAST look around his hotel room. Had he forgotten anything? He couldn't afford to do that now. Not with the buzzards on his trail. He patted his coat pocket. Yes, he had his wallet and his checkbook. He took them out and looked at them. Realized it was the second time he'd done that. Christ, was he getting senile? He chuckled to himself, shoved the wallet and checkbook back in his coat pocket.

He looked in the suitcase which was lying open on the bed. Was there anything else he'd need? No, of course not. He'd already checked that too. He shut the suitcase, locked it, stuck it back on the closet shelf. Humming softly, he looked around the room again. Anything else? No, just his room key which was lying on the night table. He picked it up and went out the door.

He took the elevator down to the lobby and dropped off his key at the front desk. Through the front window he spotted Carl Jenson hanging out on the sidewalk. He chuckled to himself. Jenson again. Easy pickings. Christ, almost too easy.

Walsh came out the front door and walked along 57th Street to the subway entrance. The whole time he never looked back once. He didn't need to. He knew Carl Jenson would be there.

Jack Walsh went down in the subway, walked the long corridor to the token booth. Although he had money in his pockets, he ducked under the turnstile out of force of habit. Fuck the transit system.

He walked up the ramp to the Broadway downtown local. The platform was fairly crowded for that late in the morning, which meant a train must be almost due.

Walsh walked to the far uptown end of the platform. There were two bums hanging out in the corner, one lying in a blanket, the other sitting propped up against the wall. Walsh walked over, squatted down, talked to them.

A train pulled into the station. Walsh stood up, turned, faced the train.

But he didn't get on. He just stood there, calmly, patiently waiting.

The doors closed, the train pulled out.

Jack Walsh sat down. He swung his legs over the edge of the platform. He hopped down onto the tracks.

His foot hit one of the ties and he pitched forward onto his hands and knees.

He wasn't hurt. He stood up, dusted his hands off.

And walked into the tunnel.

# 14

MARK TAYLOR STUCK HIS HEAD in the door. "I got good news and bad news, Steve."

"Oh?"

"My men called in. The good news is, Jack Walsh is very much alive."

"Oh yeah?"

"Yeah. He came out the front door grungy as ever and large as life about an hour ago."

"So, what's the bad news?"

Taylor sighed. "They lost him."

"Shit."

"Yeah."

"Was he wise?"

"Yes and no."

"What the hell does that mean?"

Taylor shrugged. "Well, I doubt if he spotted my men. But Carl Jenson was following him. I'm sure he was wise to him. Anyway, he ditched Jenson at the same time he ditched my men."

"How'd he do it?"

"Easy as pie. He went down in a subway station, waited till a train came through, then hopped down on the tracks and walked into the tunnel."

"You're kidding."

"Not at all. Very simple, but very effective. If you ever want to ditch someone, I highly recommend it."

Steve grinned. "I'll bet. So no one wanted to follow him?"

"They may not have wanted to, but they sure as hell did."

"Oh yeah?"

"Yeah. Jenson hesitates a moment, then he hops down and walks into the tunnel too."

"And your men?"

"Went right in after him."

"So?"

"So, I don't know if you're familiar with the underground in

New York. My men sure as hell weren't. But they sure got an education. It's all connected down there. The subway system connects with the sewer system, which connects with abandoned unfinished tunnels, which connects with subbasements —it's a whole goddamned labyrinth. I don't want to bore you with details, but suffice it to say my men got hopelessly lost. They also got totally freaked out, and they both swear they'll never do that again, even if it cost them their jobs.

"At any rate, they lost Walsh and they lost Jenson. And it's a cinch Walsh lost Jenson too, if that's what he was after. 'Cause apparently he knows his way around down there. After all he's been living there for months."

"Great," Steve said. "So what are you doing now?"

"Well, I got one man staking out the hotel in case he comes back, and the other staking out the subway system in case he comes back the way he came in." Taylor shrugged. "Figure that's the best I can do."

Steve grimaced, "Yeah, but it's probably a lost hope. If he went to the trouble to ditch Jenson, he's not gonna show up in any of the obvious places." Steve thought a moment, then shook his head. "No, call your men in, Mark. I just wanted to see what Walsh was gonna do. Well, he's done it. He's called all the family members in for conferences, and now he's gone back to the subway and ditched 'em. That sounds to me like he's checking out."

Taylor nodded. "It does to me too."

"Well, that's that," Steve said. "Anything else?"

"As a matter of fact, yeah."

"Oh?"

"Julie Creston."

"What about her?"

"I found her."

"Oh yeah? Where?"

Mark Taylor frowned and shook his head. "I'm embarrassed to tell you. And here I got men out scouring the country, looking for her under one alias or another. And look where she turns up."

"Where?"

Taylor reached into his hip pocket, pulled out a rolled up copy of TV Guide, and flopped it on the desk. "There. In next Sunday's *Murder, She Wrote.* Listed in the additional cast, playing a small but featured role under the same stage name you gave me. It seems when she left New York she moved out to L.A. and kept on working. That didn't bother Walsh's relatives none, cause they didn't give a damn what she did as long as she wasn't around him. So they weren't gonna bother her. She moved out there, got a small flat in L.A. and she's been working ever since. Nothing much, you understand, just enough to pay the rent. And even then, only with some waitressing on the side."

"Well now that's interesting," Steve said. "Anyone talk to her?"

Taylor shook his head. "That's what I wanna ask you. She's not there. She's on location. She landed a week's work on a picture shooting in the mountains around Denver. So you want me to have someone track her down on the set or wait till she comes home?"

Steve waved his hand. "Shit, let it go. You track her down in Denver, it makes it too much of a big deal. She's that much less willing to talk. Plus she'll be flustered, what with people showing up on the set. It's not urgent. You got her pegged, we can get her any time."

"O.K.," Taylor said. "Well, just wanted to keep you up to date on your millionaire bum."

"Gee, thanks," Steve said. "You get any more good news, just trot it on over."

"I'm not gonna have anything more, now you pulled my men off the job."

"You still got a leak at headquarters, don't you?"

"Yeah."

"Put a bug in his ear with the name Jack Walsh. You may get something yet."

Taylor frowned. "Like what?"

"How the hell should I know? Frankly, I hope you get nothing. I just got a bad feeling about this."

"You and me both. I mean, I hate to lose the business, but I can't tell you what a relief it will be to tell my men I'm pulling 'em out of the subway system."

"I'll bet," Steve said. "But all the same, I can't help feeling that's where they ought to be." Steve shook his head. "Damn. I just wish I knew what that lunatic was up to."

# 15

JEREMY GAVE HIGH-FIVES TO the two seniors, then stuck his hands in his pockets and watched them walk off down the hallway. Out of the corner of his eye he watched Beth Killmore, who was standing with a girlfriend halfway down the hall. He wondered if she caught that action—the seniors treating him like an equal, slapping him high-fives. Surely she'd think that was cool.

Jeremy had a real thing for Beth Killmore. Even though she herself wasn't cool. Even though she was an A student. Even though she was straight-laced, didn't party, and had a good reputation. But Jesus, what a killer bod.

He wondered if she knew it. He wondered if she knew she drove boys nuts. She certainly drove *him* nuts. And shit, she was only a sophomore, for Christ's sake. He was a junior and then some. Christ, had she *seen* him with those two seniors?

The bell rang. Damn, always the fucking bell. He had to get upstairs. And he hadn't even got his book out.

He walked down the hall to his locker, spun the combination, opened the door. He took out his backpack, unzipped it, started to fumble through.

A hand grabbed his shoulder. Aw shit, the principal? What now?

He swung around with an angry scowl on his lip.

"Well, now, you don't look pleased to see me."

Jeremy blinked at the ragged beggar in front of him. "Uncle Jack."

"The one and only. Footloose and fancy free. And thanks to you, I understand."

"What are you doing here?"

"Dodgin' teachers, mainly. Come on, my boy, we gotta get out of here."

"What?"

"Let's go. Let's go, before they throw me out on my ear."

"Go where?"

"What does that matter, as long as it's out of here? This place gives me the creeps, you know? You ever notice that?"

"Yeah."

"Yeah, I'll bet you do. Well come on, boy, we gotta go."

"Sure. But where? Why? What's going on, Uncle Jack?"

"A lot of things, my boy, a lot of things. As it happens—Oh shit, here comes a teacher."

Walsh spun Jeremy around. "Let's go this way. We get separated, get out best you can and meet me out front. You'll have to look around, 'cause I may be hidin'. Don't worry though, I'll spot you."

"Yeah, but—"

But Jack Walsh was already heading down the hallway. Jeremy hurried to catch up with him.

Jeremy was so distracted by Uncle Jack he walked right past Beth Killmore without even seeing her. He glanced back over his shoulder to see if they were being followed, and found her staring after him.

Good lord. What would Beth Killmore make of this?

# 16

JOE BISSEL SNIFFLED TWICE, opened a bleary eye. Somewhere in his alcohol-dulled brain something stirred. Danger. Intruders.

Which wasn't right. This was his spot. He'd staked it out himself. The far end of the station platform in a little alcove just behind the dumpster. It was his and no one had any right.

He opened both eyes now. Blinked. Focused. Christ, what the hell was that? Green hair? Shit. Give me a break. Green hair?

The bleary eyes focused on the other man. At least he was normal. Your typical homeless. But even they could be dangerous, and . . .

The eyes cleared. Oh. It's all right. It's Jack.

Jeremy grabbed Walsh's arm. "Uncle Jack."

"Yeah?"

Jeremy pointed. "Someone there."

Walsh turned, looked. "Oh, that's all right. That's Joe. Don't mind us, Joe. Go right back to sleep."

"Uncle Jack. What the hell are we doing here?"

"Safest place we could be, my boy."

"Yeah, but—"

"But nothin'. You been up top for a while, you get to like it down here."

"Uncle Jack—"

"Hold on, my boy. We got work to do."

"Work?"

"Yeah."

"I don't understand."

"Course you don't. Cause I haven't told you yet."

Jeremy took a breath. Maybe this wasn't such a hot idea after all. "Uncle Jack—"

"Now, now, my boy. I haven't really lost my marbles. That's what you're thinkin', isn't it? The old man's lost his marbles. Well, not at all, my boy. Crazy? Crazy like a fox. See here now."

"What?"

"You did me a favor, my boy. And now I'm going to do you a

favor. And then you're going to do me another favor. Maybe that's not equal, but maybe it is."

Jeremy frowned. "Uncle Jack—"

Walsh held up his hand. "Jeremy. You're young. You're impatient. You want everything to make sense. The thing is, things don't always make sense. And those that do, well sometimes they ain't worth nothin'. Just relax and enjoy the ride."

"Ride?"

"You're far too literal, my boy. Now sit down. We got work to do."

Walsh eased himself down, leaned up against the wall of the subway. After a moment's hesitation, Jeremy did the same.

"Fine. Good," Walsh said. "Now, let's talk about these favors. You did me the big one, gettin' me out of the nuthouse. Gettin' the lawyer you went to. Damn fine job."

"It just seemed to me—"

"I know it did, my boy, and you were right. And that was a hell of a favor and now I'll do one for you. Then you'll do one for me and we're quits.

"Now, to the business at hand."

Walsh dug in his overcoat pocket, pulled out some sheets of paper folded in thirds. He looked over at Jeremy. "You got a pen?"

"No."

Walsh shook his head. "Always carry a pen. Let that be a lesson to you. You never know when it might get you a million bucks."

"What?"

"Never mind, my boy. Just happen to have one."

Walsh fished in his coat pocket, pulled out a ballpoint pen. "Now then, something to write on. That's the thing I didn't bring. Something to write on. Well, this will have to do."

Walsh hunched over, spread the paper flat on the floor of the subway platform.

"Now pay attention, my boy, to what I'm going to do."

Behind them, the eyes of Joe Bissel focused blearily, uncomprehendingly on the scene, as Walsh took the ballpoint pen, poised it over the paper, and began to write: "I, Jack Walsh, being of sound mind and body, . . ."

# 17

STEVE WINSLOW'S VOICE WAS-
drugged with sleep. "Hello?"

"Steve? Mark."

"What?"

"Mark. It's me. Mark. Mark Taylor. Steve?"

"Yeah, Mark. Hello?"

"Steve. Wake up."

Steve Winslow hunched himself to a sitting position. He rubbed his head. "Yeah, Mark. What time is it?"

"One-thirty."

"Shit."

"Yeah. Sorry. But I thought you'd want to know."

"What?"

"Pipeline from headquarters called. Cops brought in a John Doe."

"Don't tell me."

"That's right. Just I.D.'d him as Jack Walsh."

"No shit. Suicide or accident?"

"Murder."

"Murder? You're kidding."

"Not at all."

"How'd it happen?"

"Guy didn't have all the details, but apparently the cops figure it as a thrill-kill."

"Thrill-kill?"

"Yeah. Murder for kicks. It's the new craze with kids. Wilding, you know?"

"Yeah, yeah," Steve said impatiently. "So what's the dope?"

"Well, part of the craze is pickin' on the helpless and the homeless. So that's what the cops think happened here."

"Where's here?"

"The subway."

"Shit."

"Yeah, it would be the subway, wouldn't it? Anyway, here's the dope. It was in the subway. Sixty-sixth Street Station.

Broadway line. Uptown platform. North end. Bum sleeping behind a dumpster."

"So?"

"So someone poured gasoline over him, set him on fire."

"Jesus Christ."

"Yeah."

"When'd it happen?"

"Ten-thirty, eleven, somewhere in there. Homeless man, John Doe. Then they pulled an I.D. Seems the guy had a wallet in his pocket, one of the credit cards in the middle hadn't melted too bad to read. So they come up with the name Jack Walsh."

"Oh shit."

"Now," Taylor said. "The reason I called you is, as far as I know, the name means nothing to them. The cops, I mean. Jack Walsh, it's just a name. They don't know who he is. Just another homeless man, they got no other motive, they put it down as a thrill-kill, and—"

"I got you, I got you," Steve said. "Jesus Christ, what a mess. You said the 66th Street Station?"

"Right."

"Meet you there."

# 18

Steve Winslow paid off the cab at 66th and Broadway and headed for the subway station. Ordinarily it would have been faster just to take the subway there from the West Village where he lived, but at two in the morning it was apt to be a long time between trains and Steve was too impatient to wait.

Steve went down the subway steps, bought a token, went through the turnstile. The platform was more or less deserted, as it should have been at two in the morning. At the far uptown end, a lone cop stood in front of a section of platform that had been cordoned off with a yellow "Police Scene" tape.

As Steve stood looking, a voice said, "Psssst."

Steve looked around and saw Mark Taylor and Tracy Garvin standing just out of sight in an alcove just downtown from the token booth. He walked over.

"Hi, Mark, Tracy."

Taylor jerked his thumb in Tracy's direction. "Thought we might need her."

"Thought I might kill him if he didn't call me," Tracy said. "Remember when he forgot the last time."

"Yeah, yeah," Steve said. "So what's the scoop?"

"Nothing doing," Taylor said. "I pumped the token clerk. Media's come and gone. It was too late to make the eleven o'clock news, but they shot footage for tomorrow. Treating it as a thrill-kill, like I said. Speculation is, teenagers out for kicks."

"Speculation?"

"Yeah. No hard facts. Just guesswork."

"What about the cops?"

"Long gone. Wrapped it up, posted a man, and split. Just routine once the news crews left."

"Yeah, fine," Steve said. "But what do they know?"

Taylor shrugged. "Just what I told you. No more, no less. They put it down as a thrill-kill of a homeless man. They've identified him as Jack Walsh, but as far as I know, the name means nothin' to 'em. Jack Walsh, John Doe, all the same to them."

Steve jerked his thumb. "What about the cop down there? You make a pass at him yet?"

Taylor shook his head. "Thought I'd wait for you. See how you wanted to play it."

Steve frowned. "We go ask him questions, he'll wanna know who we are. When he finds out, he won't talk."

"We don't have to tell him."

"Yeah, but I hate that, and it's not going to get us anywhere."

Steve turned, peered at the cop down the station. Turned back, thought a moment. "The cop looks young and impressionable. Tracy, why don't you go down there, get him interested in your bod, see what he has to say?"

Tracy gave him a look. "I consider that an obnoxious, sexist remark."

Steve shrugged. "You're right. You don't have to do it."

Tracy grinned. "What, are you nuts? Be right back."

She turned and walked down the platform. While Steve and Mark surreptitiously watched, Tracy walked up to the young cop and started talking to him. From what they could see, she was doing just fine.

She was back in five minutes.

"So," Steve said.

"Snowed him completely," Tracy said. "He wanted my phone number."

"I'm sure he did. What about the murder?"

"Strangely enough, he wasn't that interested in the murder. I had to convince him I *was.*"

"And?"

"He still didn't know that much. Just like Mark said—thrill-kill. Splash the guy with gas and set him on fire."

"Yeah, but who?"

"Teenagers."

"Teenagers. Black or white?"

"Apparently white."

"Oh yeah?" Steve said. "And how does he know that?"

"There must be a witness of some kind. The guy didn't know, but that's the only way it figures. Because of what he said."

Steve looked at her. "You're doing this to pay me back for the sexist remark, aren't you? I mean, there's a punch line to this, right?"

"Yeah, and you're not going to like it."

"Oh shit."

"What?" Taylor said. "What are you talking about?"

"That's it, isn't it?" Steve said. "That's why he thinks it's teen-agers and how he knows they're white. Right?"

"You got it," Tracy said. "The story from the witness is real garbled. The cop didn't know who the witness was, or what he said. Only one thing stood out."

"For Christ's sake," Taylor said. "Will you tell me what it was?"

"Only one thing makes any sense, Mark," Steve said.

Tracy nodded. "That's right. All the guy knew was, it was something about green hair."

# 19

JEREMY DAWSON SLUMPED down on his tailbone in his desk chair, stretched his feet out, lolled his head back, and paid no attention whatsoever to the algebra teacher who was droning away at the blackboard. Who needed algebra anyway? Christ, he was gonna be rich.

Jeremy chuckled softly to himself. He closed his eyes, conjured up a vision of scantily dressed young ladies adorning his luxury yacht, pouring him champagne and sticking copious quantities of cocaine up his nose. Beth Killmore was there too, reserved and disapproving at first, but slowly taken in by the affluence of the setting, the magnetism of the young millionaire. She was his now, to do with as he pleased. Ready and willing to serve his every whim.

If he'd let her. If he wanted. If he deigned to let her stay.

Jeremy chuckled again, gloried in his indifference. There she was, throwing herself at him, and he really couldn't care less. After all, the ball game was on the color TV the girls had set up on the deck of his yacht, the Mets were up and she could damn well wait.

Which she didn't want to do. What a pain in the ass. Teasing, wheedling, calling out his name.

"Jeremy. Jeremy!"

The voice was not Beth Killmore's. The yacht vanished. Reality set back in. Jeremy blinked, opened his eyes.

Miss Swain, the algebra teacher, was standing looking down at him. Oh shit, he was in for it now. The principal's office again? He was in no mood for that today, and—

Jeremy saw the two men standing next to her. The two men in suits and ties. Clean cut, grim, purposeful. Holy shit. Narcs? Was it possible? Were they busting him?

The taller of them stepped forward. "Jeremy Dawson?"

"Yeah."

The policeman flipped open his wallet, showed his badge. "Come with us, please."

"What? What are you talking about?"

"Just come with us, please."

Jeremy drew back in his seat. "Hey, man. No way."

The cop shook his head. "Listen, it'll be easier if you cooperate."

"Says you," Jeremy said. "I ain't done nothin', and I ain't goin' nowhere."

The tall cop sighed. "All right, if that's the way you want it."

He reached in his pocket and pulled out a pair of handcuffs. "Jeremy Dawson, you're under arrest. You have the right to remain silent. If you give up the right to remain silent . . ."

# 20

MARK TAYLOR TOOK A SIP FROM his paper cup of coffee, leaned forward, set it on Steve Winslow's desk, and flipped open his notebook. He frowned and shook his head. "Bad news all around."

"How so?" Steve said.

"The bottom line is the cops picked up Jeremy Dawson half an hour ago."

"Shit."

"Yeah. They showed up at his school, snagged him right out of class."

"How'd you get that so fast?"

"My man saw it happen."

"Oh?"

"Yeah. I sent two men out to the school, trying to get a line on Jack Walsh's movements yesterday. My man was in the right place and actually saw it go down."

"What happened?"

"Two plainclothes cops come down the hall escorted by an academic looking gentleman with the word "principal" written all over him. They go into the classroom. Two minutes later the cops come out escorting Jeremy between em'."

"In handcuffs?"

"Yeah."

"Was he talkin'?"

"What?"

"Jeremy. Was he talkin'? Protesting? Sayin' anything?"

"No. The way I get it, he was just walking between 'em lookin' absolutely stunned."

"Well, that's something."

"Incidentally, my men got what they came for, which don't matter much now, with the kid's arrest. Still, it's a confirmation."

"Of what?"

"That Jack Walsh was there yesterday. At least two students saw an old bum prowling the corridors. I got no one saw him actually leave with Jeremy, but it's a cinch he did, cause I found a kid says Jeremy cut his last class."

"Oh shit."

"Yeah, it's a mess all right. And if the cops got onto Jeremy, that means they know who Jack Walsh is. I mean, they're on to the fact he's got money and the whole bit."

Steve sighed, rubbed his head.

Tracy Garvin looked up from the notes she'd been taking. "Where does that leave you?" she said.

Steve looked up. "What?"

"Well," Tracy said. "Jack Walsh was your client. He's dead. Maybe I'm not understanding this, but what's your involvement now?"

Steve shook his head. "Except for the fact I haven't got a client, my involvement's the same as when I started."

"Which is?"

Steve shrugged. "The hell of it is, I don't know. Perhaps none. On the other hand, I could be an accessory before and after the fact to fraud."

"How's that?" Taylor said.

"In case someone shows up with a holographic will purporting to be entirely in Jack Walsh's handwriting. Then I'm in one hell of a position, 'cause I have every reason to believe that will would be fraudulent."

"Right," Tracy said.

"And that's just the legal aspect of it. The fact is, I got Jack Walsh out of Bellevue and now he's dead. If I hadn't interfered, he'd still be alive."

"You can't look at it that way," Taylor said.

"Oh yeah? How the hell am I supposed to look at it?"

Steve picked up an envelope from his desk, reached in and pulled out a check. "This came this morning. Five thousand bucks from Jack Walsh for services rendered."

"You feel bad takin' it?" Taylor said.

Steve smiled. "Yes and no."

"What does that mean?"

"Yes I feel bad, and no I'm not takin' it."

Taylor stared at him. "Why not?"

"Relax, Mark. I'm not so high principled as all that. The fact is, the check's worthless."

"What?" Taylor said.

"Why?" Tracy asked.

"Because Jack Walsh is dead. That freezes his account. You can't cash a check on a dead man."

"Oh shit," Taylor said.

"So it's worse than I thought," Tracy said. "You got no client and you just lost your fee. Plus you got detectives working overtime on this thing."

"Hey, easy," Taylor said. "You trying to get me fired?"

"No, I'm just pointing out—"

Steve held up his hand. "I understand. This may not be good business practice, but it's what I want to do. Stay on the job, Mark, until I tell you different. The fact is, I fucked up, and I'm gonna do what I can to straighten things out."

"With a dead client and no fee?"

Steve nodded. "Unfortunately, that's the case."

The phone rang. Steve scooped it up. "Steve Winslow . . . Uh huh . . . Uh huh . . . sit tight, I'll be right there."

Steve hung up the phone and stood up. "O.K., that changes the situation. Get ready to swing into high gear, Mark. Tracy, I still don't have a fee, but now I got a client."

"Oh?"

"That's Jeremy Dawson calling from the lockup. The cops just gave him his one phone call."

"They charge him?" Taylor said.

"Sure thing."

"What'd they charge him with."

"What do you think? The murder of Jack Walsh."

# 21

JEREMY DAWSON LOOKED through the wire mesh screen of the visiting room of the lockup. "You gotta get me out of here, man."

Steve Winslow smiled. "That may not be so easy."

"Hey, man, like don't say that. I gotta get out of here."

"I understand. But you happen to be charged with murder."

"Yeah, but I didn't do it."

Steve smiled. "That's what they all say."

Jeremy stared at him. "Hey, man, whose side are you on?"

"Your side, of course. I'm just telling you how the police see it."

"Yeah, well they see it wrong."

"So what's right?"

"Huh?"

"Look, I know you wanna get out of here. I'll do the best I can. But I don't wanna give you any false hopes. We have a serious situation here. The police seem to think they have a case. So what you gotta do is calm down, stop thinkin' about how much you wanna get out of here, and tell me what happened. If you do that, you just might get out of here, but stop thinkin' about that for now."

Jeremy rubbed his hand over his green mohawk. "Yeah, easy for you to say. I'm the one sittin' here."

Steve shrugged. "I could always come back later."

"What?" Jeremy said.

"All right, look," Steve said. "You're a kid. You're also an orphan. Your relatives ain't much, and you probably had a hard life. I'm sure you're an expert at complaining and telling people how you been fucked over. But the point is, I don't want to hear it. You're up against a murder now. The prosecutor isn't gonna give a shit about what's fair or unfair or the whole bit. And if we get that far, a jury isn't gonna care either.

"So take a deep breath, get all that shit out of your mind, and let's talk about what happened."

Jeremy stared at Steve for a moment. Then he lowered his

head. Steve smiled slightly as he noticed Jeremy actually *was* taking a deep breath.

Jeremy looked back up at Steve. "O.K. Shoot."

"Fine," Steve said. "Start with yesterday. Uncle Jack find you?"

"Yeah."

"Where?"

"In school."

"When? Where? How'd it happen?"

"O.K.," Jeremy said. "It was in the morning. Around eleven-thirty. In between class. I was in the hall just, uh, just hangin' out. I went to my locker to get my books and there he was."

"Uncle Jack?"

"Yeah."

"What'd he do?"

"Well, he was actin' kinda funny. I mean, he always was kinda funny, but even for him, you know?"

"Yeah, I know," Steve said. "Go on."

"So he's thankin' me for getting him out of Bellevue, and he wants me to go with him."

"Where?"

"He won't say. Just I done him a favor, he's gonna do one for me."

Steve raised his eyebrows. "Oh yeah?"

"Yeah. But he don't say what. It's just, we gotta get out of here."

"So?"

"So we start down the hall and Uncle Jack spots a teacher. He says, 'Meet me out front,' and scoots around a corner and I lose him. So after that I'm playin' tag in the hallways with the teacher, and I finally get outside."

"And he's there?"

"Yeah, well he's behind a parked car and he hisses to me."

"What happens then?"

"We get out of there, we take a bus to Manhattan."

"Who pays?"

"Him."

"He had money?"

"Yeah."

"How much?"

"I don't know. He's wearin' this big old floppy coat, he fishes in the pocket, pulls out a couple of dollars. We take the bus."

"To where?"

"Port Authority."

"What happens then?"

"We walk over to Times Square, go down in the subway station."

"What happens there?"

"He won't pay, he says, 'Fuck the Transit system.' He pushes me under the turnstile, hops under himself." Jeremy looked up. "Which is stupid, right? There's a cop right there in the station. He doesn't see, but he could, you know?"

"Yeah. So?"

"So we go down, catch the Number One up to 66th Street. We get out there, walk to the end of the platform. There's an old bum sleepin' there behind a dumpster and he wakes up, but Uncle Jack knows him, says it's cool. So we sit down there."

"What for?"

"Yeah, that's what I'm wondering. All he's told me is, I did him a favor, he's gonna do me one, then I'm gonna one more for him."

"So what happened?"

"He whips out a pen and paper and writes a will."

Steve blinked. "What?"

"He writes out a will. Turns out that was the favor. Some favor. He asks for a pen and when I don't have one, he makes some crack about how you should always carry a pen, you never know when it's gonna get you a million bucks. Then he sits down and he writes out a will."

"Did you read it?"

"Yeah."

"So what did it say?"

"He leaves his money to me. All of it."

Steve sighed and rubbed his head. "Jesus."

"Yeah," Jeremy said. "Real shocker. But that's the thing. That's why I called you. I can afford a lawyer, right? He's dead, I'm his heir, I got lot of money comin', right?"

"Holy shit," Steve said. He shook his head.

"What's the matter?"

"What happened to the will?"

"He gave it to me."

"He gave it to you?"

"Yeah. That was the other favor. He'll do me a favor, then I'll do him another one. That was it. To hold onto the will for him."

"Where's the will now?"

"Cops have it."

"What?"

"I had it on me when I was arrested. The cops took all my possessions, so they have it now."

"Oh shit."

"What's the matter? They won't lose it. Safest place for it."

"Yeah, sure," Steve said dryly. "All right, let's hear the rest of it."

"The rest of it?"

"Yeah. What happened then."

Jeremy shrugged. "Nothin'. That was it."

Steve looked at him in exasperation. "No, that isn't it. You're in jail charged with murder. I'm trying to find some way to get you out. Let's go on. Uncle Jack wrote the will and he gave it to you. Was that there in the subway station?"

"Right."

"So what happened next?"

"Nothin'. I took the will and I left."

"When?"

"What do you mean, when? Right then. When he gave it to me."

"He didn't want you to stick around?"

"No. He told me to take the will, put it in a safe place, say nothin' about it to no one."

"And did you?"

"What?"

"Did you tell anyone?"

"Christ no. Why would I do that?"

"I don't know. I'm just asking."

"No, I didn't."

"All right. So you left him there in the subway station?"

"That's right."

"What'd you do then?"

"What does it matter?"

"I won't know until I hear. I'm a lawyer. I gotta know the facts. What did you do then?"

"Well, by then it was afternoon, too late to go back to school. Not that I would have anyway. So I took the subway back downtown, caught a bus back to Jersey."

"And went home?"

Jeremy's eyes shifted. "Not right away."

"Where'd you go?"

"Down by the school. Newsstand there. Went in and played a few video games."

"That where the school kids hang out?"

"Yeah."

"See any of them there?"

"Yeah. Why?"

"I dunno. Happen to mention to 'em you were gonna be rich?"

"Christ no. Why the hell I do that?"

"It's not every high school kid finds out he's gonna be a millionaire. It's the type of thing you might mention."

Jeremy's eyes were wide and innocent. "Hey. Uncle Jack told me tell no one."

"I understand."

"Well, that's what I did."

"Fine. So what'd you do then?"

"Hung out a while and went home."

"What time was that?"

"Why is it important?"

"Cause Uncle Jack is dead."

Jeremy winced. He shook his head. "Shit, that's so hard to understand."

"Yeah. So what happened when you got home?"

"Whaddya mean?"

"You see anyone?"

"Just Carl Jenson."

"You talk to him?"

"He talked to me."

"Oh?"

"Yeah. He heard me come in, he came out pissed as hell."

"Why?"

"School called. Told him I skipped out, was cuttin' class."

"What did he say?"

"Wanted to know where I'd been, wanted to know if I'd seen Uncle Jack."

"What'd you tell him."

"Told him to go fuck himself." Jeremy shrugged. "Carl's a moron."

"Why'd he ask about Uncle Jack?"

"Whaddya mean?"

"What do you think I mean? Did he know something, or was he just taking a shot in the dark? I'll spell it out for you. Maybe someone at the school saw you with Uncle Jack. So when the school called and said you were cuttin' class, they might have mentioned you left with some old bum. I'm wondering if you could tell that from anything he said."

Jeremy thought about it. "I don't know. I'm not really sure. Like I said, I didn't talk to him, just told him to go get fucked, and walked out of there."

"What did you do?"

"I went upstairs, took a shower, changed."

"And did you go out again?"

"When?"

"That night."

"Yeah, actually I did."

"What time?"

"Around seven."

"Where'd you go?"

Jeremy's eyes flicked again. "I went to the movies."

"You go with anyone?"

"No, I went by myself."

"What'd you see?"

"A teenage picture. 'Heathers.' "

" 'Heathers?' What's it about?"

"Teenage suicide and murder. Good picture. Kind of funny."

"What time was the picture?"

"Eight o'clock."

"Where was it playing?"

"In Teaneck."

"You were at a movie in Teaneck from eight o'clock till when?"

"Got out about nine-thirty. Hung out for a while. Didn't feel like goin' home."

"What time did you *get* home?"

"I don't know. Twelve. Twelve-thirty."

"Anyone see you come in?"

Jeremy grimaced. "Yeah. Aunt Claire."

"Oh?"

"Yeah. She's in the living room watchin' the Johnny Carson show. She heard the door, jumped up to bawl me out."

"For what?"

"Skippin' school."

"I see. So she knows you came in around midnight?"

"Somewhere between twelve, twelve-thirty. Couldn't have been later than that 'cause the Carson show was still on."

"Tell me something. Did *she* mention Uncle Jack?"

"Huh?"

"When she bawled you out about skippin' school—did she mention him?"

"No, she didn't."

"Good."

"Why?"

"Cause then it's more likely the school didn't. O.K. Did you go out after that?"

"No, I didn't."

"What'd you do?"

"Went to bed."

"And then what?"

"Whaddya think? I went to sleep. I got up the next morning and went to school. Next thing I know, two cops show up and drag me out of class."

Steve looked at him for some time. "And that's all you know?"

"Yeah."

"From the time you left your uncle early yesterday after-noon you never saw him again?"

"That's right."

"And last night you went to a movie called 'Heathers,' hung out in Teaneck until midnight and went home?"

"That's right."

"And you have no idea who killed Uncle Jack or why?"

Jeremy looked at him. "Hey, how could I?"

"Damned if I know," Steve said.

They sat in silence.

Jeremy stirred. "Well, come on. Can you help me?"

Steve shook his head. "I'm damned if I know that either." He took a breath, blew it out again. "But if you want me, kid, I'm your lawyer."

# 22

TRACY GARVIN LOOKED UP FROM her desk when Steve Winslow came in the front door.

"Get me Mark, Tracy," Steve said. "We are in deep shit."

"Yeah, that's what Mark said."

"Oh?"

"Yeah, he said to call him as soon as you got in. He's got bad news, and more coming every minute."

"He say what?"

"No, he was on another line. But I'll tell you, he didn't seem happy."

"That makes two of us. Give him a call, get him down here."

Steve Winslow pushed open the door to his inner office, went in and flopped down in the chair at his desk. He sighed and rubbed his forehead. Jesus Christ, what a fucking disaster. Defending some sniveling punk kid who looked like he stepped out of a science fiction magazine. Christ, what was he thinking of? He hadn't even told the kid to ditch the hair. Have to shave it off, more than likely. Maybe it would grow back before trial. If not, better shaved bald than that fucking green fringe.

Steve chuckled. Christ, what a hypocrite he was. Going into court with his own long hair, looking like a refugee from the sixties, but damned if he'd let his client look like teenagers did now. Well hell, he had good reason, didn't he? The kid's liberty was at stake. He'd be guilty of malpractice if he didn't advise the kid according to his best interests.

If he wasn't guilty of malpractice already. For giving Jack Walsh advice. For letting him write that fucking holographic will.

The door opened and Tracy Garvin ushered in Mark Taylor.

"The shit's hit the fan, Steve," Mark said.

"Yeah, same here. I just hope it's the same shit."

"Did Jeremy tell you about the will?"

"Yeah."

"Good. Then that's no surprise. My pipeline from headquarters's been checking in all morning, and that's the first thing he got."

"All I know is Jack Walsh made a holographic will leaving everything to Jeremy Dawson and gave it to Jeremy to keep. You got anything more than that?"

Taylor shook his head. "That's the scoop on the will, all right."

"Any chance of seein' a copy?"

"Not a prayer. The cops have it sewed up tight, and they won't give it out till the D.A. says so. And from what I gather, that won't be until they show it to the grand jury."

"At which point I'll be able to get a copy," Steve said. "Big deal. Is that the bad news?"

"That's just for starters. You know Walsh picked up Jeremy at his school yesterday?"

"Yeah. They got witnesses to that?"

"Sure thing. And that ain't the half of it. They got a witness saw them in the subway station."

"66th Street Station?"

"Yeah."

"What time?"

"That's the only saving grace. No one's sayin'. And you'd think if it was around the time of the murder, they would."

Steve frowned. "Yeah, maybe. Who's the witness?"

"That's hush-hush, and that's the other good news. The cops won't say."

"Oh?"

"Right. And the way I figure, that means it's unreliable. Speculation is it's most likely another homeless."

Steve frowned. "I see. Is that it?"

Taylor shook his head. "Wish it were. I saved the worst for last."

"What's that?"

"The kid's a crack dealer."

Steve Winslow's jaw dropped open. "What!?"

Mark Taylor shook his head. "Sorry to be the one to bring it to you. But that's the word. Jeremy Dawson sells crack."

"You sure?"

"No, I'm just reporting what my men dug up."

"No, damn it, I mean what's the source? Has he ever been busted? Does he have a record?"

"No, not unless you count bein' suspended from school. But as far as a police record, he's clean."

"What about the school suspension—they catch him with the stuff?"

Taylor shook his head. "No, the way I get it, some honor student ratted on him. The principal called him in and suspended him for two days."

"Did he admit it?"

"Would you expect him to?"

"No."

"Then he probably didn't. I don't know. This is all just gossip. We haven't interviewed the principal yet. So far, we're pokin' into this very low key."

"The cops know this?"

"I'm sure they do. I have no direct confirmation, but it's the sort of thing they don't miss."

Steve shook his head. "Jesus Christ."

"Puts you in a hell of a position, doesn't it?"

"That's putting it mildly."

"Still gonna represent him?"

"I told him I would."

"That was before you knew this."

"So?"

"So the kid lied to you. At least, held out on you. Got you to represent him under false pretenses."

"What if he did?"

"I'm saying you got a perfect right to back out."

"Why? Because the kid didn't say, 'By the way, I happen to be a crack dealer?' Can you imagine any teenager in the world who would?"

"I can't imagine any teenage *crack dealer* who would. Which is the whole point. The kid's a loser. You wanna stick up for a crack dealer? In this day and age, that's just askin' for it. Particularly someone in your position."

Steve looked at him. "And just what's that supposed to mean?"

Taylor took a breath. "Look, Steve. You only had two cases.

Your last one, you did real good. You did real good on both of 'em, but the last one, you came off *lookin'* good. Your first case, frankly, you came off lookin' like a schmuck."

"Thanks a lot."

"Look, you know what I mean. You turned things around in terms of your career. Now you got a chance to move forward. Defendin' a crack dealer ain't gonna help."

"You're missing the point, Mark. I'm not defending him for selling crack. I'm defending him for murder."

"What's the difference?"

Steve took a breath. "There's a big difference if he didn't do it. Even the scum of the earth's entitled to a fair trial. If he didn't kill his uncle, he shouldn't go to jail for murder just because he happens to deal crack."

Taylor held up his hands. "Yeah, sure. He's presumed innocent until proven guilty. He's entitled to a fair trial. He has the right to a lawyer. There's just no reason that lawyer has to be you."

Steve looked at him. He chuckled.

"What's so funny?" Taylor said.

"Nothing. I just said almost the same thing to someone just the other day."

"So?"

"So," Steve said, "I told the kid I'm gonna represent him, I'm gonna represent him. So he held out on me and he's a less than model citizen. What else is new? In an ideal world, you'd be able to like your clients. In real life it doesn't happen that way. Because if they were such good people to begin with, they probably wouldn't *be* clients."

"So you're gonna represent him?"

"Sure I'm gonna represent him. And I'm gonna get him off, too. If that makes me look bad to some people, well that's just tough."

"You really think you can get him off?" Tracy put in.

"I don't see why not. Cops don't have that much of a case. They got the will for motivation, that's the biggie. And the fact that he was seen with his uncle. For one thing, that was much earlier in the afternoon. For another thing, the witness is totally unreliable.

"And then there's the cause of death. I'd hate to be in the prosecutor's shoes trying to argue that one. He waits until he falls asleep and then douses him with gasoline and sets him on fire? In a subway station no less?" Steve shook his head. "No, what they got so far won't do it. It's not enough that he was seen with his uncle. They need someone who saw him set the body on fire. Or at least someone saw him buy the gasoline. Have they got anything like that?"

Taylor shook his head. "Not so far. If they do, they're not letting it out."

The phone rang. Tracy Garvin reached out, picked it up. "Steve Winslow's office . . . Uh huh. Just a minute." She handed the phone to Mark Taylor. "It's for you."

Taylor took the phone, said, "Mark Taylor here." He listened for a couple of minutes, punctuating the conversation with dull, toneless 'uh huhs,' and hung up the phone with a look on his face that would have done credit to a mortician.

"Well?" Steve said.

Taylor took a breath. "Look, Steve," he said. "Are you committed to defend this kid no matter what?"

"I already told you that."

"Well then you just got a major kick in the balls. The cops got a search warrant for Jeremy Dawson's school locker. You know what they turned up? Twenty-eight vials of crack, some drug paraphernalia and a thirty-two-caliber automatic."

"What!?" Steve said.

"That's right. He's heavy into drugs, and I do mean heavy. Now I don't know if he was really playin' with the big boys, or if the gun was just for show, but in any event he had it."

"Shit."

"Yeah," Taylor said. "And you don't know the half of it. They just got the report back from the medical examiner. He determined the cause of death."

"So?" Steve said. "The cause of death was burning and/or asphyxiation, right?"

"The cause of death," Mark Taylor said dryly, "was a thirty-two-caliber bullet fired directly into the back of the head."

# 23

a sulky kid.

"You left a few things out, Jeremy."

Jeremy said nothing, kept his head down.

"You didn't tell me you dealt crack. You didn't tell me you had a gun."

Jeremy shifted slightly, continued to look at the floor.

"You don't seem surprised I know all this. Did the cops talk to you?"

No response.

"I asked you a question. The cops talk to you?"

"Yeah."

"What'd you tell 'em?"

Jeremy raised his eyes then, defiantly. "Just what you told me. I got nothin' to say, talk to my lawyer."

"That's all?"

"Yeah, that's all."

"But they didn't let up. They kept after you. They kept asking you questions. They show you vials of crack?"

"Yeah."

"They show you a gun?"

"Yeah."

"They ask you where you got them?"

No response.

"Hey, kid, wake up. This is not high-school time. I'm not a teacher askin' you why you were late for class. This is a murder here. If they nail you for it, it's gonna be a little worse than bein' kept after school. So quit sulking, grow up and answer some questions. Did they ask you where you got them?"

"Yeah."

"What did you tell them?"

"See my lawyer."

"That's all?"

"Yeah."

"You didn't answer any questions, you didn't try to explain anything?"

"Hell no."

Steve Winslow was sure he hadn't. Some kids' reaction would be to try to lie their way out of it. Jeremy's would be to pull himself into his shell and sulk.

"O.K., fine," Steve said. "You did good. I didn't want you to talk, and you didn't talk. The problem is, now you got in the habit. And I need you to talk to me. So let's shift gears here, get yourself into your talking mode, 'cause you got things to say."

Jeremy looked at him, hostile, defiant. Steve Winslow wanted very much to walk out. He fought the urge.

"O.K. Now, where did you get the gun?"

"Shit."

"Hey, I'm your lawyer. You can tell me anything. If I'm going to help you, you *have* to tell me things. The prosecutor's gonna throw the evidence at you, and I gotta fight it. I can't do that unless I know what's up. Now where did you get the gun?"

Jeremy snuffled. "Connection."

"What?"

"My connection. For crack."

"Who's that?"

Jeremy shrugged. "Black guy from Harlem."

"He gave it to you?"

"Sold it to me."

"What's his name?"

"Dunno."

"You're dealing with the guy, you don't know his name?"

"Calls himself the Main Man. It's not his name though."

"No shit. So he sold you the gun?"

"Yeah."

"For how much?"

"Seventy-five."

"Seventy-five bucks?"

"Yeah."

"Why'd you need a gun?"

No answer.

"Damn it, these are the questions that count. Why'd you need a gun?"

"He said I might need it."

"Your connection?"

"Yeah."

"It was his idea?"

"Partly."

"What do you mean, partly?"

"Well, I mentioned I might want to have one."

"Oh, did you?"

"Yeah."

"Why?"

"I dunno."

"And he thought you might need one?"

"Yeah."

"Why would he think that?"

"I dunno."

Steve looked at him a moment. "I do. You want to be a big man, you're trying to impress the guy, act tough. You tell him you need a gun."

Jeremy said nothing.

"Anyway, he got you one."

"Yeah."

"This drug dealer—the Main Man—how old is he?"

"I dunno. Fifteen, sixteen."

Steve shook his head. "Jesus Christ." He took a breath. "So tell me about the gun."

"What about it?"

"You ever fire it?"

"What's that got to do with it?"

"You ever fire the fucking gun?"

"Hey man, easy. What's the big deal?"

"The big deal is, you're up for murder. You may not understand these questions, but you don't have to. You're a stupid kid who don't know shit. I'm the lawyer who's gotta get you out of here. You want me to do that job, then do me a favor. Stop thinking. Don't think at all. You know why? You're not good at it. It just gets in the way. So stop trying to figure out why I'm asking the questions, and just answer the fucking things."

Jeremy's face reddened. "Hey, fuck you."

Steve smiled. "Son of a bitch, I got a rise out of you. Good.

Now, while I have your full attention—did you ever fire the gun?"

"Yeah."

"When?"

"When I got it."

"When was that?"

"I dunno. A month ago."

"Why'd you fire the gun?"

"I wanted to."

Steve raised his hand. "Hey, kid, I don't care how much crack you do, you can't be that dumb. Why'd you fire the gun is a question asking for an explanation. What'd you fire it at, did you fire it at a person? If so, did you hit him, kill him? Where and when did this happen? Shit, Jeremy, just for fun, try to answer my questions like a human being. Now tell me about firing the gun."

"I was just practicing."

"Where?"

"Junkyard."

"Where?"

"Queens."

"When?"

"Right after I got it."

"Why'd you do it?"

Jeremy shrugged. "Just to test it out."

"How many times you fire it?"

"Once."

"Why only once?"

"It was cold. It stung my hand."

"Were you wearing gloves?"

"Yeah. And it was awkward with the gloves."

"Well, that's good."

"What?"

"That you were wearing gloves. If you didn't fire it again, there won't be powder marks on your hands."

"Oh."

"So did you fire it again?"

"No."

"That was the only time?"

"Yeah. What's this about powder marks on my hands?"

"When you fire a gun, it leaves powder traces on your hand. A paraffin test can show that you fired one."

Jeremy looked interested. "So if there's no powder traces on my hands, it'll prove I didn't do it?"

"No, they'll say you were wearing gloves."

"Oh."

"But it's better than if there was, you got it?"

"Yeah."

"It's still bad. If it turns out it was your gun killed your uncle —and I'll bet it was—you're in deep shit. It was your gun, you kept it in your locker, your uncle winds up dead, you were seen with your uncle, the gun is found in your locker. Add that up and tell me how it looks to you."

"I didn't do it."

"So you say. No one's gonna take your word for that. We have to deal with the facts. Now if it was your gun did it, who could have done it but you?"

"How the hell should I know?"

"Well, who has the combination to your locker?"

"No one."

"No one?"

"Yeah."

"Now that can't be right."

"Why not?"

" 'Cause if it is, they got you dead to rights on a murder rap, and nothing I can do is gonna save you. So let's think about that. Who has the combination to your locker?"

Jeremy frowned. "Shit, I don't know."

"Maybe you gave it to a friend or a relative."

"I don't remember."

"Great. Well, maybe someone had to pick something up for you from school."

"Not that I know."

"O.K., we'll do it another way. You got the combination written down somewhere?"

"Yeah."

"Where."

"Piece of paper."

"I figured that. Where's the piece of paper?"

"In my wallet."

"You carry the combination to your locker around in your wallet?"

"Yeah."

"What's it say on the paper?"

"The combination."

"I know that. What else. Does it say, 'Jeremy Dawson's locker combination?' "

"No, just the string of numbers."

"Three numbers?"

"Yeah."

"With dashes between 'em?"

"Yeah."

"And this was on a piece of paper folded up in your wallet?"

"Yeah."

"So anybody looked in your wallet, they would find it."

"Who's gonna look in my wallet?"

"You tell me."

"How the hell should I know?"

"You ever lose your wallet, you leave it lying around?"

"No."

"You're not bein' much help."

"What can I tell you? If I don't know, I don't know. There's no way you can prove someone saw my wallet."

"I know that. I can't prove it. I have to raise the inference someone did."

"What does that mean?"

"That it was possible. That it could have happened. You see?"

"I guess so."

"Well, could it have happened?"

Jeremy thought a moment. "Yeah, I guess so."

"Good. You have some time to think, you try to figure out who, why, when, where. Now let's talk about your uncle."

"What about him?"

"You came to my office, asked me to get your uncle out of Bellevue."

"Yeah. So?"

"That seemed a nice gesture for a high school kid. I remember what you said at the time. He wasn't crazy, he didn't belong there, you liked him, you wanted him out."

"That's right."

"Is it? I could buy that before I knew who you are. Coming from a crack dealer, it sounds like a crock of shit."

"Hey, man—"

"Do me a favor. Don't 'hey man' me. I'm gettin' really sick of it. Your uncle—he used to give you money?"

"Why?"

"Just answer the question. He used to give you money?"

"Yeah. I told you. He was a nice guy. He liked me."

"But after he moved out, he didn't see you, he didn't give you money no more."

"Yeah."

"So, that must have been tough on a kid who likes crack. A kid who deals crack just to have some around. A kid who likes to be a big shot.

"And then your uncle gets locked up in Bellevue, and your relatives try to grab the cash, but they never treated you well and you know you're not going to get any. And it occurs to you, hey if you got your uncle out, he'd be very very grateful."

Jeremy said nothing.

"Didn't it?"

"What if it did?"

"Grateful enough to write a will?"

"Hey, man, that was a shock to me. I never even thought of it."

"No, I'll bet you didn't. A spot of cash would have been a lot more handy."

Jeremy looked at him. "Hey man, why are you doing this? You're not my father, you're my lawyer. We're supposed to be discussing a murder rap."

"That we are," Steve said. "I'm just trying to get a message across to you, and I gotta hammer it, because frankly you aren't that swift.

"Let me tell you something about murder trials. It's not just the facts of the case. The prosecution's gonna try to paint a picture of you for the jury. And they're gonna have a lot to work with. The way I'm makin' you sound—that's nothing compared with what the prosecutor's gonna do. Everything you ever did, they're gonna paint it with a greedy, selfish motive. You don't like how it sounds coming from me, think how it's gonna sound coming from them. Think how's it's gonna sound to a jury."

Jeremy looked at Steve defiantly for a few moments, then dropped his eyes to the floor.

"Now," Steve said. "I gotta get the facts. I can raise an inference about the gun, but that's all. If it's your gun, it's bad. Then we gotta concentrate on the alibi. Now, your alibi is a picture show and a soda shop where no one saw you.

"Let's start with the picture show. You keep the stub?"

"No. Why would I do that?"

"Who cares why? The fact is, if you had it would help. I take it you didn't?"

"No."

"The ticket girl remember you?"

"No, why should she?"

"I don't know. How many green haired customers you think she gets?"

"More than you'd think."

Steve sighed. "You're probably right there. Jesus Christ, I feel a hundred years old.

"All right, look. I'm gonna check your alibi out. Till I do, be damn sure you don't mention it to the cops."

Jeremy's eyes shifted.

Steve winced. "Oh shit."

Jeremy shifted in his chair.

"Damn it, you told me you didn't tell the cops anything."

"I didn't tell them nothing important. But they were saying I was on the subway that night. All I said was I wasn't."

"I told you not to say anything."

"I didn't say anything. They just said I was on the subway, and I said no, I wasn't."

"Jesus Christ."

"What's so bad about that?"

"And then they wanted to know where you were?"

"Yeah."

"And you told 'em you were at the movies?"

"Yeah."

"Jesus Christ."

"What's wrong with that?"

"If you really were at the movies, nothing. If you weren't, you just slit your throat."

"I was at the movies."

"What was the name again?"

"What?"

"The name of the movie."

" 'Heathers.' "

"What's it about?"

"What do you care?"

"What do you think?"

"I told you. It's a teen comedy."

"About what?"

"It's about this crazy chick and this guy who talks like Jack Nicholson go around killing people and making it look like suicide."

Steve looked at him. "That's a comedy?"

"Yeah. It was funny."

"O.K., I'll check it out. Now, here's what we're gonna do. First of all, I'm going to waive extradition and get you transferred to New York."

"Why would you do that?"

"In the first place, the cops got enough on you to extradite you anyway."

"Oh."

"In the second place, it's a pain in the ass to have to come all the way to Jersey every time I want to talk to you. I'm just telling you so when they move you, don't be upset."

"Here's another thing. They let you shave in here?"

"Yeah."

"Good. Next time they do, shave off the fucking hair."

"You're kidding."

"No."

"Why?"

"I gotta sell you to a jury. It's gonna be hard enough without dealing with that."

Jeremy thrust out his jaw. "Hey man, this is America. I got a right to a fair trial. They got no right to judge me on how I look."

"Right," Steve said. "And if you believe that, I have this land in Florida."

"Well, it's true, isn't it?"

"Yeah, and it's also true someone sometimes wins the lottery. But I wouldn't wanna bet on that person being you."

"That's bullshit, man. I didn't do it. No one's gonna find me guilty 'cause of how I look. I ain't cuttin' my hair for that."

Steve took a breath. "All right, how's this? The prosecution's gonna put someone on the witness stand and say, 'And did you recognize the man you saw walking in the subway station with Jack Walsh?' and the witness will say, 'Yes sir, it's that kid right there with the green hair.'"

Jeremy thought that over. He frowned. "You may have a point."

# 24

MARK TAYLOR WAS STILL ON the phone when Steve Winslow pushed open the door. He covered the mouthpiece. "Sit down, Steve. I got stuff comin' in now." Into the phone he said, "Uh huh. Go on." He listened for a minute, said, "O.K., keep on it," and hung up.

"Glad you're here, Steve, this thing is moving fast."

"What you got?"

"The biggie is, it's the kid's gun."

"The murder weapon?"

"No question about it. The bullets match."

"Shit."

"Well, it's what you expected, right?"

"Yeah, but you can always hope. What else?"

"I understand you just waived extradition."

"Right."

"How come?"

"Frankly, I was tired of running over to Jersey."

"Makes sense. Anyway, they're putting together a grand jury, getting ready to indict Jeremy Dawson for murder."

"Yesterday's news, Mark. All of that's just routine. You got anything fresh?"

"Well, word is Harry Dirkson's gonna handle the case himself."

"Oh yeah?"

"Yeah. And that's opened up a bit of speculation."

"Over what?"

"Is the D.A. getting involved personally just because the victim was a millionaire, or is it just because you happen to be attorney for the defense."

"You're trying to tell me Harry Dirkson doesn't love me?"

"That's putting it mildly. The word is he's so pissed off about what happened in the Harding case, he can't resist taking a shot at you in a case where he's got your client dead to rights."

"He doesn't have my client dead to rights. He's got circumstantial evidence. It's bad, but it's still just circumstantial."

"Yeah, well he's also got the eyewitness."

"What eyewitness?"

"The one who saw Jeremy and Jack Walsh together in the subway station."

"There really was such a witness?"

"Yeah, there was."

"That's not good."

"Well, it's not as bad as it could be. It turns out we were right about the witness bein' a bum."

"Oh yeah?"

"Yeah. That's unofficial, by the way. The cops aren't letting it out, but my man managed to get it. So that's good news. The guy's a wino. His identification's not gonna be that strong. You should be able to rip him apart on cross-examination. So that's good."

Steve frowned. "Yes and no."

"What do you mean?"

"It's a two-edged sword—the guy being a derelict, I mean. Yeah, sure, I can cut him up on the witness stand. But the jury's not gonna like it. 'Cause a guy like that's basically defenseless. If I tear into him, it's like picking on a cripple. Sure, I can raise some doubts about the identification. Maybe even get the guy's testimony struck out. But in the eyes of the jury, I'm a big bully picking on a helpless man, and the result is I wind up antagonizing them and prejudicing them against the defendant."

Taylor frowned. "I hadn't thought of that."

"Yeah, well I bet Dirkson has. He's probably happy as a clam the guy's a bum."

"You mean you're not going to try to break down his identification?"

"I've got to. That's my job." Steve frowned and rubbed his head. "So here's a job for you. Get one of your men to take some pictures for me."

"Pictures?"

"Yeah, and then have him blow 'em up to eight-by-ten glossies."

"Pictures of what?"

"Kids with green hair. At least five of them. Head shots. Shot from the same angle. Similar photos, you got it?"

"Yeah."

"And not just green hair. Green mohawks."

"I understand. Anything else?"

"Yeah. First off, get a shot of Jeremy Dawson. Have the photographer use that picture as a model for the other ones."

"Where am I gonna get that?"

"Are you kidding me? It'll be on the wire services. They're indicting him for murder. It'll be on the front page of the *Daily News.*"

"Yeah, right. Anything else?"

"Yeah. Check on all the relatives. Check 'em for alibis. See what they were doin' that time of night."

"Now that I like."

"Why?"

"Routine, time consuming, and expensive."

Steve frowned. "Yeah."

"What's the matter?"

"Well—"

"Don't tell me you haven't got a retainer?"

Steve shrugged. "My client's a teenage kid."

"Shit, that's right."

"On the one hand, he hasn't got a dime. On the other hand, he's got a holographic will that makes him the sole heir to millions."

"What about that? Can the will stand up? Is it legally binding?"

Steve shrugged. "I haven't seen it yet."

"Yeah, but as a general rule—can a handwritten will knock out a prior one drawn up by lawyers?"

"It can if it's drawn right." Steve smiled. "And if you'll recall, Jack Walsh consulted me about how to write the will. So if I knew what I was talking about, the will should stand up.

"Except for one thing."

"What's that?"

"One little law I forgot to mention. Not that it would have done Jack Walsh any good."

"Oh yeah? What?"

"A person convicted of murder can't inherit from his victim.

If Jeremy Dawson killed his uncle, it doesn't matter what that will says, he can't touch a dime."

"Shit, that's right."

"Which puts me in the unique position of handling a murder case on a contingency basis. If I get Jeremy Dawson off, he inherits and I get paid. If he's convicted, he can't inherit and I get zilch."

Taylor shook his head. "Shit, what a bummer."

"Yeah. So get going on the other relatives. Come up with someone else who could have killed the guy."

"I'll try, Steve, but Jesus."

"What?"

"Well, Jeremy's the one who was seen in the subway, he's the one who inherits, and it was his gun. Now, I can try to make a case against one of the others, but let me tell you, it sure don't sound good."

"I'm not asking you to make a case, Mark. That's my job. I'm just asking you to get the facts."

"Yeah, and you're paying me out of your own pocket. That's the part I don't like."

"Don't worry about that. I have every intention of being paid for this case. Now, you got anything else?"

"Yeah. It's just incidental now, but I got a line on Julie Creston."

"Oh?"

"Yeah. She finished filming, showed up back in L.A. My contact out there looked her up. Frankly, what with the murder and everything, I'd forgotten to call him off. I didn't think of it till he reported in. I'm sorry, cause it's an unnecessary expense, and—"

"Screw the expense, Mark." Steve held up his hands. "Let me make something clear. I either take a case or I don't. The size of the retainer doesn't matter. If I take a murder case, I'm gonna go all out. As far as you're concerned, I want you to investigate this as if I had a hundred-thousand-dollar retainer. Don't stint on anything. 'Cause frankly, the case looks pretty bad, and I need all the help I can get. You got it?"

"Yeah."

"O.K. So what about Julie Creston?"

"Well, the guy looked her up, asked her about Jack Walsh."

"And?"

"And she didn't want to hear from him. Acted like the name was poison. She's out there, she's got a new life, a new career, she's livin' with someone, the name Jack Walsh's just a big embarrassment to her."

"Oh?"

"Yeah. And she don't want her boyfriend hearin' about him, either. She took the detective out in the hall, gave him an earful. According to her, Jack Walsh is a slime and a shit, and she wants nothing to do with him."

Steve held up his hand. "Wait a minute, wait a minute. When was this?"

"I don't know the exact time. It was earlier today."

"Today?"

"Yeah."

"But she's talkin' as if Walsh was still alive. Didn't your man tell her he was dead?"

"He didn't know, Steve. The guy's in California. And this is an assignment left over from last week. I'd completely forgotten about it till the guy phoned in his report."

"I see," Steve said. He frowned. "So this Julie Creston—she still doesn't know Jack Walsh is dead?"

"That's right."

"But your man in L.A. said she hates his guts?"

"Yeah."

"All right. Fine. Look, call him up and tell him to make another pass at her. Only this time give her the dope. Tell her what happened to Walsh. See how she reacts."

"Sure," Taylor said. "But what for?"

Steve went on as if he hadn't heard him. "And tell him to trace her movements. Find out when she finished filming. And find out when she went back to L.A. And whether she went straight back, or whether she had time to make a side trip somewhere, specifically to New York."

Taylor stared at him. "Are you kidding me?"

"Not at all. Here's a woman who hates Jack Walsh. From what your man says, she'd like to see him dead. Let's find out how much."

"Steve, that's mighty thin. I mean, Walsh didn't dump her, the relatives got in the way. Maybe she blames him and thinks it was his fault, but still. I mean, that was a year ago, she's out there in California now, she doesn't profit from his death, and—"

"How do you know?"

"Huh?"

"How do you know she doesn't? Jack Walsh wrote one holographic will. What's to have stopped him from writing another one? When your man tells her Walsh is dead, have him ask her how it affects her. Find out if she expects to inherit in any way. Who knows, how do we know she isn't holding a handwritten will Walsh made out a year ago when they were all lovey-dovey?"

Mark Taylor had trouble meeting Steve Winslow's eyes. "I'll do it, Steve, but Jesus. I mean—"

Steve smiled and held up his hand. "Hey, Mark. I'm not crazy and I'm not stupid. You know and I know that didn't happen. But I'm trying to get the kid off. Reasonable doubt, that's all I need."

Taylor sighed. "Yeah, Steve. But I think the operative word is reasonable."

"Hey, Mark. You just get me the data. I'll make it sound reasonable."

# 25

TRACY GARVIN STOOD AND
watched while Steve Winslow read through the facsimile of
Jack Walsh's holographic will. Steve finished, set the paper on
his desk, leaned back in his chair and frowned.

"Well?" Tracy said.

Steve shook his head. "It's all wrong."

"What do you mean?"

Steve tipped the chair forward, pointed to the will. "This
will. It's all wrong."

"What's wrong with it?"

"Have you read it?"

Tracy shook her head. "No. I knew you were waiting for it.
As soon as it arrived, I brought it in."

"All right," Steve said. "Listen to this."

He picked up the will and read, " 'I, Jack Walsh, being of
sound mind and body, do hereby revoke all prior wills and
make this my last will and testament.' "

Steve looked up from the will. "He now puts in the date,
specifying not only February 26th, but February 26th at 2:30
P.M."

"What's wrong with that?" Tracy asked.

"Nothing. It's just odd. People date a will. They don't usually
put the exact hour."

"So he was a precise man."

"He was also a lunatic. At least, arguably. And an insane
man cannot write a will. Not and have it binding. Putting the
time on is odd, and anything odd is suspect.

"But that's nothing," Steve said. "Listen to the rest of it. 'I'm
writing this will in the 66th Street Station of the Broadway
Number One line. It pleases me to do so. I think it a nice touch
that a document affecting the transfer of so much money
should be executed at the very spot where indigents sleep.

" 'Having revoked all prior wills, I now dispose of my property as follows:

" 'To my relatives, Rose Tindel, Pat Grayson, Claire Chesterton, and Carl Jenson, I leave the sum of one thousand dollars

each, in the hope that they will use it to pull themselves together and find themselves and their lazy, worthless spouses work.

" 'The rest, remainder and residue of my property I leave as follows:

" 'To Jeremy Dawson, who though only a boy, has exhibited the attributes of consideration, concern and kindness. It was he who came to me in my hour of need, and he who saw fit to look out for my welfare. He is deserving, and this shall be his reward.

" 'I hereby appoint the Chase Manhattan Bank to act as trustee for Jeremy Dawson until he shall reach the age of twenty-one, at which time they are to turn over the entire principal to him without restriction or reservation. I appoint the bank *sole* trustee, and specifically state that none of the aforementioned relatives, Rose Tindel, Pat Grayson, Claire Chesterton, Carl Jenson, or the aforementioned spouses, Jason Tindel and Fred Grayson, shall have any say whatsoever in the trust, nor have any right to use any of the monies contained therein for any purpose whatsoever.' "

Steve looked up from the will, shook his head, said, "And that's it."

"So what's wrong with that?" Tracy said.

"Everything," Steve said. He picked up the will, handed it to her. "Here. Take a look."

Tracy took the will, looked at it and frowned. "Seems O.K. to me."

"Yeah, well there's something missing."

"Really? What? No, don't tell me." She looked at the will again and then her eyes widened. "Son of a bitch."

"Got it?"

"Yeah. The signature."

"Right."

"He didn't sign it."

"No. And that's very odd, because it's one of the things we specifically talked about."

"Yeah, I remember."

"I told him writing his name at the top could be construed as a signature, but to make sure there's no mistake, sign it at the bottom."

"Suppose he misunderstood you?"

"Not that man. He's sharp as a tack."

"So why'd he do it?"

"I don't know. Maybe he didn't."

Tracy frowned. "What do you mean?"

"Well, take a look. Jack Walsh was writing in longhand. The handwriting is spread out and nearly fills the page."

"So?"

"So what if there's a page 2?"

Tracy looked at him. "You think there is?"

"It's possible there *was.*"

"All right, well what if there was? What difference would it make?"

"It might make a lot," Steve said. "Look at the way the will is worded."

"What do you mean?"

"Particularly the residuary clause. Notice, he doesn't say, 'All the rest, remainer and residue of my estate I leave to Jeremy Dawson.' Instead, he says, 'All the rest, remainer and residue of my estate I leave as follows:' Then there's a colon. Then he starts a paragraph, 'To Jeremy Dawson, etc., etc.' "

"What's the difference?"

"Big difference. Suppose on page 2 there's another short paragraph about how the trust is set up and how the other relatives can't get their hands on it, ending with a semicolon. And then the next paragraph begins, 'To my beloved such-and-such.' "

"You mean there could be another heir? He could have left his money to two people?"

"Exactly. And the way this will is worded, that's not really such a long shot."

"Well, if that's true," Tracy said, "what happened to page 2?"

"There's two possibilities. One, Jeremy destroyed it so he'd inherit the whole thing."

"Is he smart enough to do that?"

"Hard to tell. He's smart in some ways, dumb in others. He's a tough kid to read."

"What's the other possibility?"

"Jack Walsh gave it to someone else."

"Why would he do that?"

"How should I know? The man was eccentric. It might have amused him. And then there's a third possibility."

"What's that?"

"He might have kept it himself. In which case it burned up with him."

"Shit. You really think he did?"

"I think it's a good possibility. I keep trying to get in the man's mind. And I know from the questions he asked me he was planning something exactly of that sort. If the will isn't found right away, and the prior will gets probated, and then the new will shows up. Well, it's a just slight wrinkle on that to what if half of the will gets probated and then the other half shows up."

"You mean—"

"Exactly. I think it's entirely possible Jack Walsh wrote out a second half of the will, which he planned to stash somewhere with someone, to be mailed to me or the police or the bank at some later specified date."

"If that's true, then we'll never know."

"Right, and—"

Steve broke off at the sound of the outer door opening and closing. "Someone in the outer office."

"I'll see who it is," Tracy said.

She went out, returned moments later.

"Jason Tindel to see you."

"Oh? Is he on the warpath?"

"Not with me. He seemed perfectly polite and respectful."

"This should be fun. Show him in."

Tracy went out and came in ushering Jason Tindel.

Tindel immediately held up his hands in a conciliatory gesture. "I'm not angry," he said.

"Oh?"

"No. That was some job you did to me on the witness stand. But I understand you were only doing your job. There's no hard feelings."

"I'm glad to hear it. So what can I do for you?"

"It's about Jeremy, of course."

"Oh?"

"Yes. The family's very concerned. At first we thought it was ridiculous, but now it appears there actually is something of a case."

"The police seem to think so."

"That's absurd. Jeremy wouldn't do anything like that. Not to Uncle Jack. Now Jeremy is a bit wild. He's been in scrapes before. There's some things I wouldn't put past him. But not this."

"I'm glad to hear it," Steve said. "But why are you here?"

Jason frowned. "To offer my support, of course. The whole family's support."

"Oh?"

"Well, I would think you'd need help in this. From what I hear, the police happen to have a pretty good case. Well, we happen to know a few things about Jeremy's background, his history, that could assist you in putting together the defense."

"Such as what?"

"Well, Jeremy hasn't always been mentally stable. There's been incidents in the past, things you could bring up that would show diminished responsibility."

A grin spread over Steve's face. "Diminished responsibility?"

"Yes."

"You've seen the will, haven't you? Jeremy's will?"

Jason Tindel frowned. "Yes. Why?"

"And you plan to contest it, don't you?"

"Well, of course I do," Jason said.

"On what grounds?"

"Lots of grounds. When Jack Walsh made that will, he was not of sound mind. There's also the question of undue influence. There's also the fact that the will isn't signed."

"Sounds like good grounds to me," Steve said. "I assume a lawyer pointed them out to you?"

"I spoke to my lawyer, yes."

"Yeah, I was sure you had," Steve said. "The moment you used the term, 'diminished responsibility.' And your lawyer advised you you could contest the will on those grounds?"

"Well, yes he did."

"And he also told you you couldn't be sure of winning, didn't he?"

Jason frowned. "What's that got to do with it?"

"It's got everything to do with it," Steve said. "I was wondering why you were here. Then you said 'diminished responsibility' and I knew. Because I know the next thing your lawyer told you. And that's even if you couldn't knock out Jeremy's will, it still wouldn't matter if Jeremy got convicted of murder. 'Cause a murderer can't inherit from his victim. That's why you're in here offering me support, and that's why the support isn't anything that's gonna get Jeremy off. It's the type of stuff to get the sentence reduced once he's convicted. 'Cause you don't care how long he goes to jail, just as long as he's convicted and it knocks out his will."

Jason Tindel looked totally nonplussed. "Well, now . . ." he said.

"Well now, indeed," Steve said. He smiled. "Well, anyway I'm glad you're not angry. I'm not angry either." Steve pointed. "But if you wouldn't mind doing me the favor, would you please get your ass out of my office?"

# 26

STEVE WINSLOW SMILED AT Jeremy Dawson through the wire mesh screen in the lockup. "I like your haircut."

Jeremy's eyes flashed. "Hey, fuck you," he said. He ran his hand over his bald head. "I feel like a freak."

Steve had trouble keeping a straight face. He shrugged. "Well, there's freaks and there's freaks."

"Hey, I don't need your abuse. You said shave it off and I shaved it off. But I feel stupid as hell."

"Relax. Bald is sexy. Remember Yul Brynner."

"Who?"

Steve groaned. "Never mind." He waved his hand around the lockup. "So how do you like your new surroundings?"

"Jail is jail, man. When am I gonna get out of here?"

"Small problem there. You've been indicted for murder."

"Yeah, well what about bail?"

"You can't make bail."

"Why not? I just inherited a million bucks."

"Yeah, well that's another thing."

"What is?"

"Where's page 2, Jeremy?"

"What?"

"You know what. What happened to the second page?"

"What second page?"

"The will, Jeremy. The second page of the will."

Jeremy stared at Steve Winslow. "What the fuck are you talking about?"

Steve frowned. He'd been watching Jeremy's reactions closely. Jeremy Dawson seemed utterly baffled. Either his confusion was genuine, or the kid was one hell of an actor.

Steve Winslow couldn't tell which. And, he figured, with anyone else he probably could. But this punk kid, this bald teenager staring up at him, this stupid street-smart crack dealer, he couldn't read at all.

Steve sighed. "There's a problem with the will, Jeremy."

"What do you mean? What problem?"

"The will isn't signed."

"What are you talking about? I saw him write it. He wrote his name on it."

"He didn't sign it at the bottom."

"What the hell difference does it make?"

"Maybe none. But the point is, your relatives are contesting it."

"Can they win?"

"I don't think so."

"So what's the problem?"

"The problem is they're contesting it. Whether they can win or not is a moot point. That means it's not important, it doesn't matter. What's important is they're contesting it at all."

"Why?"

"Because until the will contest is settled, the will can't be probated and you can't inherit."

"Oh."

"Which means you can't touch the money, and I can't use it to pay your bail."

"Shit."

"Exactly. Which means right now the only way for you to get out of here is to have twelve people stand up and say 'not guilty.' So forget the will, forget the money, forget the bail. Beating the rap, that's the only thing now."

Jeremy held up his hands. "Wait a minute, wait a minute. I can't forget the will. Now, you say they're contesting it—how can they do that?"

"Any relative can contest a will."

"No, I mean what are they claiming?"

"First of all, that the will isn't signed."

"It *is* signed."

"It's a debatable point. I'm gonna debate it in court. I don't need to debate it with you."

"But isn't it a point you can win?"

"Nothing's certain. Let's just say we got a good shot."

"O.K. What else do they claim?"

"They'll claim undue influence."

"What does that mean?"

"That you were with your uncle when he wrote the will, that you coerced him into writing it."

"Bullshit. It was all his idea. I didn't even know he was doing it."

"I understand. I'm just telling you what they'll claim."

"Well, they're wrong."

"And I will so inform the judge. I'm on your side, Jeremy. You don't have to argue this with me."

"Yeah, right. What else will they claim?"

"That Jack Walsh wasn't of sound mind when he made the will."

"Wait a minute. That's been decided. You proved he was."

"A judge ruled him sane then. It doesn't mean one now will rule he was."

"But—"

Steve Winslow held up his hands. "Look, kid. I'm trying to help. But I talk to you, and I can't help feeling, 'My god, am I here all alone?' Now I understand, a million bucks is a lot of money, you're interested, you wanna know if you're gonna get it.

"But get this through your thick head. If you're convicted of murder, one, you're going to jail and two, you ain't getting a cent. So get your head out of the clouds, stop thinking about the damn money, and give me some help with this damn murder case."

Steve stopped and rubbed his head. "Now, you've had time to think about it. Who had the combination to your locker? Who could have taken the gun?"

Jeremy sighed and shook his head. "There's no one."

"Nobody ever picked up something for you after school?"

"No."

"No one you ever asked to do you a favor, to get something out of your locker for you?"

"No."

"What about the movie?"

"What?"

"The movie. And afterwards. Your alibi. You remember anyone who saw you, anyone at all?"

"No, I don't."

"Think. You must have seen someone."

"Well, I didn't."

"The whole time?"

"Yeah."

"You didn't see anyone?"

"No."

Steve sighed. "Christ, you're a big help."

Jeremy shrugged. "Hey, I'm sorry."

Steve looked at him. He shook his head. "No, you're not," he said. "But let me tell you something. When District Attorney Harry Dirkson gets you on the witness stand—" Steve pointed his finger, "—*then* you'll be sorry."

# 27

his notebook.

"O.K., here's the dope. Alibis, get your alibis, red-hot alibis. The way it stacks up, the women got 'em and the men don't."

"Oh?"

"Yeah. Claire Chesterton, Pat Grayson and Rose Tindel all alibi each other. Convenient as all hell, but it probably all checks out. The three of 'em were on a shopping spree in the afternoon. Not that they did much shopping. If you want some cash receipts to back it up, they probably don't have 'em. What they were doin' was touring shopping malls. Browsing here, browsing there. Bloomingdale's, Conran's, places like that. I don't think they bought a thing. Frankly, I don't think they got much money. But they spent the afternoon doing it. Then they caught dinner at one of the mall shops, and went to the movies."

"You're kidding."

"No. Why?"

"Don't tell me they saw a film called 'Heathers?' "

"Christ, no. Not their cup of tea. They saw 'Rain Man.' "

"Oh."

"Yeah. There's a big RKO Tenplex on Route 4, that's where they went. Went there, got home about ten-thirty."

"And?"

"And what?"

"Murder could have been as much as an hour later. What did they do till then?"

"Puttered around the house and went to bed. Why?"

"Well, Jeremy Dawson says he came home and found Claire Chesterton watching TV."

"Right."

"So I'm wondering what happened to the other two."

"They went up to bed."

"Is that confirmed?"

Taylor looked slightly exasperated. "Not in any way that will stand up in court. But can you imagine any one of the three of 'em taking off at ten-thirty at night, getting to Jeremy's school, securing the gun, getting into Manhattan, finding Jack Walsh and plugging him, and then setting the body on fire—well, just between you and me you're gonna have a little trouble selling it to a jury."

"I know, Mark. I don't think it happened. I just want to be able to raise inferences."

"Well, you'll have a lot better time with the men."

"What have you got on 'em?"

"Nothing. That's the beauty of it. Zero, zilch, nothing. I don't know where they were, but I know where they weren't. And they weren't home."

"Until when?"

"At least until 12:30. 'Cause that's when Claire Chesterton turned off the Carson show and went to bed."

"And they were all out?"

"All of 'em."

"Together?"

"There your guess is as good as mine. Problem is, what with this will contest thing they're on the other side and won't give us the time of day.

"So here's what we got. The night before, the three guys were on guard duty at Jack Walsh's hotel. Last man on was Carl Jenson, Walsh went down and ditched him in the subway. Last time we've seen Jenson, last time we saw Walsh. Now, we know Jenson arrived home sometime during the day. We know that only from what Jeremy Dawson told you. He got home in the afternoon, Jenson was there, bawled him out for skippin' school. Jeremy went out again and Carl Jenson must have left sometime after that, 'cause he wasn't there when the women got home. As to where he was, your guess is as good as mine, 'cause all he'll tell my man is to go fuck himself."

"Nice."

"On the other men, I know even less. You'll recall Jason Tindel had the first shift the night before. He staked out the Holiday Inn until three in the morning. After that, he presumably went home and got some sleep. So we assume he got up some time the next day and went out, but no one knows where, and he ain't talkin'.

"Now, Fred Grayson had the three A.M. till eight shift. Presumably he went home, slept the morning, and then went out too. Whether he went with Jason, we don't know. What we do know is the two of them were gone all day long and neither of them got back before twelve-thirty at night."

Steve thought a moment. "That could be good."

"How so?"

"Well, let's look at the facts. Jason and Fred had the night shift, staking out the hotel. They've gone home and they've gone to sleep. Carl Jenson's on duty. The guys are home sleeping, the women have gone out. Jack Walsh takes off and loses Carl Jenson in the subway tunnel."

"Right."

"So what would naturally happen then?"

"Carl Jenson calls the others, tells them Jack Walsh got away."

"Right," Steve said. "And they organize a search party and go looking for him. And they're gone all day and don't get back that night."

"Yeah. So?"

"So what if they find Jack Walsh and kill him?"

"With Jeremy Dawson's gun?"

"Sure, which Jason Tindel found a week before when he dropped by the school to pick up something Jeremy left behind."

Taylor frowned. "That's mighty thin."

"Reasonable doubt, Mark. That's all I need."

"Yeah, sure," Taylor said without enthusiasm. He looked at his notes again. "And then we have Julie Creston."

"Oh?"

"Yeah. I checked out her alibi 'cause you told me to do it. But quite frankly it was a bitch and a waste of time, and I feel bad about it 'cause I ran up a lot of expenses on it and—"

"I told you, forget the money. I just want results."

"Well, you got 'em, and they ain't worth shit. Except you can cross Julie Creston off your list, which I think you could have done without going through the charade."

Steve shook his head. "I wanted it done. Just give me what you got."

"O.K." Taylor referred to his notes. "Julie Creston finished filming February 24th. She caught a plane from Denver back to L.A. that night. Set down in L.A. ten-thirty P.M. Airline confirms ticket in her name was used. Now, I knew that wouldn't satisfy you, you'd say she could have given her ticket to someone else, so I ran it down. Turns out Julie wasn't the only one finished filming that day. There were four other actors working the same sequence who finished up at the same time. All of them took the flight back together. My man in L.A. hunted one of them down, and he confirms the fact Julie Creston did indeed take the plane back to L.A. that night."

"That's the 24th?"

"Right."

"Two days before the murder."

"Uh huh. Next confirmation, morning of the 25th, Julie Creston shows up for an audition for a Burger King commercial."

Taylor looked at Steve. "Now, you're not going to like what I've got next, 'cause you'll say it isn't conclusive, but it's enough for me. The morning of the 26th, she has a luncheon appointment with her agent. Brunch, really. Eleven o'clock. Coffee and rolls. Anyway, the guy's got an audition lined up for that afternoon and she cancels it."

"Oh yeah?"

"Yeah, but don't read anything into it. I think it's just what it seems. She tells her agent she's worn out from the Denver shoot, the Burger King audition the day before went badly— she's exhausted, she's got bags under her eyes, she didn't test well, she's never going to get anything this way, she needs to take a short vacation, pull herself together."

"And that's the last you got?" Steve said.

"That's the last time I can definitely place her up until the murder. But look what you got, Steve. She left her agent twelve o'clock, noon. That's L.A. time, which makes it three P.M. here."

"That leaves her eight hours," Steve said.

"Right," Taylor said dryly. "Eight hours to get to the airport, fly to New York, get to New Jersey, steal Jeremy Dawson's gun out of his school locker, get back to Manhattan, buy a can of gasoline, find Jack Walsh on the subway, plug him and set the body on fire."

"It could be done," Steve said.

"Yeah, in a paperback thriller. And even then I don't buy it. I read that and throw the fucking book across the room."

Steve frowned. "Yeah, Mark. But there's a difference between what works in black and white and what works in the minds of a jury. They don't get a nice straight story. They're sitting there listening to volumes of testimony. They gotta sift through it, piece it together. Anything that clouds the issue, doesn't quite add up, has to be a victory for the defense."

"Yeah," Taylor said. "But Dirkson's gonna summarize the testimony and make his argument. You think that sarcastic son of a bitch can't take all that and make it sound like ridiculous bullshit?"

"I'm sure he can, Mark. You think I can't take ridiculous bullshit and make it sound good?"

Taylor looked at him. "You mean you're going after this?"

"I don't know. What's the rest of it? Your man make a pass at her?"

"Yeah, he did."

"Told her Jack Walsh was dead?"

"Yeah."

"And?"

"Didn't faze her. Other than the normal shock one would expect at hearing someone was murdered, she couldn't have cared less."

"What about the will?"

"There's no will."

"You sure?"

"Not unless she's lying—and there's no reason why she should. Look, here's what happened. I called my man, told him to go back up there and give her the news. So he does. She comes to the door. When she sees it's him again, she tries to brush him off—it's a bad time, her boyfriend's in the shower, they're taking a trip, she's packing up to go, come back some other time.

"Well, my man's a pro, he won't brush. He hits her with the fact that Walsh is dead. That shook her up, but not the way you think. It's just she don't want her boyfriend coming out of the shower and hearing this. She's not going to let my man in, but he's not leaving, so to get him out of there she goes out and has a cup of coffee with him. So they go out to a little coffee shop and shoot the shit."

"And?"

Taylor shook his head. "And it's a dead end. Jack Walsh is nothing to her. She's sorry he's dead, but she still don't like him. There's no will, he never promised her any money, she doesn't expect any money, she's not going to claim any money. She's got a new career and a new boyfriend, she doesn't want the scandal. She's been working herself ragged, now she's on vacation, she and her boyfriend are taking a trip together, and if my man does anything to queer it, she'll rip his fucking eyes out."

Steve frowned. "Did he believe her?"

Taylor looked at him. "What's not to believe. Everything she says makes sense. If there isn't a will and she's got no claims on the money, why would she jeopardize everything she's got to rush back to New York to kill a man she knew a year ago, just because she feels he let her down by not sticking up for her when his relatives ganged up on her? I mean, pardon me, but could you explain that theory to me so that it makes any sense?"

"No, I couldn't. But it doesn't have to make sense. We're collecting information, Mark. When we get it all collected, then we see what we can do about it. Now, that doesn't add up, but there's one thing about it I like."

"What's that?"

"She's packin' to leave. Flight is an indication of guilt. Always has been, always will be." Steve thought a moment. "Slap a subpoena on her."

Taylor stared at him. "What?"

"If she's taking off, I don't want her getting away. Call up your man, we'll get a subpoena served."

Taylor looked at him. "Steve, don't do this."

"Why not?"

"You know why not. There's nothing Harry Dirkson would love better than to get you for abuse of process. You subpoena this woman with no definite purpose in mind, he'll nail you to the wall."

"He can try."

"He can do more than that. You got no grounds for a subpoena. You just want to drag this woman in and make her a red herring. Which is exactly what abuse of process is all about. Dirkson will have you dead to rights."

Steve sighed. "You're probably right."

"You know I'm right. So what you wanna do?"

Steve frowned and shook his head. "I gotta fight for my client, Mark." He took a breath and blew it out again. "Serve the subpoena."

# 28

TRACY GARVIN WAS PISSED. SHE sat in Steve Winslow's overstuffed clients' chair, folded her glasses, tapped them into her other hand, unfolded them, and folded them up again, a sure sign that she was really steamed.

Steve Winslow took no notice. He had just finished giving Tracy a complete rundown of the facts of the case as he knew them. Now, utterly exhausted, he was sitting tipped back in his desk chair, his arms hanging limply at his sides, his eyes staring blankly at some small imperfection in the ceiling. He closed his eyes, raised his arms and rubbed his head as if to clear it.

"All right," he said. "Ask me questions."

This was no idle exercise on Steve's part. Tracy Garvin was sharp and he valued her input. In his previous case, she'd asked the key question, the one that turned the whole thing around. In this case, frankly, Steve didn't know what the hell to do. So he was eager to hear what Tracy had to say.

"All right," she said. "What the fuck do you think you're doing?"

That was not the question he'd been looking for. Steve Winslow's eyes snapped open. He tipped his chair down, sat up to find Tracy Garvin glaring at him.

"I beg your pardon?"

Tracy Garvin took a breath. "I'm sorry, but . . . well, I don't get it at all."

"Get what?"

"You. This case. Well . . . dammit, you."

"What about me?"

"What the hell are you doing?"

"I get the impression you're displeased."

"Dammit, don't humor me. I'm not in the mood."

"Fine. I won't humor you. Just tell me what's the matter, and then let's see what we can do about it."

"What's the matter? The matter is you. I thought I knew you. What you stood for. Now this case comes along, and I don't know you at all."

162

"Specifics."

"What?"

"Specifics. I don't know what you're talking about. If you want me to respond to this, you're gonna have to recite chapter and verse."

Tracy took a breath. "Look. The Marilyn Harding thing. We worked together on that and it was great. You did things. You took risks. You didn't like your clients much, but you fought like hell for 'em, you went out on a limb for 'em, and when you did—well, you were still on the side of the angels. I mean, what you were doing was somehow right.

"But this case." Tracy shook her head. "Here you are defending a crack dealer who's probably guilty as hell."

Steve opened his mouth to protest, but Tracy cut him off. "No, no, I know, I shouldn't say that. He's innocent until proven guilty, I just spoke heresy, I retract it. Let's not go off on a tangent. I don't want to hear you make a speech."

Tracy held up her hand. "Here's the thing. You're defending this kid and you're taking risks and doing unorthodox things again. But you're not on the side of the angels anymore. You want chapter and verse, I'll give you chapter and verse. This woman in California—this Julie Creston—you're gonna subpoena her and drag her into court. Well then, you're gonna get her name in the papers and probably fuck up her career. And what's worse, you screw up her relationship with her boyfriend. And you know and I know she hasn't got a goddam thing to do with this. She's an innocent bystander. If anything, she's a victim. She's the one who got dumped on, chased out of New York. Now you wanna drag her back to dump on her some more. Dammit, it just isn't right."

Tracy stopped, pushed her hair out of her face. "I'm sorry if that pisses you off. But that's how I feel."

Steve sighed. "I understand. I suppose I'd like to feel the same way. But I can't. I can't allow myself the luxury. I've got a job to do. I may not like it, but it's my job, so I gotta do it. If I didn't do my job, I'm a lousy lawyer, I should quit practicing law."

He held up his hand. "Now, I know that doesn't mean anything to you. You've been talking from the heart, and I'm giving you cold lawyer bullshit. O.K. Stop for a minute. And if you don't mind, let me take exception to what you're saying."

"Say anything you want. That's why I brought it up."

"I know. But you're not gonna like what you're gonna hear."

"I figured that."

"O.K. First off, you're young."

Tracy bristled.

"Scratch that," Steve said. "Unfair, not relevant. First off, you're a romantic."

Tracy opened her mouth to protest again.

"Yeah, I know," Steve said. "That hurts you even worse. But it shouldn't. Basically, I'm a romantic too. I just have to stifle it."

"What the hell are you talking about?"

"I'm trying to explain something. It's not particularly easy. Let me take a stab at it. When I say you're a romantic, I mean you have a lot of ideas about good and bad, right or wrong. You read a lot of books. There's heroes and villains. The good prosper, and the bad get their comeuppance.

"Well, I have no argument with that. That's the way it ought to be. But real life isn't a storybook, and when you start thinking of it as one, you're doomed to disappointment.

"Now take this case. You see Julie Creston as the embodiment of good. The poor wronged woman. The underdog. Cruelly and heartlessly separated from the man she loves. In romantic terms, she would be loving and true, Jack Walsh would be a kindly old man, and the two of them would live happily ever after. You don't really believe that, but that's the image you can't get out of your head, and it colors your thought.

"Now, what's frustrating the hell out of you is the reality doesn't live up to the fantasy. Because in real life, Jack Walsh was a cunning, vindictive lunatic. And Julie Creston gives every indication of being a cold, calculating gold digger who's always been looking out for number one. She doesn't give a hang about Jack Walsh, she couldn't care less that he's dead. Her one interest in him was always money, and since she sees no chance of getting any, she'd just as soon wash her hands of the whole affair so it doesn't mess up her current gravy train."

"That's not fair," Tracy said.

"I know it's not fair. But it's how I have to look at it. And your next argument is, I'm just doing it to help some crack dealer. Well, that's true, and if he was charged with selling crack, I wouldn't lift a finger to help him. But he's charged with murder. And if he didn't do it—"

"But he did," Tracy said. "Oh, I know I shouldn't be saying that, but, dammit, he did. Everything points to it. The gun. The witness. Everything. And what evidence do you have that he didn't? Just his say so. The word of a crack addict. Someone you wouldn't trust to tell you the time of day."

"This is true."

"Then why are you doing it?"

"I'm his lawyer, and I can't quit."

"Why not?"

"All right, look. I didn't have to take the case, but I did. I didn't know he was a crack dealer then, but that's neither here nor there. The fact is, I took it. And once I take a case, I can't quit. It would be an open admission I thought my client was guilty. And it's not my place to make that judgment. That's up to a jury. Once I take a case, it's my duty to present that case to a jury and let them decide."

"Fine, but do you have to ruin some woman's life to do it?"

"Hey. There's no halfway. I either take a case or I don't. Let me ask you something. Suppose my client was some nice, clean-cut kid that you thought was innocent—would you still be asking me to lay off?"

Tracy's eyes faltered, but just for a moment. "Yeah, I probably would."

"Why?"

"What do you expect to prove with this woman?"

"I don't know."

"That's why. Because you don't know what you're doing. You have no definite purpose in mind. It's a shot in the dark, a gamble. If you come up with something, great. But if you don't, you're guilty of abuse of process and you just might get disbarred."

"You're telling me I shouldn't risk that?"

"You know you shouldn't."

"Maybe. But I think if Jeremy Dawson were that clean-cut kid you thought was innocent, you just might think I should."

"I don't think so."

"But you're not sure?"

"Dammit," Tracy said. "What difference does it make? It's what you call a moot point, Counselor. Never mind the what-if, let's deal with the facts. The facts are Jeremy Dawson is a lying, teenage punk crack dealer."

"Yes, but is he guilty? Answer me that. You may think so, but do you know it? Can you judge the case for me now? Can you tell me there's no reason in the world for me to defend this kid, because you know for a fact that he's guilty?"

"Of course not."

"There you are. He's my client and I'm gonna defend him. And what's more, I'm gonna get him off."

The phone rang. Tracy got up and answered it. "Steve Winslow's office." She handed the phone to Steve. "Mark Taylor."

Steve took the phone. "Yeah, Mark, what you got?"

"More bad news, Steve."

"Yeah, let's have it."

"No go on the subpoena."

"How come?"

"Julie Creston's gone."

"Shit."

"Yeah. My man went out to serve her, just missed her. Remember she was packing to go? Well, she left on her vacation."

"For how long?"

"You got me. My man pumped the landlady, she didn't know."

"Shit. Can you find out where she went?"

"I did, but it don't help us a bit."

"Why not?"

"Turns out she went to Rio."

"You're kidding."

"No. And last time I checked, Rio was outside the jurisdiction of the court."

"No shit. All right, Mark, have your man bribe the landlady to tip us off when she gets back."

"Has been done."

"O.K. Good work."

"Just routine. Then there's the other thing."

"What's that?"

"Jeremy Dawson's alibi."

"What about it?"

"I've been trying to come up with someone who saw him at the movie, 'Heathers.' Well, I finally found one."

"That's great."

"No, it isn't. I got a kid that will swear absolutely he saw Jeremy Dawson there. He couldn't miss the green mohawk. He was in back of him in the popcorn line."

"So?"

"So, it wasn't the night of the murder. It was the previous Saturday night."

"Are you sure?"

"The kid is. His parents won't let him go to the movies on school nights. Just on weekends."

"Oh, shit. Do the cops know this?"

"Sure do. In fact, my leak at headquarters was how I got it."

"Damn."

"Yeah. I'm sorry. Just thought you'd want to know."

"Thanks, Mark. Keep me posted."

Steve hung up the phone.

Tracy Garvin was looking at him with anxious eyes. "Well?"

Steve managed a grin. "Well, I'm off the hook with you."

"What?"

"Julie Creston. She left for Rio on vacation. They couldn't serve the subpoena. That point has become moot."

"No, dammit," Tracy said. "The other thing after that. When you looked like your world had just collapsed."

"Oh," Steve said. "The cops got a witness will swear Jeremy Dawson was at the film 'Heathers' the previous Saturday night."

"Oh shit," Tracy said. "How bad is it?"

"It's the worst. Jeremy Dawson told the cops he was at that movie. It's an admission against interest, and it's admissible. Look what's gonna happen now. Dirkson will put on all the circumstantial evidence showing motive, method and opportunity. Then he'll call the cop to the stand and have him testify

Jeremy Dawson gave him the alibi he went to the movies. Then he'll call the kid to the stand and prove that Jeremy lied. Then Dirkson will smile at the jury and rest his case right there."

"Oh Jesus," Tracy said. "And what will happen then?"

"Then," Steve said, "I won't have a fucking prayer."

# 29

DISTRICT ATTORNEY HARRY Dirkson began his opening statement with the punch line. "Ladies and gentlemen of the jury. We expect to prove that on the 26th of February the defendant, Jeremy Dawson, killed the decedent, Jack Walsh, by shooting him in the head with a loaded gun."

Dirkson paused to let that statement sink in. "We shall prove it beyond a shadow of a doubt. We shall prove it by eyewitness evidence, by circumstantial evidence, and by ballistics evidence. By eyewitness evidence we shall prove that Jeremy Dawson was seen with the decedent, Jack Walsh, in the very spot where he was murdered. By circumstantial evidence we shall prove that Jeremy Dawson was the only one who could have killed Jack Walsh. By ballistics evidence we shall prove that the shot which killed Jack Walsh came from Jeremy Dawson's gun.

"Why did Jeremy Dawson kill Jack Walsh? For money. The motive was money. In fact, millions of dollars.

"Here is the situation. Here are the facts, as we shall lay them out for you. And they require a bit of explanation, because they are somewhat extraordinary.

"Within the last year the decedent, Jack Walsh, had sold his house and gone to live on the subway system. Why? That is the question you must answer. One logical explanation would seem to be that the man was insane. That was the conclusion reached by his nearest living relatives, Rose Tindel, Pat Grayson, Claire Chesterton and Carl Jenson. They, fearing Jack Walsh had taken leave of his faculties, and hoping to conserve his estate, had him committed to Bellevue. If so, you might ask, why is he not there now? The answer is simple. You see, Jack Walsh had another relative."

Dirkson paused, wheeled his bulk ponderously around, and raised his arm dramatically to point at Jeremy Dawson. "Him. The defendant. Jeremy Dawson. The young man sitting before you."

Dirkson paused, ran his hand over his bald head, wheeled

back to look at the jury. "Ladies and gentlemen of the jury, we expect to show that Jeremy Dawson, with the aid of his attorney, Steve Winslow, connived to have Jack Walsh released from Bellevue. Why did he do so? You can draw your conclusions from what happened next.

"Now, some of this is conjecture, but this much we know. The following day, February 26th, the day of the murder, Jack Walsh was spotted in the corridor of Jeremy Dawson's high school. He was seen by several students and one teacher. At least two students saw Jeremy Dawson and Jack Walsh together. We haven't been able to find anyone who saw the two of them leave together, but the following facts are known. From that point on, the point at which he was seen with Jack Walsh, Jeremy Dawson cut all the rest of his classes and was not seen anywhere on the high school premises for the rest of the day.

"He *was* seen, however, later that day, with Jack Walsh in the very subway station where Walsh was killed.

"What else do we know? We know that Jack Walsh was shot in the head, and the body set on fire."

Dirkson paused and looked at the jury again, let them see the horror and repugnance he felt at the very thought. "That's right, ladies and gentlemen. Set on fire.

"Why was that done? Well, once again, you must answer that question for yourselves. But to aid you, I must point out that the burning of the body effectively disguised the entrance wound of the fatal bullet, and had it not been for the thoroughness of the medical examiner in performing the autopsy on the corpse, the bullet lodged in the brain might have been totally overlooked, in which case the murder might have been written off as a thrill-kill, a random crime against the homeless, a wilding incident.

"But the bullet was discovered. And where did that bullet come from? The ballistics expert will testify beyond a shadow of a doubt that that bullet came from a particular gun. We have that gun, and we shall introduce it here in evidence. And where did the police recover that gun which we shall prove to be the murder weapon? They recovered it on February 27th, the day after the murder, from the school locker of the defendant, Jeremy Dawson. The locker to which only he had the combination."

Dirkson paused, smiled at the jury. He shrugged his shoulders in an apologetic way. "But I have digressed. I was talking about motive. What motive would Jeremy Dawson have had for killing Jack Walsh? Well, when Jeremy Dawson was arrested by police officers on the afternoon of February 27th, he had in his possession a piece of paper. We have that piece of paper, and shall introduce it in evidence here in court. And what is that piece of paper? It is a document, which a handwriting expert shall testify is entirely in the handwriting of the decedent, Jack Walsh. And what type of document is it? It is a will. A will written by Jack Walsh. A will dated February 26th, the very day he was murdered. A will leaving the bulk of his estate—an estate which can be valued in the millions of dollars —to none other than the defendant, Jeremy Dawson."

Dirkson paused, smiled again. "Ladies and gentlemen of the jury, I'm not going to insult your intelligence by belaboring these facts. They are simple, straightforward and self-evident. I shall lay them before you, prove each and every one of them by competent evidence, and expect a verdict of guilty at your hands."

Dirkson smiled one last time, bowed, and with a flourish, walked back to his chair and sat down.

Judge Grimes, slight, pale, relatively young, but already with a reputation for ruling his courtroom with an iron hand, turned to Steve Winslow. As he had during jury selection, Judge Grimes restrained himself from frowning at the young attorney who had seen fit to show up in his courtroom in a corduroy jacket, blue jeans and long hair.

"Does the defense wish to make an opening statement?" Grimes inquired.

Steve Winslow paused. He glanced at Jeremy Dawson sitting next to him. Jeremy looked pretty good in a suit and tie. His hair had grown in just enough to look like a very short crewcut rather than just a skinhead.

Steve glanced at the jury, found that they were looking at Jeremy too.

Which was a very bad sign. The jurors were not looking at

him, the attorney, to see what argument he was about to make. No, they were looking at the defendant. Which, Steve well knew, was an indication of how well Dirkson had scored. Dirkson's argument had been convincing, and the jurors had made up their minds. And now their interest was entirely on Jeremy Dawson. Because Dirkson had sold them on the concept, and human nature being what it was, they couldn't help being fascinated.

They were looking at a murderer.

Steve knew he should do something. Break the mood. Try to win the jury back. But in the light of Dirkson's overwhelming argument, for the moment he couldn't think of anything to say. And he knew better than to flounder around, to do something inadequate or ineffectual. Better to let it go.

He smiled confidently, and, as if it had been his plan all along, said, smoothly, "We will reserve our opening argument until we begin putting on our case, Your Honor."

Judge Grimes nodded. "Very well. Mr. Dirkson. You may proceed. Call you first witness."

"Thank you, Your Honor."

Dirkson rose. He glanced down at the papers on the prosecution table, as if looking for the name of the witness, though actually he knew perfectly well who he wished to call. As he did, he turned and looked over at the defense table. Steve Winslow was, of course, looking at him, and their eyes met. When they did, Dirkson smiled, a smug winner's smile.

There was no mistaking the meaning of Dirkson's look.

"Gotcha," was what it said.

# 30

FOR HIS FIRST WITNESS, DIRK-
son called Maria Martez, who cited six years experience as an
officer for the transit police.

"Now, Officer Martez," Dirkson said. "On the night of February 26th, between the hours of ten and eleven, could you tell us
where you were stationed?"

"Yes, sir. I was patrolling the uptown Number Two express
on the Broadway line."

"Did you observe anything out of the ordinary at that time?"

"Yes, I did."

"Could you tell us when and where this happened and what
it was?"

"Yes. I was riding uptown on the Number Two train. We
went through the 66th Street Station. That's not an express
stop, so the train doesn't even slow down. Well, actually, it
slows down a little, because the track curves right after that.
You know, there's that big curve between there and the station
at 72nd. Which *is* an express stop. So the train is slowing down
for that too.

"Anyway, going through the station—I was standing in the
car on patrol. And out the window I saw what looked like a fire
in the station."

"Where in the station?"

"On the uptown side. The extreme north end of the platform."

"And what did you see?"

"A fire."

"And what can you tell us about the fire?"

"Not much. I saw flames and that's all. You gotta understand.
This is the far end of the station. The very end of the platform.
After the train passes that, it goes right into the tunnel on the
way up to 72nd Street. See what I'm saying? If the fire had
been in the middle of the station, I could have looked back
down the platform and watched it as we went by. But this was
the very end of the platform. I see it, and the next second we're

by it and into the tunnel. So when I look back, I can't see a thing."

"I understand. But in that short amount of time, just what did you see?"

"I saw fire on the platform. That's all I could tell."

"Let me ask you this. Did you see any people on the platform?"

"No, I did not. And I don't think there were. 'Cause if there had been, they'd have seen the fire and reported it, and nobody did, and—"

Judge Grimes held up his hand. "One minute." He looked down at the defense table. "Mr. Winslow, you're not objecting here."

"No, Your Honor."

"Yet this witness is testifying to opinions, surmises and conclusions which she has drawn that are obviously based on hearsay testimony."

"I understand, Your Honor. But this officer strikes me as a competent and honest witness, and her opinions seem sound, logical and reasonable to me. I find it hard to object to something I agree with."

Judge Grimes frowned. "Well, the court will interpose an objection for you. I don't intend to have the record cluttered up with testimony of this type." To the court reporter he said, "Leave in where she said she didn't recall seeing anyone in the station. Everything after that can go out." He looked up again. "Proceed, Mr. Dirkson."

"Yes, Your Honor. Officer Martez, what did you do then?"

"I left the train at 72nd Street, called the token clerk at 66th, and called the police and the fire departments."

"What did you do then?"

"Took the local back down to 66th."

"And when you got there, what did you observe?"

"The police and fire departments had already arrived."

Dirkson smiled. "Thank you. No further questions."

Steve Winslow did not cross-examine.

For his next witness, Dirkson called Leon Dokes, who testified to being one of four firemen who responded to a report of a fire in the 66th Street Station.

"And when you got there," Dirkson said, "what did you see?"

"There was a fire going on the north end of the uptown platform."

"How big a fire?"

"Not that big. Perhaps the size of a small bonfire. But it was burning steadily. And the flames were high."

"Was there anyone there at the time?"

"Yes, sir."

"Who was that?"

"Two radio patrol officers who had already responded to the call."

"Were the officers attempting to put out the fire?"

"No, sir. They are not equipped to do so, and that's not their job."

"So what were they doing?"

"Blocking off that area of the platform and making sure no one got too close."

"You say making sure no one got too close—then there were other people in the station?"

"Yes, sir. There were about a half a dozen passengers there waiting for the train."

"And the police were keeping them away from the fire?"

"That's right."

"I see. And what did you do then?"

"The four of us proceeded to put out the fire."

"And how did you do that?"

"With the portable extinguishers we wear on our backs."

"You were able to do so?"

"Yes, sir."

"You had no particular problems putting out the fire?"

"No, sir."

"How long did it take you to do so?"

"Not long. Two, three minutes."

"Fine," Dirkson said. "Now, let me ask you this. Could you tell what it was that was burning?"

"No, sir."

"And why was that?"

"As I said, the flames were high. That made it hard to see what they were consuming. There was a small mound on the platform, and that's what was burning. That was the best we could tell."

"Before you extinguished the fire?"

"Yes, sir."

"And after you extinguished it?"

"Then I looked closer, and was able to distinguish that what had been burning was the body of a man."

"A man?"

"That's right."

"What did you do then?"

"Alerted the police officers and told them to phone for an EMS unit."

"Emergency Medical Service?"

"That's right."

"Were you there when the EMS unit arrived?"

"Yes, I was."

"When was that?"

"Approximately ten minutes later."

Dirkson nodded. "Thank you. That's all."

Again, Steve Winslow declined to cross-examine.

Next, Dirkson called Phil Kestin of the Emergency Medical Service unit, who testified to responding to the call from the 66th Street Station.

"And what time was it when you arrived?" Dirkson asked.

"Approximately 10:55."

"And what did you find when you arrived?"

"The police and fire departments were already on the scene. The section of the platform had been cordoned off."

"What section was that?"

"The north end of the uptown platform."

"And what did you find there?"

"I found the body of a man."

"Was he alive?"

"He was not."

"The man was dead?"

"Yes."

"How do you know he was dead?"

"I examined him."

"You yourself?"

"That's right."

"How did you make that determination? You felt for a pulse and there was none?"

The witness hesitated, frowned, said, "I determined that there was no heartbeat. But in response to your question, I think I have to explain my answer."

"Certainly," Dirkson said. "Please explain to the jury in your own words, how you determined the man was dead."

The medic turned to the jury. He was a young man, with a boyish, open face. His manner radiated sincerity. From Dirkson's point of view, he was a good witness.

"What you have to understand," he said, "is the extent of the injuries. The body had been badly burned. It had not just been burned. It had been charred. It was barely recognizable as that of a human being. So to feel for a pulse under those circumstances—well, the question is not really applicable. I determined that there was no heartbeat. I determined that there was no breath. I determined that there was no life. But frankly, one look was enough to see that there couldn't have been."

It was effective. Steve Winslow watched the faces of the jurors as the young medic spoke, and he could see that they were shocked and moved as they drank in the horror of the scene.

Dirkson prolonged the effect by pausing a moment before asking, "And did you take the body to the hospital?"

"No, I did not."

"Why not? Because you'd already determined the man was dead?"

"No, sir. I didn't have to make that decision."

"Why not?"

"Because the medical examiner arrived and took over."

"Thank you. No further questions."

Judge Grimes said, "Mr. Winslow?"

"No questions, Your Honor."

Jeremy Dawson tugged at Steve Winslow's arm. "Hey man," he hissed, "aren't you gonna do anything?"

"Not till it'll do some good."

"But—"

"Shhh."

Dirkson called Robert Oliver of the Crime Scene Unit to the stand. Officer Oliver testified to arriving at the 66th Street Station and processing the crime scene for evidence, which consisted largely of taking pictures.

"And do you have those photographs in court?" Dirkson asked.

"Yes, I do."

"Would you produce them please?"

"Certainly," the witness said. He reached in his briefcase and pulled out a file folder of eight-by-ten photographs.

"Object to the pictures," Jeremy hissed.

"Why?" Steve whispered back.

"They're gonna piss off the jury."

"That they are."

"So object to them."

"I can't. They're legal evidence. They're admissible."

"Can't you even try?"

Steve took a breath. "Look," he hissed through clenched teeth. "The pictures won't do you half as much harm as you're doing yourself by constantly grabbing me by the sleeve and looking like your world just collapsed. Now sit back and shut up. The bottom line is, if we act like we're afraid to let the jury see those pictures, you might as well change your plea to guilty right now."

Jeremy glared at Steve, but subsided in his seat.

Judge Grimes, noting the byplay between them, said, "Did Counsel hear the question? The prosecutor has asked that these pictures be marked for identification."

"May I see them, Your Honor?"

"Certainly," Dirkson said. He took the pictures, passed them over.

Steve leafed through them. They were truly gruesome. Jeremy, looking at them over Steve's shoulder, seemed about to say something, but managed to sit still.

Steve handed the pictures back. "No objection, Your Honor. And if the witness will testify that these are indeed the pictures he took, I will stipulate that they may be received in evidence."

"Very well," Judge Grimes said. "The photographs may be considered in evidence as People's Exhibits One A through—

what have you got there?" he asked the court reporter, who was marking the photographs.

"One minute," the court reporter said. "That would be A through K."

"Fine," Judge Grimes said. The pictures are now in evidence as People's Exhibits One A through K."

"Thank you, Your Honor," Dirkson said. "With the court's permission, I would like to show the exhibits to the jury at this time."

"No objection, Your Honor," Steve said.

"Very well," Judge Grimes said. "Bailiff."

The bailiff took the file of photos, handed them to the first juror, who looked at the top one, pulled it off the stack and passed it along. Within minutes the eleven photos had been spread out and were snaking their way through the twelve jurors and four alternates in the box.

Dirkson watched this with satisfaction. The reaction of the jury was exactly as he had anticipated. Some winced. Some scowled. And by the time they had finished, all of their faces were hard.

When the photographs had been returned, Dirkson again approached the witness.

"Now then," he said, "did you examine the clothing of the decedent?"

The witness frowned. "Yes and no."

"What do you mean by that?"

"Well, as you can see by the photographs, the clothing had all but been consumed by fire. I examined what remnants remained."

"Could you describe them, please?"

"Yes, sir. The decedent had been dressed in a long, heavy overcoat. Most of it had burned away, leaving only the charred outline of the fabric. However, there was a discernible bulge that remained. On investigation it proved to be—or at least at one time had been—a pocket."

"I see. And was there anything in this pocket?"

"Yes, sir."

"And what was that?"

"The charred remains of what appeared to be a leather object."

"And did you retrieve that object?"

"Yes, I did."

"And identify it?"

"Yes, sir."

"And what was it?"

"On inspection, it proved to be a wallet."

"A wallet?"

"Yes."

"And do you have that wallet here in court?"

"Yes, I do."

The witness reached into his briefcase again and produced a plastic evidence bag. In it was what might have been a wallet, though it was now impossible to tell.

"I ask that this wallet be marked for identification and received in evidence as People's Exhibit Two."

"No objection."

"So ordered."

"Now," Dirkson said. "Did you examine the contents of that wallet?"

"Yes, I did."

"And what did you find?"

"Several papers too charred to be legible, and a gooey mass of what appeared to be plastic."

"Referring to the gooey mass of plastic—do you know what that proved to be?"

"Yes, I do."

"Could you tell us please?"

"Yes, sir. The plastic came from several credit cards, which under the extreme heat had melted and fused together."

"Were you able to distinguish between the credit cards?"

"In most cases, no. But one in the middle of the pack was not so badly damaged and I was able to separate it from the rest."

"And what did it prove to be?"

"It was a Visa card."

"And was the name on the card still legible?"

"Yes, it was."

"And what was that name?"

"Jack Walsh."

"Do you have that card here in court?"

"Yes, I do."

The witness reached in his briefcase, produced another evidence bag holding a credit card.

"I ask that this card be marked for identification and received in evidence as People's Exhibit Three."

"No objection."

"So ordered."

The court reporter marked the exhibit.

"That's all," Dirkson said.

"Mr. Winslow?" Judge Grimes said.

"No questions."

Jeremy Dawson gave Steve a look, but held his tongue.

Dirkson next called the medical examiner to the stand. A thin, white-haired, bespectacled man, he gave his name as Murray Abraham, cited his rather extensive qualifications, and testified to being summoned to the 66th Street Station on the night of the crime.

"And what time did you get there?" Dirkson asked.

The medical examiner pushed his glasses up on his nose with a long finger. "Eleven-oh-two," he snapped.

Some of the jurors smiled. After the horrors Dirkson had been dragging them through, they were ready for any relief. The prissy preciseness of the medical examiner was affording them the opportunity, and they were gratefully seizing it.

"I see," Dirkson said. "And can you tell me what you found there?"

"I found the body of a man."

"Was he alive?"

"He was dead."

"You pronounced him dead at the scene?"

"Yes, I did."

"There was no question in your mind?"

"None at all. Nor would there have been any question in yours. The man was dead."

"Now listen carefully, Doctor. What was the *apparent* cause of death?"

"The man had apparently burned to death."

"I see. Did you make that determination then?"

"Certainly not," the medical examiner snapped. "You said apparent cause of death, and that is how I answered the question. The man had apparently burned to death."

"Did you subsequently determine the *actual* cause of death?"

"Yes, I did."

"Fine. We'll get to that in a moment," Dirkson said. "First, can you tell me what you did at the scene of the crime?"

"Yes. As I said, I made a preliminary examination of the body and pronounced the man dead. I indicated to the officers of the Crime Scene Unit that it was highly likely that the man had met his death by criminal means. Then I waited while the Crime Scene Unit investigated and took photographs, and then ordered the body transferred to the morgue for autopsy."

"And who performed that autopsy?"

"I did."

"You performed the autopsy personally?"

"That is correct."

"And had the decedent met his death by burning?"

"As I've already stated, he had not."

"And did you determine the actual cause of death?"

"Yes, I did. The cause of death was a bullet which had penetrated the back of the skull and lodged itself in the decedent's brain."

"A bullet?"

"That's right."

"And did you remove this bullet from the brain of the decedent?"

"Yes, I did."

"I see. And tell me, Doctor, would you know this bullet if you saw it again?"

"Yes, I would."

Dirkson strode back to the prosecution table, picked up a small evidence bag.

"Your Honor, I ask that this be marked for identification as People's Exhibit Four."

When the court reporter had marked the exhibit, Dirkson handed it to the witness.

"Doctor, I hand you a bullet and ask you if you have seen it before?"

The medical examiner took the plastic evidence bag in his hands. He turned it over, examining the bullet.

"Yes, I have."

"Can you tell us when and where?"

"Yes, sir. That is the bullet I removed that night from the brain of the decedent."

"And how do you identify the bullet, Doctor?"

The medical examiner held up the plastic bag and pointed. "By my initials, which I scratched on the base of the bullet with a small etching tool."

Dirkson nodded his approval. "Very good, Doctor. Now then, you've stated that this bullet was the cause of death?"

"That's right."

"How do you know that? How do you know he died from the bullet wound rather than the burning? Or in other words, how do you know he was first shot and then the body burned, rather than the other way around?"

"I know that from my autopsy. An examination of the body showed that the man was dead before the body was set on fire."

"Oh really? And how could you tell that?"

"There were several factors, easily recognized by a trained pathologist." The medical examiner sniffed and said somewhat condescendingly. "I shall point out those most easily understood by a layman. For one thing, live flesh burns differently than dead flesh. Even more conclusive was the condition of the lungs."

"What about them?"

"There was no smoke in them. And if the man were alive when he was set on fire, there would have to be. He would have inhaled, and smoke would have gotten in the lungs. But he didn't inhale. Therefore he wasn't breathing. Therefore he wasn't alive."

"I see. So the bullet wound had to come first?"

"That's what I just said."

"And was the bullet wound extensive enough to cause death?"

"Absolutely. There was severe trauma to the brain. The man simply could not have lived."

"Not even for a little while? What I'm getting at, Doctor, is it possible that the bullet merely rendered the man unconscious, put him into a coma, and it was the fire that actually killed him?"

The doctor shook his head impatiently. "A comatose man still breathes. Smoke would have entered the lungs. That didn't happen." Dr. Abraham held up one finger. "There is no question. The bullet killed him. The body was dead when it was set on fire."

Dirkson nodded gravely, as if attaching great weight to the doctor's remarks. "I see, Doctor. Tell me, did you determine the time of death?"

"I did."

"And what was the time of death?"

"The decedent met his death between the hours of ten and eleven P.M. on February 26th."

Dirkson nodded. "Thank you, Doctor. No further questions."

Judge Grimes looked at the defense table. "Mr. Winslow?"

Steve hesitated just long enough to let the doctor think he was going to get away. Then he rose to his feet. "I have one or two questions, Your Honor."

Steve stepped out from behind the table and crossed to the witness stand.

The jurors watched with some interest. This was the first witness Steve Winslow had seen fit to cross-examine, which magnified its importance.

"Between the hours of ten and eleven, Doctor?"

"That's right."

"That's a rather precise time frame, isn't it?"

"Yes, it is."

"How were you able to be so accurate?"

"Because I saw the body so soon after death. I was on the scene at 11:02. I performed the autopsy shortly after midnight."

"I see. And when did you determine the time of death? At 11:02 when you first saw the body, or shortly after midnight when you performed your autopsy?"

"When I performed my autopsy, of course."

"You determined the time of death solely from medical factors?"

"Of course."

"Well, Doctor, I'm just a layman, but as I recall, one of the factors in determining the time of death is post mortem lividity, is that right?"

"It is, but—"

"Just answer the question, Doctor. Post mortem lividity *is* one of the factors used in determining the time of death, is that right?"

"Yes."

"Fine. Now, as I understand post mortem lividity, a dead body has no pulse, therefore after death, the blood stops circulating and tends to gravitate to the lower portions of the body, causing a reddish tinge to appear on the skin. Is that right?"

"Yes, but in this case—"

"In this case that would not be a factor, am I correct? Because it takes time for post mortem lividity to develop and sufficient time had not elapsed, and even if it had, the body was so badly charred the lividity would not have shown. Is that right?"

"Yes," Dr. Abraham snapped. "That was what I was about to say before you interrupted me."

"So," Steve said, "in this case post mortem lividity told you nothing, and was not a factor used in determining the time of death?"

"No, it wasn't."

"Then there's rigor mortis, also used in determining time of death. As I understand it, when the body has been dead for a sufficient time, rigor slowly sets in and the body becomes stiff. Then after sufficient time, rigor leaves the body, and it slowly relaxes again. Is that right?"

"Yes, it is. But—"

"But in this case sufficient time had not elapsed for rigor to even begin to set in, is that right?"

"Yes, it is."

"So, rigor mortis was not a factor in determining the time of death?"

"No, it wasn't."

"I believe another means is by stomach contents. Since digestion ceases when a person is dead, by examining the contents of the stomach and determining how far digestion has progressed, one can determine fairly accurately how soon a person died after eating a particular meal, is that right?"

"Yes, it is."

"Did you examine the stomach contents of the decedent?"

"Yes, I did."

"What did you find?"

"I found the partially digested remnants of a frankfurter with mustard and sauerkraut."

"I see. Were you able to determine when the person died relative to when they ate the hot dog?"

"Yes, I was."

"And how long was that?"

"Based on the progress of the digestion, I was able to postulate that the decedent ingested the food approximately four hours before his death."

"Four hours?"

"That is correct."

"I see. And you estimate the time of death between ten and eleven. The median time would be ten-thirty. Four hours prior to that would be six-thirty. So then is it your opinion that the decedent ate the hot dog at approximately six-thirty P.M. on the night of the murder?"

"Approximately six-thirty." The doctor smiled a thin smile. "Six-thirty is a median time, as is ten-thirty. I would say my findings indicate the man ingested the food sometime between six and seven o'clock, just as I say he died sometime between ten and eleven. Six and seven and ten and eleven are, of course, extreme limits, the times within which the events *might* have occurred. However, as to when the events are most likely to have occurred, the optimum time of ingestion of the frankfurter was around six-thirty, and the optimum time of death around ten-thirty."

"I see, Doctor. Thank you for you clarification. Now let me ask you this. Do you know of your own personal knowledge when the man ate the hot dog?"

Doctor Abraham shifted in his seat. "I do not know when the food was ingested, no."

"Well, aside from your own personal knowledge, did anyone *tell* you when the decedent ate the hot dog?"

"Objection, hearsay," Dirkson said.

"I'm not asking what the man was told," Steve said. "I'm asking *if* anyone informed him."

Judge Grimes frowned. "Sustained as to form. You may rephrase the question."

"Very well," Steve said. "Doctor, aside from your personal knowledge, did you learn when the man ate the hot dog from any other source?"

"No, I did not."

"I see," Steve said. "That's very interesting. So when you say the man ate the hot dog between six and seven, you are deducing that from your examination of the stomach contents alone, is that right?"

"That is correct."

"You are saying, this man died approximately four hours after eating the hot dog. I fix the time of death between ten and eleven and therefore he ate the hot dog between six and seven. Is that right?"

"Exactly. As I have already stated."

"I know you have, Doctor. But what I'm getting at is this. Since you don't know when the man ate the hot dog, the stomach contents really tell you nothing in terms of time of death. In other words, in reaching your conclusions, you are taking the time of death as a given, and using it to determine when the man ate the food. You're saying the man died between ten and eleven, therefore he ate between six and seven. Instead of the other way around, which would be, the man ate between six and seven, therefore he must have died between ten and eleven. Is that right?"

"That's essentially correct."

"Essentially? I think it's totally correct, Doctor. Is it not true that if you don't know when the man ate the hot dog, the stomach contents cannot tell you the time of death?"

"Yes, that's true."

"And is it not true that you *don't* know when the man ate the hot dog?"

"Yes, that's true."

"So is it not true that in this case the stomach contents *do not* tell you the time of death?"

"Yes, that's true."

"Gee, Doctor," Steve said. "Then I guess that my assumption was *essentially* correct."

"Objection, Your Honor," Dirkson said.

"Sustained. Mr. Winslow, if we could avoid these side remarks."

"Sorry, Your Honor. So, Doctor, in this case is it not true that you could not determine the time of death from the stomach contents?"

"Objected to as already asked and answered."

Judge Grimes frowned. "I'll allow it."

"Yes, that's true."

"So," Steve said, ticking them off on his fingers. "You could not determine the time of death by post mortem lividity, you could not determine the time of death by rigor mortis, and you could not determine the time of death from the stomach contents. Tell me, Doctor, how *did* you determine the time of death."

"By body temperature."

"Oh?"

"Yes," Dr. Abraham snapped. "As I would have pointed out in the beginning, if I'd been allowed. Those three methods you mentioned are factors in determining the time of death, but they are relatively unimportant factors. Post mortem lividity is a factor, but a relatively negligible one. Rigor mortis is of some importance, but still not that accurate. Examination of the stomach contents can be of great help in determining the time of death if the time of ingestion of the last meal is known. But far and away the most accurate method of determining the time of death is by body temperature."

"And that is how you determined the time of death in this case?"

"It is."

"You took the body temperature of the decedent?"

"That's right."

"And when was this done?"

"When I performed my autopsy. At approximately 12:05, after midnight on the morning of the 27th."

"That would be approximately an hour and a half after the time you determine as the optimum time of death?"

"That is correct."

Steve paused, scratched his head. "Well, that's mighty interesting, Doctor." He turned to include the jury. "And now, for the benefit of us laymen, who have not had the benefit of your medical experience, could you perhaps explain how you use body temperature to determine the time of death?"

"Certainly," Dr. Abraham said. "Humans are, as you know, warm-blooded. During life, the body temperature is approximately ninety-eight-point-six. After death, the body begins to cool. Since the rate of cooling is constant, by taking the body temperature it is possible to determine when the body began cooling. Which is, of course, when the person died."

"A very good explanation, Doctor. And may I compliment you on not cluttering it up with a lot of technical jargon. So you say the rate of body cooling is a constant?"

"It is."

"If I'm not mistaken, that rate is one and a half degrees Fahrenheit per hour. Is that right?"

"Yes, it is."

"Well, Doctor, you stated you took the body temperature at 12:05, approximately an hour and a half after the time you fix as the time of death. Is that right?"

"Yes, it is."

"Well, let's do the math. We have one and a half degrees Fahrenheit per hour for an hour and a half. So a half hour would be three-quarters of a degree Fahrenheit, or point-seven-five degrees, if you will. So one and a half plus three-quarters equals two and a quarter degrees Fahrenheit, or two-point-two-five. As you've already stated, the body temperature is normally ninety-eight-point-six. So ninety-eight-point-six, minus two-point-two-five leaves ninety-six-point-three-five. So, Doctor, am I to assume when you took the body temperature you got a reading of ninety-six-point-three-five degrees Fahrenheit?"

Dr. Abraham tugged at his shirt collar. "No, sir. That is incorrect."

"Oh really? I thought we agreed that the body cools at one and a half degrees Fahrenheit per hour."

"Yes, we did."

"And did you state that the body temperature is ninety-eight-point-six?"

"Yes, I did. But—"

"I'm a little confused, Doctor. And I'm sure some of the jurors are too."

"Objection."

"Sustained."

"Sorry, Your Honor. I'll confine myself to my own confusion. Are you telling me, Doctor, that my mathematics is incorrect?"

"No, I'm not. But—"

"I'm not? Then I am correct in saying that if the body cools at one and a half degrees per hour, if you examined the body an hour and a half after death, the body temperature should have been ninety-six-point-three-five. Isn't that right?"

"No, sir. That is not correct."

"And why not Doctor? Is there something wrong with my math?"

"No, there's nothing wrong with your math. The problem is, you're making a false assumption."

"Oh? And what is that?"

"That the body temperature of the decedent was ninety-eight-point-six."

"Oh? I thought you said it was."

"No. I said that was the general case."

"Are you saying that was not the case here?"

"Of course."

"And why was that?"

Dr. Abraham smiled condescendingly. "You're forgetting, Counselor, that the body was burned. Naturally, that would raise the body temperature."

Steve Winslow feigned surprise, as if that thought had never occurred to him. "Oh, I see, Doctor. Thank you for pointing that out to me. So, you're saying the body temperature of the victim was *higher* than ninety-eight-point-six when he died? Therefore it was higher than ninety-six-point-three-five when you took his temperature?"

"That is correct."

"What *was* the actual body temperature when you did your autopsy?"

"Ninety-eight-point-two."

"Ninety-eight-point-two? Then, if the body had cooled two-point-two-five degrees, then the temperature at the time of death would have been a hundred-point-four-five. Is that right?"

"Approximately."

"The temperature at the time of death was a hundred-point-four-five?"

"I said approximately. It's impossible to be that accurate. But the body temperature was somewhere around a hundred and a half degrees Fahrenheit."

Steve pursed his lips and shook his head. "Wow, that's interesting, Doctor. A hundred-point-five degrees?"

"Approximately."

"Gee, Doctor, where did you get that figure?"

"I just told you."

"Yes, you sure did. Tell me something, Doctor. Isn't this just like the hot dog?"

"I beg your pardon?"

"It's exactly like the hot dog, isn't it. You don't *know* the temperature at the time of death. You didn't *take* the temperature at the time of death. You weren't *there* at the time of death. You took the temperature at the time of the autopsy. That temperature was ninety-eight-point-two. Now you say the man died an hour and a half earlier, so when he died his temperature must have been a hundred and a half. In other words, you *assume* the temperature was a hundred and half because you *assume* the man died at ten thirty. And you *assume* the man died at ten thirty, because you *assume* the temperature was a hundred and a half. Is that right?"

"That's not fair."

"I didn't ask you if it was fair, Doctor. I asked you if it was accurate."

"It is not accurate. I determined the time of death by medical means."

"And those medical means include a wild guess as to what the body temperature was at the time of death, don't they, Doctor?"

"Objection to the characterization, 'wild guess'," Dirkson said.

Steve Winslow chuckled. "I'll withdraw the question, Doctor." He smiled at the jury before adding. "I can understand why the prosecutor wouldn't want you to answer it."

# 31

"So," Taylor said, "why is the time element so important?"

Mark Taylor, Tracy Garvin and Steve Winslow were catching lunch at a small diner near the courthouse. Steve, exhausted from the morning session, had ordered a round of coffee to start, and the waitress had just delivered it and taken their sandwich orders.

Steve took a sip of coffee, grimaced at the bitter taste, shook his head. "It isn't," he said.

Mark Taylor took a sip of coffee, made a face, dumped more sugar in. "Why is it none of these places ever wash the pot?" He took another sip, found it only slightly more to his liking. "I don't understand. What do you mean, it's not important?"

Steve shrugged. "It doesn't matter. The doctor says he died between ten and eleven. He's probably right. But even if he's wrong—say the guy died between nine and ten—what does it matter? Jeremy Dawson could have killed him between nine and ten just as well."

"So what's the big deal?"

"No big deal."

Mark Taylor took a sip of coffee, frowned, shook his head. "I don't know what's pissing me off more, you or this coffee. If the time element's no big deal, why did you make such a big stink about it?"

"Because it's there."

"What?"

Steve sighed. "You tell him, Tracy."

Tracy shrugged. "The way I see it, he couldn't care less about the time element. He's just trying to win the sympathy of the jury. Just like with the female transit cop."

Steve grinned. "Oh, you caught that?"

Tracy gave him a look. "How could I miss it. It was shameless. You got six women and three Hispanics on the jury, so you take an Hispanic woman cop and make a speech about her intelligence and honesty." Tracy shook her head. "I tell you, when I heard that I said, 'Shit, he must really be in trouble now.' "

Steve nodded. "Well, you're absolutely right. Dirkson's got me by the balls. I'm in a situation where I have to use every trick I can." Steve turned back to Mark Taylor. "So, no, Mark, the time element don't mean shit. But tell me, did you like my cross-examination of the doctor?"

"I'll say," Taylor said. "It was right on. That's why I figured it had to mean something."

"Well, it doesn't. But you liked it, huh?"

"Yeah."

"Well, the jury liked it too. I knew they would. I mean, here's an arrogant, pompous, condescending doctor, and the jury just loved to watch me rip his can off. We scored points for it.

"And that's what it's all about now. Dirkson has such a damn good case on the one hand, and such a horrifying one on the other. I mean, you should have seen those pictures. This is not just a murder. This is a gruesome murder. Dirkson's drenching the jury in horror, and they're lapping it up. The best I can do now is lighten the mood. It ain't easy, and I gotta score points any way I can. That's why I was so brutal with the doctor."

"Yeah, I see that," Taylor said. "So now what?"

Steve shrugged. "More of the same. And it's only gonna get worse."

"How come?" Tracy asked.

"Well, more than likely next up is the derelict who saw Jack Walsh and Jeremy Dawson together. He's gonna make the identification, I'm gonna have to shake it. And it's gonna be a bitch. The jury loved me for tearing into the doctor. They'll hate me if I tear into this guy."

"So what you gonna do?" Tracy asked.

"Anything I can. You got those pictures, Mark?"

Taylor tapped his briefcase. "Yeah. Right here."

"What pictures?" Tracy asked.

"Head shots," Taylor said. "Kids with green hair."

"Oh, I didn't see 'em," Tracy said. "Can I take a look?"

"Sure," Steve said. "Pass 'em over, Mark. But keep 'em covered," he cautioned Tracy. "It'd be just our luck to have someone from Dirkson's office walk by."

Taylor opened the briefcase, took out a manila envelope, passed it over to Tracy.

Tracy pulled out the photos, leafed through them. They were eight-by-ten color glossies of teenagers with green mohawks. Tracy flipped through the pictures, stuck them back in the envelope, and looked up at Steve.

"Are these different kids, or are they all the same guy?"

Steve grinned. "You just made my day. Nice work, Mark."

Tracy handed the envelope back to Mark Taylor and frowned. "Yeah, good, but I don't get it. You may be able to confuse the hell out of the witness, but isn't that just what you said you didn't want to do? Isn't that gonna piss the jury off?"

"Depends how it's done," Steve said. "I gotta tread lightly and try to reverse the field."

Tracy frowned. "I don't know what that means. Tell me something. Was one of those pictures Jeremy Dawson?"

Steve grinned again. "That's the second best thing I've heard all day."

Tracy frowned and shook her head. "I don't like this. I don't like this at all."

"Why not?"

"You know why not. I mean, everything you're doing—the pictures, the doctor—it's not to prove a point. It's to confuse the issue. It's to try to throw up a smoke screen to keep the facts from getting out. Dammit, it's the classic case you hear about. It's the clever defense attorney using his legal education to help some criminal beat the rap."

"I can't think that way."

"Why not?"

"I have a premise, a given, a bottom line. That bottom line is, Jeremy Dawson did not kill Jack Walsh. That's the assumption on which I'm operating. The prosecution says he did, I say he didn't."

Steve paused, took a sip of coffee. "And let me tell you something. If you didn't like the doctor and the photos, you are in for a rude shock." Steve held up his finger. "Because I promise you, I am going to use every trick in the book to get Jeremy Dawson off."

# 32

WHEN COURT RECONVENED,
Dirkson stood up and said, "Call Joseph Bissel."

In the back of the courtroom, Mark Taylor nudged Tracy
Garvin. "This is it."

"Huh?"

"Joe Bissel. That's the derelict."

Tracy Garvin watched with some interest as Joseph Bissel
walked to the stand. The prosecution had certainly done everything in their power to clean him up for court. He'd had a
shave and a haircut. He was dressed in an inexpensive, but
clean and presentable suit.

He was also sober, which had to be a big victory for the
prosecution. Tracy couldn't help wondering exactly how they'd
managed that. An occasional slight tremor now and then as he
walked up the aisle with the court officer was the only real
indication of what this man had once been. Otherwise, he
seemed a perfectly ordinary, if somewhat pale and emaciated
fifty-five-year-old man.

Joseph Bissel took the oath, seated himself on the witness
stand.

Dirkson rose and approached him. "Your name is Joseph
Bissel?"

The witness tugged at his shirt collar, snuffled slightly. His
manner indicated nervousness, but not fear. His face was long
and lean. His eyes, though slightly sunk in, were wide and
trusting. The overall impression he made was good—a simple,
honest man.

"Yes, sir," he said.

Dirkson smiled. "And where do you live, Mr. Bissel?" he
asked gently.

Joseph Bissel tugged at his shirt collar again. "I don't live
anywhere."

"No?"

"No. I guess I'm what you'd call one of the homeless."

"I see," Dirkson said. He glanced at the jury, and there was
sympathy in his look. Dirkson's entire manner was different

196

than it had been with any other witness. He was gentle, considerate, solicitous.

Kind.

This is a man who can be easily bruised, Dirkson's manner seemed to say. And *I* am not going to be the one to do so.

"Tell me, Mr. Bissel. Where do you sleep?"

"When it's warm, I sleep in the park. When it's cold, I sleep in subway stations."

"In subway stations?"

"Yes."

"And were you sleeping in a subway station on February the 26th?"

"February the 26th?"

"Yes."

The witness shook his head. "I know you've asked me this question before. As I've told you, I don't know the date. I can only tell I was sleeping in the subway on the day of the fire."

Dirkson nodded his approval, emphasizing the witness's honesty and integrity. "Yes. The day of the fire. That's the day we are interested in. You say you were sleeping in the subway on the day of the fire?"

"Yes, I was."

"And what subway station was that?"

"The 66th Street Station."

"Are you sure?"

"Yes, I am."

"How can you be sure?"

"Because that's where I usually stay. There and 28th Street."

"On the Broadway line?"

"Yes."

"How can you be sure you were at 66th and not 28th?"

"I happen to remember. I was at 28th Street first. But someone was there. Sleeping in my spot. I didn't want to wake him. So I caught the train to 66th."

"And what did you do there?"

"Went to my usual spot. No one was there, so I lay down and went to sleep."

"And where is your usual spot?"

"North end of the uptown platform. There's a dumpster there. A little alcove behind it. That's where I sleep."

"And you went there that day?"

"That's right."

"And what did you do?"

"Like I said. I went to the alcove on the platform. No one was there. So I lay down and went to sleep."

"Did you wake up at any time that day?"

"Yes, I did."

"Tell us about it. How did that happen?"

"There was someone moving around. I heard voices. And someone stepped on my foot."

"That woke you up?"

"Yes."

"Why?"

The witness snuffled. Frowned. "Danger. That's why. People mean danger. Have to be alert. I got nothin' to steal, but even so. Some people wish you harm. I sleep light. Someone there, I know."

"So, in any event, you woke up?"

"Yes, I did."

"What did you see?"

"First thing I saw was scary. Woke me up more."

"Scary? And why was that?"

" 'Cause it was strange. It was a kid with green hair."

"Green hair?"

"Yes. And it wasn't just that it was green. It was cut funny." Joseph Bissel ran his hands along the side of his head. "You know. Like an Indian."

"You mean a mohawk?"

"That's right. Mohawk."

"I see. That does sound scary," Dirkson said. "So that terrified you, because you didn't know what it was?"

Bissel shook his head. "No. I knew what it was. A teenager. They wear their hair like that. I knew. That's why I was scared. Teenagers scare me."

"I see," Dirkson said. "Tell me. This teenager—the one with the green hair—was he alone?"

"No, sir."

"There was someone with him?"

"Yes, sir. There was an old man."

"And did you know the man?"

"Yes, I did."

"And who was he?"

"Jack Walsh."

"Jack Walsh? Then you knew Jack Walsh?"

"Yes, I did."

"Where did you know him from?"

"From the subway. He was one of us. He used to sleep down there."

"You're sure it was Jack Walsh?"

"Yes, I am."

"Did you speak to him?"

"No, but he spoke to me."

"What did he say?"

"Just something like, 'It's all right, Joe, go back to sleep.' "

"I see. And did you?"

"Did I what?"

"Go back to sleep?"

Joseph Bissel shook his head. "Not right away."

"What did you do?"

"I watched them."

"Jack Walsh and the kid with green hair?"

"That's right."

"And what did they do?"

"They were talking."

"Could you hear what they were saying?"

"Some of it I could."

Dirkson looked up at the judge. "Some of this may be hearsay, You Honor, but I believe what Jack Walsh said at the time would be part of the *res gestae*."

"So far there's been no objection, Counselor," Judge Grimes said. "Why don't you proceed, and we'll argue this if and when there is one."

"Thank you, Your Honor. And what did you hear Jack Walsh say?"

"I only got the gist of it."

Dirkson smiled. "The gist is all we want. What was it?"

"Something about how the boy had done him a favor, and now Jack was gonna do one for him."

"Was that all?"

"That's all I remember. There was some talk about a pen."

"A pen?"

"Yes."

"Do you remember what it was?"

"No, I don't."

"All right. And what did you see them do?"

"Well, they sat down on the platform." Joseph Bissel frowned. "Actually, I think I heard this after they sat down on the platform—what I just told you, I mean. If that matters."

Dirkson smiled. "I don't think it does, but thank you for pointing it out to us. And did you see them do anything else?"

"Yes, I did."

"And what was that?"

"Well, he—Jack Walsh—he took some paper out of his pocket and started writing on it."

"Do you know what he was writing?"

"No, I don't."

"Did you see *how* he was writing?"

"Yeah. He spread the paper flat on the platform, and was bent over writing on it."

"And the boy with green hair?"

"He was watching him write."

"I see," Dirkson said. "And the man who was writing on the paper—this was Jack Walsh, whom you've known personally for some time?"

"That's right."

"And the other person—the boy with green hair—had you ever seen him before?"

"No, I had not."

"Have you ever seen him *again?*"

"Yes, I have."

"And do you know who he is?"

"Yes, I do."

"Is he in this courtroom?"

"Yes, he is."

"Could you point him out for us, please?"

"Yes, sir."

Joseph Bissel raised his arm and pointed. "That's him, right there."

"Let the record show that the witness is pointing at the defendant, Jeremy Dawson. Now, I want to be certain about this," Dirkson said. "You're saying that the boy you saw on the subway platform, the boy with Jack Walsh, when Jack Walsh was writing on the paper—that boy was Jeremy Dawson, the defendant sitting right there?"

Joseph Bissel nodded. "That's right. That's him. In the subway station he had green hair. He don't have green hair now, but that's him all right."

Dirkson nodded. "And this was the 66th Street Station, the Broadway line?"

"That's right."

"And this was on February 26th?"

Bissel shook his head. "That I don't know. I just know it was the day of the fire."

Dirkson nodded approvingly. "Thank you very much, Mr. Bissel." Dirkson turned to Steve Winslow. His smile was smug and his eyes were hard. "Your witness."

In the back of the courtroom, Tracy Garvin bit her lip. Steve had said it was going to be hard, but she hadn't quite understood just how hard. And in light of the way Dirkson had handled the witness, Tracy didn't really see anything that Steve could do.

Judge Grimes looked down at the defense table. "Mr. Winslow, do you care to cross-examine?"

Steve Winslow rose. "I do, Your Honor. But before I do so, I have a motion that had best be made outside the presence of the jury."

Judge Grimes frowned. "Will this take long?"

Steve smiled. "The motion is brief, Your Honor. But I imagine the ensuing argument might be lengthy."

Judge Grimes took a breath. "Very well. Bailiff, if you will escort the jurors to the jury room."

After the jurors had been led out, Judge Grimes said, "Proceed, Mr. Winslow."

"Thank you, Your Honor. At this time I would like to move

that the testimony of the witness, Joseph Bissel, be stricken from the record, and the jurors be instructed to give it no weight."

Judge Grimes blinked.

Dirkson lunged to his feet. "Oh, Your Honor—"

Judge Grimes held up his hand. "One moment, Mr. Dirkson. Mr. Winslow, I assume you have some grounds for making your motion?"

"Certainly, Your Honor. It appears that the entire testimony of the witness, Bissel, is for the purpose of establishing that my client and the decedent were seen together at the scene of the crime." Steve Winslow shot a glance at Dirkson. "Though I note the prosecutor has not made any attempt to show that the *time* they were seen there was even remotely near the time of the murder."

"That's no grounds for such a motion," Dirkson put in. "If the witness doesn't know the exact time of the events he was describing, that's a matter to be brought out on cross-examination. But that in no way should affect the admissibility of the evidence, or preclude what I brought out on direct examination."

Judge Grimes nodded. "I think Mr. Dirkson is essentially correct, Mr. Winslow."

Steve Winslow bowed. "Yes, Your Honor. I apologize. That was a side issue, which I shouldn't have even brought up. Mr. Dirkson jumped in before I could get to my argument.

"My objection is this: the testimony of Joseph Bissel is for the purpose of implicating my client in the crime."

Judge Grimes smiled dryly. "That is the purpose of a murder trial."

"Yes, Your Honor. But a murder trial must be conducted according to the rules of evidence. And Mr. Dirkson has not yet shown the *corpus delicti*. And it is an elemental rule of law that the *corpus delicti* must be proven before any evidence can be introduced for the purpose of linking the defendant with the commission of the crime."

Dirkson was on his feet again. "Your Honor, Your Honor, this is utterly absurd. The *corpus delicti is* proven. We have showed evidence that the decedent died as a result of a gunshot wound to the head. Now I admit that Counsel also had grounds to argue that the decedent died from burning, but he didn't do that. The medical examiner testified that death was due to the gunshot wound to the head, and could *not* have been from burning. Mr. Winslow could have cross-examined him on those points, but he chose not to do so. Therefore, the only testimony in evidence is to the fact that the decedent died from the gunshot wound. Since that testimony is uncontested, there is no grounds for Mr. Winslow to be raising the point at this time."

Judge Grimes nodded. "I think that is essentially correct, Mr. Winslow."

Steve smiled. "I think so too, Your Honor. But I'm afraid you and Mr. Dirkson misunderstand the point of my objection. My client has been accused of the crime of murdering Jack Walsh. So far, all the prosecution has shown is that the decedent died as the result of a gunshot wound to the head. Which I readily concede. What the prosecution has *not* shown—which is the reason the *corpus delicti* has *not* been proven—is that the man who died of a gunshot wound to the head is, indeed, Jack Walsh. The prosecution certainly can't introduce any evidence tending to link my client to the murder of Jack Walsh, unless they first show that Jack Walsh is, indeed, dead."

"Your Honor, Your Honor, there *is* evidence," Dirkson protested. "The testimony of Officer Oliver, of the Crime Scene Unit, who examined the credit card of Jack Walsh."

"Which doesn't identify the body, Your Honor. From the testimony now in court, for all we know the decedent could be some derelict who happened to have stolen Jack Walsh's wallet."

"That's utter nonsense, Your Honor," Dirkson said. "That's the wildest fantasy. You can't prove that."

"I don't have to," Steve said. "I don't have to prove Jack Walsh is alive. You have to prove him dead."

"I've proved him dead, Your Honor."

"You've proved *someone* dead," Steve said.

Dirkson took a breath. "Now, look here."

Judge Grimes banged the gavel. "Gentlemen, that's enough. I've heard enough to understand Mr. Winslow's contention.

Mr. Winslow, I must confess at first I thought your motion entirely without merit. But on reflection, I see that this is a matter that requires some consideration."

Judge Grimes turned to the prosecutor. "Mr. Dirkson. In light of Mr. Winslow's objection, I must ask you, do you have any evidence whatsoever that the body of the decedent was that of Jack Walsh?"

Dirkson took a breath, "Your Honor has seen the photographs."

"Yes, I have."

"Then you understand why I have not brought anyone forward to positively identify the body."

"I understand that. It still does not obviate you of the necessity."

Dirkson ran his hand over his head. "I understand."

"What about fingerprints?" Judge Grimes said. "Were you able to get fingerprints from the deceased?"

Dirkson grimaced and shook his head. "No, Your Honor. The hands were too badly burned."

"What about the teeth? Have you attempted to match dental records?"

"We have, Your Honor. And there we have some corroboration, though it is inconclusive."

Judge Grimes's eyes narrowed. "Why is it inconclusive?"

Dirkson held up his hands. "No, no, Your Honor. There is no inconsistency. The fact is, the records match absolutely. They're just not of that much help. The dental record of Jack Walsh shows that he wore dentures. He had no teeth. The burned body found in the subway station also had no teeth. So the dental records are absolutely consistent. Unfortunately, that's not as conclusive as if the man had some teeth on which work had been done, so we'd be able to show several points of similarity. As it is, we have only one point of similarity, the lack of teeth. However, in the face of the preponderance of the other evidence in the case, I would think that should be sufficient."

"Sufficient for what? To prove a certainty, or indicate a likelihood?" Steve said. "You could also reason this way: Jack Walsh was a man, the decedent was a man, therefore the decedent was Jack Walsh."

Judge Grimes's gavel cut off Dirkson's angry retort. "That will do. Mr. Dirkson, do you have any other evidence that the body of the decedent was that of Jack Walsh?"

"Not at the present time, Your Honor. I had not anticipated this problem would arise. I need time to look into the matter, to confer with my associates. At this point, I'd like to request a continuance."

"Any objection on the part of the defense?"

"None, Your Honor."

"Very well," Judge Grimes said. "That would seem to be the proper course of action. I must confess, I myself need time to look into the aspects of the defense attorney's motion." Judge Grimes banged the gavel. "Court is adjourned until ten o'clock tomorrow morning."

# 33

TRACY GARVIN PUSHED THE hair out of her eyes, leaned forward in her chair and said, "Is it true?"

Steve Winslow was slumped back in his desk chair. After court he'd had a long and frustrating session with Jeremy Dawson, yielding practically nothing new. Jeremy remembered vaguely that there'd been a bum sleeping on the platform when Uncle Jack had written the will, but he had no idea at all whether the clean, spruced up gentleman he'd seen in court was actually the grubby man he'd seen there. Not, Steve realized, that knowing the answer would have done him any particular good—he simply wanted to know.

Nor had Jeremy Dawson been of any help on any of the other points Steve raised. Jeremy's answers had all been so typically teenage punk, that as usual, had it not been for the wire mesh screen, Steve would have had a hard time restraining himself from giving him a good, swift kick in the butt.

Steve had returned to the office in a foul mood, pushed past Tracy Garvin, gone into his office and collapsed in his chair to try to think.

Tracy Garvin wasn't about to let him. She'd followed him right in, pulled up a chair determinedly and popped the question.

Steve Winslow opened his eyes to find Tracy Garvin glaring at him. "Is what true?"

Tracy snatched off her glasses, folded them up. "Dammit, you know what. Jack Walsh. The body. Is it him?"

Steve sighed. "How the hell should I know?"

Tracy glared at him. "I know you don't know. I mean what do you think? What you said in court—was it all bullshit? Or do you think it might be true? I mean, I know what you're doing. You're stalling because you don't want to cross-examine the witness. But is that all it is, or do you think there's some truth to it?"

Steve shrugged. "You're right on both counts. Yeah, I don't wanna cross-examine the witness. And do I think the body could be someone else?—yeah, I think it's a good shot."

"Why?"

"Because of Jack Walsh."

Tracy frowned. "Don't get cryptic on me, say what you mean."

Steve tipped his chair forward, leaned in on the desk. "All right, look. We know Jack Walsh. We know what kind of a man he was. He was a nut, but he was a clever nut. There was a method to his madness. And I look at this murder, and the whole thing is so typically Jack Walsh."

"How so?"

"O.K., take the will. He gets the kid out of school, takes the kid down in the subway and writes the will. Presumably leaves everything to the kid. Just the sort of thing that will drive the rest of the relatives bananas. Not twenty-four hours later he's dead, the kid's got the will, and the relatives *do* go bananas. And the will is drawn without a final signature so it may or may not be legal, and even if it is, the kid may not be able to inherit because he may be found guilty of murdering Jack Walsh. From the point of view of a vindictive madman who wanted to get back at his relatives, it couldn't be better."

"But that would have to mean—"

Steve nodded. "That he did it himself. Exactly. This is what I've been looking for all along. Someone who could have done this crime besides Jeremy Dawson. Someone with motive, method and opportunity. Well, the motive is clear. Method and opportunity? Well, the big stumbling block is Jeremy Dawson's gun which was in Jeremy's locker. But if somehow Jack Walsh had the combination to that locker—which isn't that far-fetched a premise—well, Jesus Christ, here he was on the day of the murder hanging out in the hallway of Jeremy Dawson's school."

"You mean he could have taken the gun?"

"Sure he could. I've been pounding Jeremy Dawson over the head all afternoon, trying to get him to remember if he saw the gun in the locker before he left with his uncle that afternoon.

And wouldn't you know it, the fucking kid can't remember.
Yes, he opened the locker before he left with his uncle. No, he
can't remember for sure whether he saw the gun."

"So you think Jack Walsh—"

"It's not what I think," Steve said. "It's a case of what *might*
have happened. I have to create reasonable doubt. To explain
the facts of this case by a reasonable hypothesis other than
that of guilt. Well, that's the hypothesis. Say Jack Walsh takes
the gun. Gets Jeremy down there, writes the will. Sends Jeremy away. What happens then? Jack Walsh finds some old
bum—probably has the guy already lined up. The require-
ments aren't that rough. Has to be an elderly white man about
Jack Walsh's size and weight, and he's gotta have no teeth. So
what does he do? He takes the man to the 66th Street Station,
gives the man his coat with his wallet in the pocket. Probably
gets the man drunk so he passes out. Then he probably waits
until an express is going through the station so no one will
hear the shot, and he takes Jeremy Dawson's gun and plugs the
guy in the back of the head. Then he douses the body with
gasoline, sets it on fire, and gets out of there. Sometime later
that night he breaks into the high school, sticks the gun back in
the locker, and takes off free as air, leaving his relatives to stew
over the results."

Steve shrugged. "And there you are. A reasonable hypothesis
other than that of guilt."

"Yeah," Tracy said. "Very reasonable. You're trying to prove
the corpse committed the murder."

Steve smiled. "There is that one small drawback."

The phone rang.

Tracy leaned forward, scooped it up. "Steve Winslow's office." She listened a moment, said, "O.K., come on down," and
hung up the phone. "Mark Taylor. Says he's got something
hot."

"Good or bad?"

"He didn't say."

"Christ, let it be good for once. It's about time we got a
break."

Tracy looked at him. "Are you serious? About Jack Walsh, I

mean. About Jack Walsh doing all that? I mean, do you really believe it?"

Steve shook his head. "Hell, I don't know. Tracy, I'll tell you honestly, I sift through the facts, and I make up this bullshit off the top of my head, and sometimes I think it's right. Sometimes I think it's true." Steve took a breath and looked her right in the eye. "And sometimes I'm just like you. Sometimes I think Jeremy Dawson's a lying little punk who set the whole thing up and killed Jack Walsh to feed his crack habit. I have to put that behind me, 'cause I'm his lawyer and I can't think that way. But if you want the truth, the truth is I'm insecure and I always have doubts, and defending this case is not exactly my idea of a good time."

They looked at each other for moment.

Tracy said, "Hey look, I'm sorry if—"

"Forget it. I understand you not liking this case. But do me a favor. Every time you get too pissed off at me for what I'm doing for Jeremy Dawson, ask yourself how you'd feel if I was defending that rich guy's son who killed his girlfriend."

Mark Taylor opened the door to find the two of them looking at each other.

"Am I interrupting something?"

"Not at all," Tracy said. She straightened up and shoved on her glasses. "Steve's just giving me his new version of the case. It turns out the corpse committed the murder."

Taylor looked at Steve. "That's the angle?"

"That's it. You got anything that'll help?"

Taylor flopped into the clients' chair, shook his head. "No, and you're not gonna like what I got. Pipeline got the word from headquarters. Dirkson's all in a dither about the question of identity. Turning the place upside down trying to get something that'll stick. Medical examiner's workin' overtime on the body, looking for something he missed. Cops are interrupting him every five minutes trooping people in there to look at the body, even though they know it's a lost hope. And Dirkson's questioning everybody he can get his hands on."

"Yeah? So?"

"So they got something. I don't know what it is, but they got something. Lids on, so my man can't find out what. Only one thing he knows for sure."

"What's that?"

Taylor grimaced. "Hate to rain on your parade. They I.D.'d the body as Jack Walsh."

# 34

JUDGE GRIMES LOOKED DOWN
from his bench at Steve Winslow and Harry Dirkson. "Gentlemen. Since yesterday I've gone over the testimony of the witness, Joseph Bissel, and considered Mr. Winslow's motion. I am now prepared to rule. However, as I now understand it, Mr. Dirkson has some new evidence which could render my ruling moot. Nonetheless, here is the situation. With regard to the motion to strike the testimony of Joseph Bissel, it is at least in part denied. An examination of his testimony shows that it is not true that the sole purpose of the testimony was to implicate the defendant, Jeremy Dawson, in the crime. Indeed, the greater part of his testimony, that he saw Jack Walsh in the subway station on February 26th, that he personally observed Jack Walsh writing something on a piece of paper, is not only relevant and admissible, but is actually part of the circumstantial evidence which the prosecution can use for making a case that the body found in the station was indeed Jack Walsh. Therefore, the only part of the testimony in question is that where Joseph Bissel identifies the man he saw in the subway station with Jack Walsh as the defendant, Jeremy Dawson."

Judge Grimes paused and frowned. "I have given the matter careful consideration because I must say frankly I believe it to be a close point. However, I find that I must hold with the defense attorney and rule that the prosecution does not have sufficient grounds to introduce the evidence at this time. I am therefore striking the testimony regarding the identification of Jeremy Dawson from the record. However, I am prepared to reinstate it, if and when the prosecution produces sufficient evidence to warrant my doing so. However, I am striking it from the record at this particular time.

"Now, with regard to matters of procedure. Mr. Winslow, Mr. Dirkson has concluded his direct examination of the witness. You now have the right to cross-examine. But naturally, only on that portion of the testimony which now remains in the record. If you do, and Mr. Dirkson then makes an additional showing which results in the reinstatement of the remainder of Joseph Bissel's testimony, you would at that time be given an opportunity to cross-examine on that. That being the case, I ask you if you would care to cross-examine the witness now, or whether you would care to defer your cross-examination until such time as it is determined whether the remainder of his testimony is to be reinstated."

Steve smiled. "Your Honor, in the event that his testimony is *not* reinstated, rather than cross-examine, I think I would find I had another motion to make."

Judge Grimes smiled. "I'm sure you would, Mr. Winslow. Though if the *corpus delicti* is *not* proved, the motion to dismiss would not be necessary.

"Now, Mr. Dirkson. Are you prepared to proceed?"

"I am, Your Honor."

"Very well. Bring in the jury."

When the jurors had been seated, Judge Grimes said, "Ladies and gentlemen of the jury, I apologize for the delay. Allow me to explain the situation. At this time I must ask you disregard the testimony of the witness, Joseph Bissel, with regard to identifying Jeremy Dawson as the person he saw in the subway station with Jack Walsh. You are to put it from your minds, and give it no weight.

"Now, with regard to the witness, Joseph Bissel. He has not completed his testimony. The defense still has the right to cross-examine. However, he has been withdrawn from the stand at the present time so that the prosecutor may introduce additional evidence.

"We are now prepared to proceed. Mr. Dirkson."

Dirkson rose. "Thank you, Your Honor. Recall Dr. Murray Abraham."

The medical examiner entered from the back of the courtroom and took the stand. It was obvious that he was still smarting from the effects of Steve Winslow's cross-examination. He did not glance once at the defense table, and his lips were set in a firm line.

When the medical examiner had seated himself on the stand, Judge Grimes said, "Dr. Abraham. You have already testified. Let me remind you that you are still under oath. Mr. Dirkson."

"Thank you, Your Honor. Dr. Abraham, since yesterday have you performed any additional tests on the body of the decedent?"

"Yes, I have."

"Can you tell us about those tests?"

"Yes, sir. I went over the body of the decedent again with the express purpose of looking for some medical anomaly which could be used as the basis for establishing the identity of the victim."

"And did you find anything?"

"Yes, I did."

"And what was that?"

"I found a hairline fracture of the right fibula."

"For the benefit of us laymen, Doctor, just what is the fibula?"

"It is one of the lower leg bones. The smaller bone in the back of the lower leg."

"I see. And you say the victim had a hairline fracture on his right lower leg bone?"

"That is correct."

"Can you tell us anything about that hairline fracture?"

"Several things. For one, the fracture had probably not been medically treated."

"Why do you say that?"

"Because of the way it healed. The split bone is slightly askew. In other words, it healed in precisely the position it cracked. It was not set. No attempt was made to hold the bone together. From which it is apparent the leg was never put in a cast."

"I see, Doctor. But how is that possible? Wouldn't a man with a broken leg require medical attention?"

Dr. Abraham shook his head. "Not with a hairline fracture of the fibula. You see, the fibula is not the support bone. The tibia is. A person with a hairline fracture of the fibula *should* have medical attention, to make sure it heals properly and in order not to risk a permanent disability. But since it is not a support bone, a person with a hairline fracture of the fibula can walk on it. Although they are apt to experience pain and walk with a slight limp until such time as the fracture has healed itself."

"And the fracture was this type of injury?"

"It was."

Dirkson nodded his approval. "Very good, Doctor. Now let me ask you this. Can you tell us anything with regard to the time of the injury? When it occurred?"

"Only in a general way. It is obvious the injury is not recent. From the age of the calcium deposits built up around the fracture, it is clear that this is an old injury. Most likely twenty to thirty years old."

"Thank you, Doctor. That's all."

"Mr. Winslow?" Judge Grimes said.

Steve Winslow stood up. "Ah yes, Doctor. With regard to this hairline fracture—this fracture that you missed in your initial autopsy—"

The medical examiner set his jaw. "I beg your pardon," he snapped. "I did *not* miss it in my initial autopsy."

"Oh?" Steve said. "Did you find it?"

"No, I didn't, but—"

"Then you missed it, didn't you?"

The medical examiner scowled. "I didn't miss it. It wasn't what I was looking for."

"Oh? And what were you looking for?"

"I was looking for the cause of death. That is the purpose of an autopsy."

"I see," Steve said. "You didn't miss it because you weren't looking for it. Then tell me, how is it that you happened to find it this time?"

"Because I was specifically looking for it."

"And why was that?"

"You know why. The prosecution asked me to examine the body and see if I could find anything that would determine the identity."

"I see. And when the prosecution asks you to look for something, you look for it. Is that right, Doctor?"

Dr. Abraham took a breath. "As a medical examiner, that is my job."

"I see. And when the prosecution asks you to find something, you find it. Is that right, Doctor?"

"Objection," Dirkson said.

"Sustained."

Steve smiled. "Thank you. No further questions."

Steve Winslow sat down, wondering what was next. The prosecution obviously had no medical records, not with Dirkson having the doctor testify how these hairline fractures could heal without medical attention. And in his opinion, none had been given in this case. So how was Dirkson going to tie it up?

When the medical examiner had been excused, Dirkson said, "Call Carl Jenson."

Jeremy Dawson grabbed Steve's arm. "Why are they callin' Carl?"

"I don't know. Wait and see."

"Yeah, well he's a lyin' sack of shit. Don't trust him."

"Don't worry."

Steve watched Carl Jenson take the stand. In Steve's opinion, Carl did not make a good impression. He was wearing his best suit and tie, and he was clean shaved and his hair was well groomed. But there was always something about him that was not quite right.

And it showed.

After Jenson had been sworn in, Dirkson said, "Your name is Carl Jenson?"

"That's right."

"What is your relationship to the decedent?"

"Objection, Your Honor," Steve said. "Assuming facts not in evidence."

Dirkson frowned. "I beg your pardon?"

"The word 'decedent,'" Steve said.

"Sustained," Judge Grimes said.

"I'll rephrase the question, Your Honor. What is your relationship to Jack Walsh?"

"He is my great-uncle."

"How long have you known him?"

"All my life."

"How well did you know him?"

"Very well. I lived in his house most of my life."

"Very good," Dirkson said. "Then let me ask you this. Do you have any personal knowledge of any injuries Jack Walsh sustained in his lifetime?"

"Objection to 'in his lifetime,' " Steve said.

"Sustained. That phrase may go out."

Nettled, Dirkson said, "Same question, omit the phrase. Do you have any personal knowledge of any injuries Jack Walsh ever sustained?"

"Yes, I do."

"Could you tell us about that, please?"

"Yes, I could. It was a long time ago. I must have been nine or ten years old. I was living in Jack's house at the time."

"And where was that?"

"In Great Neck."

"Thank you. Go on."

"I was out in the backyard, and Uncle Jack was playing with me."

"What were you playing?"

"Baseball. Whiffleball, actually. Jack was pitching and I was hitting the ball."

"What happened?"

"I hit a popup. Uncle Jack ran to get it and tripped and fell."

"Was he hurt?"

"Yeah. He hit his leg on a rock."

"Which leg?"

"His right leg."

"What part of his leg hit the rock?"

"The bottom of his leg. Right there."

"Let the court reporter note that the witness is indicating a spot in the back of his right leg midway between the knee and the ankle." Dirkson turned back to the witness. "So what happened then?"

"Nothing. Except we stopped playing ball."

"Did Jack Walsh go to the hospital?"

"No."

"Or see a doctor?"

"No."

"Are you sure?"

"Yes, I am. I remember, I said, 'Uncle Jack, you gonna go to the doctor?' and he said, no, it was nothing. But I know he couldn't walk on it. He sat with his leg up for a couple of days. After that he limped for a while."

"And after that?"

Jenson shrugged. "It got better. You know, just like he'd sprained his ankle."

"I see. But it wasn't his ankle, was it?"

"No. It was his leg. Right there, like I said."

"I see," Dirkson said. "Thank you. No further questions."

Judge Grimes said, "Mr. Winslow?"

Steve rose. "I have a few questions, Your Honor." He crossed in to the witness. "Mr. Jenson, you testified that this incident occurred when you were nine or ten?"

"That's right."

"That would be about twenty-five years ago?"

"Yes, it would."

"You have an excellent memory."

"Thank you."

"You're welcome. Mr. Jenson, are you familiar with the provisions of Jack Walsh's will?"

"Objection, Your Honor," Dirkson said. "Incompetent, irrelevant and immaterial."

"It's always proper to show bias, Your Honor."

"Objection overruled. Witness will answer."

"Are you familiar with the provisions of the will?"

"Yes, I am."

"Are you a beneficiary of Jack Walsh's will?"

"No, I'm not."

"You're not?"

"No sir. As you well know. The only beneficiary of that will is Jeremy Dawson."

"You're referring to the handwritten will that was in Jeremy Dawson's possession when he was arrested by the police?"

"Your Honor, Your Honor," Dirkson said. "Objected to as leading and suggestive, and assuming facts not in evidence. Counsel is now going into parts of the prosecution's case which we have not yet set forth."

"Objection overruled," Judge Grimes said. He turned to the jury. "Ladies and gentlemen of the jury. Let me explain. The matters Counsel is going into now are not in evidence, and are not to be considered by you as such. You are to consider only how these matters relate to the bias of this particular witness." He turned back to Steve. "Proceed, Mr. Winslow."

"Thank you, Your Honor. The question was whether you were referring to the holographic will found in Jeremy Dawson's possession when he was arrested by the police?"

"Yes, I was."

"That was the will purportedly written by Jack Walsh on February 26th?"

"That's right."

"And you say the only beneficiary of that will is my client, Jeremy Dawson?"

"Well, actually, I'm left a thousand dollars. As are the other relatives. But I don't consider that making me a beneficiary, somehow. I consider it a slap in the face."

Steve frowned. "So, if I understand what you're saying, your contention is that you are not biased in this matter because you are not a principal beneficiary in the will?"

"Exactly."

"Fine. Then let me ask you this. Is it not true that you have already consulted a lawyer and are contesting that will?"

"Yes, I am."

"On what grounds?"

"Lots of grounds." Carl Jenson ticked them off on his fingers. "The will was made under undue influence. The will was made while Jack Walsh was not of sound mind. And the will wasn't finished. It's not even signed."

"Do you expect to win the will contest?"

"Yes, I do."

"I take it you are a beneficiary of a previous will made by Jack Walsh?"

"Yes, I am."

"As I understand it, in that previous will, you and four other relatives, including Jeremy Dawson, are the principal beneficiaries, each to receive an equal share of the estate. Is that right?"

"Yes, it is."

"And you and the other beneficiaries, excluding Jeremy Dawson, have consulted a lawyer for the purpose of contesting

the handwritten will found in the possession of Jeremy Dawson?"

"Yes, we have."

"And did that lawyer tell you that no person convicted of
murder may profit from inheritance from his victim, so if it
should be proven in court that Jeremy Dawson killed Jack
Walsh, he could not and would not inherit, regardless of any
will?"

There was a pause. Carl Jenson frowned.

"Can you answer that, Mr. Jenson?"

"I think he said something to that effect."

"Oh, you do, do you?" Steve said. "Well, let's see where that
leaves us. You are contesting the will and you expect to win. In
the event that you do, you will receive one-fifth share in an
estate worth millions of dollars. On top of that, if Jeremy Dawson should be convicted of the crime and could not inherit,
you would receive one-fourth share of said estate. But is it not
true that in any case, you will inherit that money if and only if
Jack Walsh is proven dead? To put it another way, is it not a
fact that if the murdered man found in the subway tunnel
turns out to be Jack Walsh, you stand to share in an estate
worth millions of dollars, but if the man found in the subway
tunnel is *not* identified as Jack Walsh, you don't get a dime?"

Jenson shifted on the witness stand. "I'm not a lawyer."

"No, but you've consulted one. And I'm asking you, in your
own mind, are you not aware that if that body is identified as
Jack Walsh you stand to inherit money, and if it isn't you
don't? And does that in any way color your recollection, in any
way influence your remarkable memory to come up with the
details of an unimportant and eminently forgettable incident
you claim happened some twenty-five years ago?"

"No, it doesn't. I'm just telling you what happened."

"You remember it clearly?"

"Yes, I do."

"Jack Walsh fell down and hit his leg on a rock?"

"Yes, he did."

"His right leg?"

"That's right."

"You're certain of that?"

"Yes, I am."

"Could not have been his left leg?"

"No, it couldn't."

"You remember that so clearly that you can swear absolutely that it could not have been his left leg?"

"No. It was his right."

"And the fact that if it had been his left leg you might lose a million dollars doesn't cloud your memory at all?"

"No. It was his right leg."

Steve Winslow rolled his eyes, shook his head, gave the jury the benefit of his look of utter disbelief. "Thank you so much, Mr. Jenson," he said ironically. "No further questions."

Judge Grimes took a twenty-minute recess. When court reconvened, he frowned, took a breath and said, "I have considered that matter carefully. It now appears that there is sufficient circumstantial evidence to conclude that the body found in the subway station was indeed Jack Walsh. Therefore we may consider the *corpus delicti* proven, and the prosecution may introduce evidence tending to link the defendant to the crime. Therefore at this time, the testimony of the witness, Joseph Bissel, which had been stricken from the record, shall be considered reinstated, and may be considered in evidence.

"Now, the witness, Bissel, was withdrawn from the stand in order that this new evidence might be heard. And the defense reserved its cross-examination until such time as it should be determined if his testimony was in evidence. That time is now. Return the witness, Bissel, to the stand for cross-examination."

# 35

STEVE WINSLOW COULDN'T BE-
lieve how quickly things had turned around. He'd had Dirkson
on the ropes. He'd been that close to winning a dismissal. And
then Carl Jenson stepped up to the plate and made it a brand
new ballgame. Steve had been able to show how implausible,
farfetched, and likely to be biased Carl Jenson's testimony
was, but he hadn't been able to contradict it. And taken at face
value, Jenson's testimony had done the trick. Just like that, the
body had been I.D.'d as Jack Walsh, Joseph Bissel's testimony
had been reinstated, and Steve was right back in the position
he had been fighting to avoid, that of having to cross-examine
a homeless man.

When Joseph Bissel had been seated on the witness stand,
Steve Winslow stood up. Before he crossed in to the witness,
he looked at the jury. He could read the answer on their faces,
and it was just as he'd expected. Any attempt on his part to
brow-beat this helpless man and break down his identification
was going to alienate them all.

In the back of the courtroom, Tracy Garvin could read the
situation too. Joseph Bissel's identification of Jeremy Dawson
was shaky at best. Jeremy Dawson in court was a clean-cut kid
in a suit, and Joseph Bissel had seen a punk with green hair.
Joseph Bissel didn't know the day or the time of the occurrence, so in all likelihood he had been drinking, which was
something Steve had a legal right to bring up. But if he did,
he'd lose the jury.

So what the hell could Steve do?

Steve Winslow took a moment to refer to his notes. Then he
straightened up, crossed in to the witness, and smiled. "Good
morning, Mr. Bissel."

"Good morning, sir."

"You testified yesterday, Mr. Bissel, that you saw Jack Walsh
in the 66th Street subway station on February 26th, is that
right?"

"I don't know if it was the 26th. I only know it was the day of
the fire."

221

Steve nodded. "That's fine, Mr. Bissel. I appreciate your frankness. Now, you also stated that Jack Walsh had someone with him at that time. Is that right?"

"Yes, it is."

"And I believe you also stated that that person was my client, Jeremy Dawson. Is that right?"

"Yes, it is."

"Did you also state that the person in the subway station had green hair?"

"Yes, I did."

Steve turned and indicated Jeremy Dawson. "My client does not have green hair now. So obviously you are not identifying him by his hair. Mr. Bissel, can you tell me how it is that you're certain it was my client that you saw with Jack Walsh at that time?"

Bissel nodded. "The hair is different, but the face is the same. I've always had a good memory for faces. Some people do and some people don't. But I've always been good that way." He raised his finger to point. "And that is the face of the man I saw."

"Thank you," Steve said. "One moment, Your Honor." He turned and crossed to the defense table, picked up a manila envelope and pulled out the eight-by-ten photographs. "Your Honor, I ask that these pictures be marked for identification as Defense Exhibits A one through five."

"One moment, Your Honor," Dirkson said. "May I see those?"

"Certainly," Steve said. He passed the photos over.

Dirkson took a look at the photographs. His face flushed. "Your Honor, I object."

Judge Grimes smiled. "You can't object to him marking them for identification."

"I know, Your Honor. I object to him showing them to the witness."

"The objection is overruled. Counsel may show the witness anything he likes."

"But—"

Judge Grimes held up his hand. "That will do, Mr. Dirkson."

The court reporter marked the photographs.

Steve Winslow took them and approached the witness. "Mr. Bissel, you have stated that you recognize Jeremy Dawson as being the person you saw in the subway station with Jack Walsh, that his hair was cut in a green mohawk at the time, but that you recognize him anyway because you are very good with faces. Is that right?"

"Yes, it is."

"I hand you five eight-by-ten color photographs of young men with green hair, and ask you if you can look them over and tell me which one of them is the man you saw in the subway station."

Dirkson lunged to his feet. "Your Honor, I object."

Judge Grimes frowned. "On what grounds?"

"On the grounds that this is not a proper test. Those photographs have all been carefully staged. They are all young men with green hair, and they have all been shot at exactly the same light at exactly the same angle."

"Of course they have, Your Honor," Steve said. "Otherwise, it would not be a fair test."

"It is a test designed to confuse the witness, Your Honor."

"I beg your pardon," Steve said. "Your Honor, I object to the prosecutor characterizng what I am trying to do."

Dirkson's angry retort was cut off by Judge Grimes's gavel. "That will do. The objection is overruled. The witness will answer the question."

"Thank you, Your Honor," Steve said. "Now, Mr. Bissel, if you'd just look at the pictures and tell me if you recognize the man you saw in the subway station with Jack Walsh."

Joseph Bissel leafed through the pictures, looked closely at each one. On his second time through the stack he stopped and pointed to a picture. "That's him," he said. "That's the one."

Steve Winslow leaned forward, picked up the picture, held it up in front of the witness. "This one, Mr. Bissel?"

"Yes, sir. That's him."

Steve turned with a big smile on his face. "Let the record show that the witness has identified the picture marked for identification as Defense Exhibit A–2." Steve turned back to the witness. "Thank you very much, Mr. Bissel. No further questions."

Dirkson lunged to his feet. His face looked murderous. "All right, all right," he said. "Let me see those pictures." He snatched the pictures, found the one marked A–2. He turned it over, looked at it, clenched his fist. He turned to the witness. "Mr. Bissel," he said ominously, "you are now stating that the man you saw in the subway station with Jack Walsh is the young man in this picture?"

Joseph Bissel cringed slightly. He seemed surprised and hurt at this unexpected attack from a supposed ally. "Yes, sir," he said. "That's him."

"I want you to look at the picture again. In fact, I want you to look at all the pictures again. And tell me if you can identify *any* of them as being the man you saw in the subway station. In fact, whether you can even tell one picture from the other."

"Objection, Your Honor," Steve Winslow said. "Counsel is brow-beating the witness. Mr. Bissel has already made his identification."

"Mr. Bissel was *tricked* into making his identification," Dirkson snapped. "These photographs are a trick on the part of Counsel, and are totally unfair."

"Your Honor," Steve said. "Joseph Bissel strikes me as an exceptionally competent witness, and I would certainly trust his judgment. I'm not sure I understand. Is the District Attorney taking the position that Joseph Bissel *can't* identify the person he saw in the subway station?"

"No, I am not," Dirkson said. "Your Honor, I charge the defense attorney with misconduct."

"Misconduct, Mr. Dirkson?"

"Yes, Your Honor. Counsel specifically asked the witness which one of these pictures was of the man he saw in the subway station. That was an improper statement designed to deceive the witness into believing one of the pictures he was going to see would be of that man. When in point of fact, Your Honor, *none* of these pictures Counsel has shown the witness is of the defendant, Jeremy Dawson. I assign his asking the question as misconduct."

"And I assign that statement as misconduct," Steve said. "Your Honor, the prosecutor is making prejudicial statements in the presence of the jury. In an attempt to belittle the testimony of this witness, he is making statements of fact that are not in evidence. I ask that you cite him for misconduct."

Judge Grimes banged the gavel. "That will do. Not another word from either of you. Mr. Dirkson, your remarks were out of order. I ask you to remember yourself, particularly in the presence of the jury. Now, with regard to your objections to this particular test, they are overruled. The witness has testified, and that testimony is in the record. If you would like to take exception to that testimony, if you would like to try to impeach the witness, you may do so by cross-examination. But that is your *only* remedy at the present time.

"And as for you, Mr. Winslow, I'll have no more speeches out of you. If there are any further objections on either side, simply state them in legal terms.

"Now, Mr. Dirkson. Do you wish to proceed?"

Dirkson took a breath. "Very well, Your Honor. Mr. Bissel, are you absolutely certain that the picture that you have identified is that of the man you saw in the subway station?"

"Yes, it is."

"These pictures look very much like each other. Is there no chance you could be mistaken?"

The witness frowned. "Anyone can be mistaken. I can only tell you, in my opinion, that's the man."

"But it's just your opinion."

Bissel looked puzzled. "Well . . . yes, it's just my opinion."

"Thank you," Dirkson said. "That's all."

"Mr. Winslow, do you have any further cross-examination?" Judge Grimes asked.

"None, Your Honor."

"Very well. It has approached the hour for noon recess. Court's adjourned until two o'clock."

As court broke up, Mark Taylor and Tracy Garvin pushed their way through the crowd to meet Steve coming down the aisle.

"Real good," Taylor said. "You really did it."

"Oh yeah?" Steve said.

"Yeah," Tracy said. "Look, Steve, I still don't like this case much, and I don't really approve of what you did, but I have to tell you, I felt like cheering. I mean, it was really brilliant."

"What was?"

"Turning the tables on Dirkson. I didn't think there was any way you could cross-examine Bissel without coming across as the bad guy. But you did it. You turned it around. Dirkson's the bad guy and you're Mr. Clean."

Steve sighed. "Yeah. Right."

"What's the matter?" Taylor said. "You shook the identification. Dirkson's going bananas and you came out smelling like a rose."

"Except for one thing," Steve said.

"Oh yeah? What's that?"

Steve grimaced. "Bissel's a good witness. Defense Exhibit A-2 happens to be a picture of Jeremy Dawson."

# 36

IT WAS ALL DOWNHILL FROM there. From the confidence in Dirkson's manner when he returned from lunch, it was clear that he had finally figured out just who it was that Joseph Bissel had identified. Having gotten over that hurdle gave Dirkson new confidence, and he plunged ahead with a vengeance, building up his case.

He started off with Rose Tindel, who identified a glossy eight-by-ten as being a blowup of a picture she herself had taken of Jack Walsh. With that in evidence, Dirkson, in rapid succession, called three Teaneck High students, all of whom identified the man in the photograph as the man they had seen hanging around the corridors of the high school on February 26th.

Dirkson then called Officer Hambrick of the Jersey police, who testified to being one of the officers who arrested Jeremy Dawson at his high school on February 27th.

"Now," Dirkson said, "aside from the arrest warrant, did you have any other warrant with you at that time?"

"Yes, I did."

"What was that?"

"I had a search warrant for Jeremy Dawson's locker."

"Did you serve that warrant?"

"Yes, I did."

"On whom did you serve it?"

"The principal of the school."

"And did he open the locker?"

"Yes, he did."

"Were you present when the locker was opened?"

"Yes, I was."

"And what did you find?"

"I found a gun."

"What kind of gun?"

"A thirty-two-caliber automatic."

"And would you know that gun if you saw it again?"

"Yes, I would."

"How would you identify it?"

227

"I copied down the serial number."

In short order, the gun was produced, marked for identification, and introduced into evidence.

When that was completed, Dirkson said, "And did you find anything else in the locker?"

"Yes, I did."

"And what was that?"

Officer Hambrick raised his voice. "I found seventeen vials of crack."

Dirkson expected an objection at that point. Officer Hambrick couldn't know that the vials contained crack. That was purely a conclusion on his part. At best, he could testify that they contained a white, crystalline substance. Dirkson was of course prepared with a lab analysis to prove that it was indeed crack, but expected Winslow would fight to keep that testimony from getting in.

Steve didn't, however. Even though he could see the jurors' faces growing hard at the mention of drugs, Steve knew better than to make a fight at this point. Just let it pass.

The lack of an objection threw Dirkson's timing off. He had not prepared his next question, since he had not expected to be given a chance to ask it. There was a pause, and Judge Grimes had to say, "Are you finished with the witness, Mr. Dirkson?"

"No, Your Honor," Dirkson said. "Now, Officer Hambrick, were you present when Jeremy Dawson was taken into custody?"

"Yes, I was."

"And were you present when he surrendered his personal belongings?"

"Yes, I was."

"At the time, did Jeremy Dawson have anything in his possession which you considered significant?"

"Yes, he did."

"And what was that?"

"It was a folded sheet of paper, purporting to be the last will and testament of Jack Walsh."

"And would you recognize that document if you saw it again?"

"Yes, I would."

"And how would you recognize it?"

"I wrote my initials on the back."

After the will had been produced, marked for identification and introduced into evidence, Dirkson said, "Your witness."

Steve rose. "Officer Hambrick, can you identify the young man that you arrested on February 27th?"

"Yes, of course."

"Is he in the courtroom today?"

"Yes, sir. He is the defendant, Jeremy Dawson."

"I see," Steve said. "Tell me something. When you arrested him, did he look the same as he does today?"

Officer Hambrick smiled. "He most certainly did not."

"Oh? And how was he different?"

"He had green hair."

"Green hair?"

"Yes, sir. His hair was cut in a green mohawk."

"Thank you. No further questions."

When Steve sat down, Jeremy Dawson leaned in. "I don't get it. You're trying to mix him up, right? You're trying to make him think it wasn't me?"

"Not at all," Steve said.

After that Dirkson picked up speed. He called a handwriting expert who testified that the will was indeed in the handwriting of Jack Walsh. He called the ballistics expert who testified that test bullets fired from the gun found in Jeremy Dawson's locker matched absolutely with the fatal bullet taken from the body of the decedent. He called an expert from the crime lab, who testified that a series of tests performed on samples of the charred remains of the clothing found in the subway station indicated that they had indeed been drenched with gasoline and then set on fire.

Steve Winslow did not cross-examine any of these witnesses.

And the faces of the jurors became grimmer and grimmer.

At that point, Dirkson recalled Carl Jenson to the stand.

Once Judge Grimes had reminded Jenson that he was still under oath, Dirkson rose and said, "Now, Mr. Jenson. Referring to the date, February 26th, the day of the murder, did you see the defendant, Jeremy Dawson, at any time on that day?"

"Yes, I did."

"And when was that?"

"It was approximately five-thirty in the afternoon."

"And where did you see him?"

"At home. At our house, in Teaneck."

"You and the defendant both live there?"

"That's right."

"And what happened on this occasion?"

"Well, I was in the kitchen making myself a sandwich. I heard the front door open. I went out to see who it was and it was him."

"By him, you mean . . . ?"

"The defendant. Jeremy Dawson."

"What was he doing?"

"He was coming in the front door."

"Did you talk with him at that time?"

"Yes, I did."

"What did you talk about?"

"I asked him where he'd been."

"Did you have a reason for asking that?"

"Yes, I did."

Dirkson nodded. "Fine, Mr. Jenson. Now listen carefully, because we are getting into an area where we have to be careful about the rules regarding hearsay evidence. So try to answer my questions carefully, and answer only what is asked, and try to avoid telling us what some other person, other than the defendant, may have told you. Do you understand?"

"Yes."

"Fine. With that in mind, let me ask you this. During the course of the afternoon, were you in communication with anyone from Jeremy Dawson's high school?"

"Yes, I was."

"Good. Now, you say you asked Jeremy Dawson where he'd been?"

"That's right."

"And what did he say?"

"He shrugged, and said, 'Out.'"

"What did you say then?"

"I told him I'd been on the phone with his high school, and asked him why he cut his afternoon classes."

"What did he say?"

"He didn't answer. He just made a rude remark."

"Was that the extent of the conversation?"

"No, it wasn't. I asked him if he'd seen Jack Walsh."

"What did he say to that?"

"He laughed and said, 'Where the hell would I see him?' "

"What happened then?"

"I kept pressing him, asking him questions. Finally he turned on me and he grinned and he said, 'You're really stupid, Carl. You think you're ever gonna see any of Uncle Jack's money? You better think again.' "

"I want to be clear on this. This was five-thirty on the afternoon of the day of the murder. Jeremy Dawson laughed at you and made a remark about Jack Walsh's money and your chances of ever getting it?"

"That's right."

"What happened then?"

"I asked him what the hell he meant by that and he just laughed and went upstairs."

"And then what?"

"He just went upstairs, took a shower and changed his clothes."

"What did you do?"

"I hung around, waited for him to come down."

"Why?"

"I was upset. It bothered me, what he'd said. Particularly with what was going on, or with what I thought was going on. I wanted to talk with him some more."

"And did you?"

"I tried, but he wouldn't talk. He came downstairs a half hour later, all showered and changed. I asked him what he meant by what he said, and what was going on. But he wouldn't answer. He just made some rude remarks and went out the door."

"Did you ask him where he was going?"

"Yes, I did, but he wouldn't say. He just made comments I would not repeat in court."

"Did he say anything else that you *can* repeat?"

"Yeah. Last thing he said before he went out the door."

"And what was that?"

"He turned around, he pointed his finger in my face, and he said, 'You be nice to me, Carl, 'cause I'm gonna be rich.'"

Dirkson paused and let that sink in. "And that was approximately at what time?"

"Between six and six-thirty."

"On the evening of February 26th?"

"That's right."

"That was the last time you saw Jeremy Dawson that night?"

"That's right."

"Thank you, Mr. Jenson. That's all."

Judge Grimes said, "Mr. Winslow?"

Steve rose, crossed in to the witness.

Carl Jenson eyed him warily. After Winslow's previous cross-examination of him, Jenson was bracing himself for the anticipated attack.

It didn't come. Steve's manner was not adversarial. It was polite and conversational, even friendly.

Steve smiled, held up his hand and said, "Now, Mr. Jenson. Mr. Dirkson has been scrupulously careful about the phone call you had from the school, but I think there's no need to be overtechnical here. The fact is, the school called and told you Jeremy Dawson had cut his afternoon classes, right?"

"That's right."

"Tell me, did that surprise you?"

"I beg your pardon?"

"Well, was this a novel occurrence, something new and unexpected, something you'd never dealt with before?"

"No, it wasn't."

"Jeremy Dawson had cut his classes before?"

"Yes, he had."

"On more than one occasion?"

"That's right."

"And had the school called before with regard to Jeremy cutting his classes?"

"Yes, it had."

"And on those occasions, when Jeremy Dawson got home, did you ask him where he'd been?"

Jenson frowned, hesitated a moment. "I can't remember."

Dirkson came to his rescue. "I think it's incompetent, irrelevant and immaterial, Your Honor."

"On the contrary, Your Honor," Steve said. "This witness has testified as to remarks Jeremy Dawson made to him on this occasion regarding Jack Walsh and his money. It's entirely relevant whether those remarks were special to this occasion, or whether this was something Jeremy Dawson taunted Carl Jenson with all the time."

Judge Grimes frowned. "I will allow this line of questioning."

"You say on those occasions you can't remember if you asked him where he'd been. Can you remember if on those occasions you asked him anything about Jack Walsh?"

"No, I didn't."

"Are you sure?"

"Yes, I'm sure."

"You're not sure if you asked him where he'd been, but you *are* sure you didn't ask him about Jack Walsh?"

"That's right."

"How can you be sure about that?"

"On those other occasions there was no reason to ask him about Jack Walsh."

"Oh, so you're saying on this occasion there was?"

"Yes, there was."

"And what was that?"

Jenson hesitated, took a breath. "Well, recently the family had been very concerned about Jack. He'd been acting irrationally. He'd been confined in Bellevue. He'd been released just the day before. So naturally it was on my mind."

"Yes, but what made you think Jeremy Dawson might have seen him?"

"Well, there was the phone call from the school."

"Ah, yes," Steve said. "The phone call from the school. I was wondering about that. Is it possible that when the school called to tell you Jeremy Dawson had cut his classes, they also mentioned that he had been seen with a rather disreputable looking older gentleman?"

"Yes, they did."

"You didn't mention this on direct examination."

"Objection," Dirkson said.

Judge Grimes frowned. "Objection to what?"

"Objection to that statement. Counsel is trying to make it appear there was something sinister about the witness not mentioning that fact on direct examination. When in point of fact, the only reason he didn't mention it is because it's hearsay and inadmissible."

Judge Grimes smiled. "Are *you* objecting on the grounds it's hearsay and inadmissible?"

"Not at all," Dirkson said. "I'm happy to have it in the record."

"Then we have no problem. Proceed, Mr. Winslow."

"At any rate, Mr. Jenson, that is why you questioned Jeremy Dawson about Jack Walsh at this particular time?"

"That's right."

"Now, referring to those previous occasions on which the school called you about Jeremy Dawson, did he ever make any remarks to you about Jack Walsh's money?"

"No, he did not."

"The subject never came up?"

"No, it did not."

"But you do recall other occasions when Jeremy Dawson cut classes and you were called by the school?"

"Yes, I do."

"Tell me something. Was Jeremy Dawson ever suspended from school?"

"Yes, he was. But that wasn't for cutting classes. That was for selling crack."

There was a murmur in the courtroom. Dirkson grinned.

Steve frowned. "For selling crack, you say?"

"That's right."

"Now look here, Mr. Jenson, you don't know for a fact that Jeremy Dawson was selling crack, do you?"

"Yes, I do."

"How do you know that?"

"The school caught him at it."

"Wait a minute, Mr. Jenson. *You* didn't catch him at it, did you?"

"No, the school did."

"And you only know that because you were told that, right?"

"That's right."

"But that's hearsay, Mr. Jenson. You can't testify to that."

"I don't know about that," Jenson said. "I'm not a lawyer. You asked me so I told you."

That sally drew a laugh from spectators in the courtroom. Dirkson grinned broadly, and some of the jurors smiled.

Judge Grimes frowned. "Are you asking that answer be stricken from the record, Mr. Winslow?"

"No, I'm not, Your Honor. I'd like to cross-examine the witness on it."

"It's plainly hearsay, Mr. Winslow."

"It goes to the bias of the witness, Your Honor. This witness has given material evidence on statements my client made on the day of the murder. I'm interested in any factors that might have colored his judgment."

"Very well. Proceed."

"Mr. Jenson, you don't *know* of your own knowledge that Jeremy Dawson is a crack dealer, do you?"

Jenson hesitated. "You mean aside from what someone told me?"

"That's right."

"No, I do not."

"Well, tell me something. When Jeremy Dawson was suspended for selling crack, how did you feel about that?"

"How did I feel?"

"Yes."

"I was furious, of course."

"At the school, or at Jeremy Dawson?"

"At Jeremy Dawson."

"Why?"

"Why? Are you kidding me? I suppose you *approve* of selling crack."

"No, I don't, Mr. Jenson. And I'm sure you don't either. So you were outraged, is that right?"

"Yes, it is."

"You say you don't *know* of your own knowledge he was selling crack. Then let me ask you this. Did you *try* to find out for sure if he was selling crack?"

Jenson frowned. "What do you mean?"

"After the school told you that, did you make any investigation of your own? In particular, did you search Jeremy Dawson's room?"

Jenson hesitated.

"Well, Mr. Jenson?"

"Well, as a matter of fact, I did."

"Why?"

"Why? Come on, I was living in that same house. If he had drugs in the house, he was endangering us all."

"I see. So you searched his room?"

"Yes, I did."

"And did you find any drugs?"

"No, I didn't."

"And did that make you think maybe the school was wrong?"

"No. Because he didn't have them at home. He had them at school. He was selling drugs out of his locker."

"You know that now because of what the police found in his locker, but you didn't know it then."

"Yes, I did."

"How?"

Jenson hesitated, bit his lip.

"How, Mr. Jenson?"

"I don't know. I just knew."

"How did you know?"

"Well, it stood to reason."

"Yes, it did, Mr. Jenson," Steve said dryly. "And it certainly stands to reason much more now after the police found vials of crack in his locker. Just as it stands to reason now that Jeremy Dawson must have been taunting you about Uncle Jack's money since the police found a will in his possession leaving all that money to him."

Dirkson lunged to his feet. "Objection, Your Honor."

"Sustained," Judge Grimes said. "Mr. Winslow, that is clearly improper."

"Sorry, Your Honor. Mr. Jenson, you saw Jeremy Dawson on the day of the murder?"

"That's right."

"You spoke to him about skipping school and asked him if he'd seen Jack Walsh?"

"That's right."

"He went upstairs, took a shower and changed?"

"That's right."

"And when he came downstairs to go out, you asked him where he was going and he told you to be nice to him because he was going to be rich?"

"Yes, he did."

"And the amount of money which you personally have involved in the outcome in this case has in no way colored your recollection or judgment?"

"No, it hasn't."

Steve sighed and shook his head. "Thank you. No further questions."

Judge Grimes said, "Mr. Dirkson. Any redirect?"

"No, Your Honor."

"The witness is excused. It has reached the hour of adjournment. Court is adjourned until tomorrow morning at ten o'clock."

# 37

"DO YOU LIKE TO GAMBLE, JER-
emy?"

Jeremy Dawson frowned at Steve Winslow through the wire
mesh screen. "What?"

"You a gambling man? You like to take chances?"

"What are you talking about?"

"Dirkson's getting ready to rest his case. When he does, we
got a problem."

"What's that?"

"You. You're the problem. You're a teenage crack dealer, and
people don't like that."

"Yeah, right," Jeremy said. "You tell me this now? So what
the fuck you doin', man? I sit in court and watch you, and all I
can think is what the fuck is goin' on?"

"At least you didn't grab my sleeve."

"I was too stunned. I didn't know what to do. I'm sittin'
there, you got Carl on the stand, and suddenly you're asking
him if I was selling crack."

"You didn't like that?"

"What, are you nuts? I didn't know what the hell you're
doin'. I thought you lost your mind."

"Yeah, I think Dirkson thought so too."

"So what the hell were you doin'?"

"The crack issue's in the mind of the jurors. We can't keep it
out."

"Yeah, but we don't have to hammer it in."

"With Carl, I did."

"Why?"

"For one thing, it kept me from talking about the other stuff.
The stuff you told him about Uncle Jack."

"Oh."

"You really tell him that?"

"I may have made some remarks."

"Yeah, I'll bet you did."

"Well, so what? And what's that got to do with crack? And

what's crack got to do with Carl Jenson, for Christ's sake? I mean, why you have to ask him about crack?"

"You don't think the jury liked that?"

"I know damn well the jury didn't like that."

"Yeah, well I don't like it either," Steve said. "And let me tell you something. I'm not defending you for selling crack. I'm representing you in this murder case. And I'm representing you on the will. But as far as crack goes, if the cops decide to charge you with selling it, you get yourself another lawyer. I'm not defending that."

"I'll say. God, you're like a fucking prosecutor."

"That's what you think. Wait'll a real prosecutor comes after you for crack and you'll change your tune."

"Yeah, sure."

"Most people aren't lucky enough to get a second chance, Jeremy. You're lucky enough to beat this murder rap, give up that shit and fly straight. Things work out, you'll have some bucks. Most likely you'll get a fine and probation on the drugs. You stay straight, you'll be sitting pretty."

Jeremy's face contorted. "How can you talk about that, man? They got me on this murder thing, and I didn't do it. And you're not doin' a thing to help. They keep pilin' on the evidence, you don't cross-examine half the witnesses. The ones you do, you just get me in deeper. Talkin' about crack, for Chrissake."

"Forget crack. Let's talk about the murder."

"What about it?"

"Like I said, the D.A.'s gonna rest his case, then we got a big problem."

"Yeah. So what do we do?"

"That's what I want to talk to you about."

"So talk."

"The problem is your story, Jeremy. You claim you saw this film, 'Heathers.' But the cops got a witness who saw you there the previous Saturday night."

"So? Why couldn't I have seen it twice?"

"You could, but you didn't, Jeremy. As an alibi, it's real thin. And it isn't the truth. The way I see it, you went home, you took a shower and changed. You had the will in your pocket.

You were feeling like a big man, on top of the world. You weren't about to go to the movies. No, I think you went out that night and smoked crack."

Jeremy's eyes faltered.

"And if you did, you went to your locker to get it, didn't you?"

"Shit."

"That's what you did, wasn't it?"

"What if I did?"

"The gun was in your locker, Jeremy. That's when you would have taken the gun."

"I didn't take the damn gun."

"Did you see it there?"

"When?"

"When you went to your locker to get the crack?"

A pause, then, "No, I didn't."

"You didn't go, or you didn't see it?"

"I didn't see it."

"Would you have seen it?"

"No."

"Why not?"

"Why do you think? It wasn't in plain sight. It was wrapped up."

"So you don't know if it was there?"

"No."

"But you did go to your locker to get crack that night?"

"All right. So what if I did?"

"Did you smoke it with anyone?"

"What?"

"These are not hard questions, Jeremy. Did you smoke the crack with anyone? Someone who would testify that you couldn't have been in Manhattan killing your uncle because you were smoking crack with them at the time?"

Jeremy looked at him. "Fat chance."

"Oh yeah?"

"No one's gonna do that."

"Even to get you off a murder rap?"

"Yeah, even then."

Steve shook his head. "Some close friends you got, Jeremy. You ever think about that?"

Jeremy said nothing.

"So what's his name? The guy you smoked crack with?"

Jeremy shrugged. "Phil."

"Phil what?"

"I don't know."

"Where would I find Phil?"

"You wouldn't."

"I gotta subpoena him, don't I, Jeremy?"

"Not gonna do you any good."

"You're right, it isn't," Steve said. "And you know why? I'll tell you why. 'Cause if I find this Phil, in the first place he's gonna lie, and in the second place he's a crack head, so the jury wouldn't believe him anyway.

"And it's a hell of a rotten defense. 'I didn't do it, Your Honor, I was stoned out of my head on crack.' If we try that, half the jury's gonna believe you smoked crack, got stoned out of your head and went out and killed your uncle."

"I see that."

"You do? Good. So you understand we're up shit creek as far as an alibi goes."

"I see that. So what am I gonna say?"

Steve took a breath. "Well, that's the problem. You already told the cops you were at the movies. They can prove that's a lie. You stick with the story, you look bad because the jury knows you're lying. You *change* the story, you're admitting you lied on the one hand, and on the other hand, what you gonna change it to? You wanna tell 'em you were out smoking crack?"

Jeremy's eyes narrowed. "What are you saying?"

"I'm saying we ain't got a snowball's chance in hell if I put you on the stand."

Jeremy stared at him. "You're not gonna put me on the stand?"

"What good would it do?"

"I don't know. But, Jesus Christ, we gotta do something."

"That's for sure," Steve said. "There are a lot of other ways to go, Jeremy. But they're tough on the one hand, and risky on the other. And if we try 'em, a lot of it's gonna depend on you."

"On me? What would I have to do?"

"Nothing."

"What?"

"Just that. Absolutely nothing. And believe me, it's gonna be hard. What you have to do is absolutely nothing. Just sit in your chair. And don't grab my arm. And don't roll your eyes. And don't look at me as if I've just taken leave of my senses. No matter how you feel about what I'm doing, or no matter what I do."

Jeremy stared at him incredulously.

"Yeah," Steve said, pointing. "Like that. That's exactly what you cannot do in court."

Jeremy shook his head. "You're crazy, man. You're out of your fuckin' mind."

"Maybe," Steve said. "And that's a judgment call you're gonna have to make. You're the boss, Jeremy. You know that? If you want, you can always fire me and hire a conventional lawyer. But frankly, I don't think it would do you any good."

"Why not?"

"Because the prosecution has too good a case. There's no way to beat it any conventional way."

"So?"

"So, we gotta try something else. Maybe it works, maybe it doesn't. The way I see it, it's our best shot."

"Oh yeah?"

"Yeah. If I'm your lawyer, that's how I'm gonna play it. But you're the boss. It's your call. If we lose, you're the one goin' up the river. So that's why I'm telling you what I'm gonna do, and giving you a chance to fire me if you want."

Steve shrugged. "So that's why I'm asking." He smiled, and looked him right in the eye. "You like to gamble, Jeremy?"

# 38

MARK TAYLOR LOOKED APO-
logetic. "They subpoenaed my photographer."

"Oh?"

Steve Winslow was slumped back in his desk chair, utterly exhausted from the day in court. Mark Taylor had stopped by to give him the bad news.

"Yes," Taylor said. "They'll put him on the stand and he'll have to testify that defendant's Exhibit A–2 is a picture he duped from the photos of Jeremy Dawson sent out to the wire services."

"It's all right, Mark. We knew that was coming."

Taylor flopped into the clients' chair. "They subpoenaed him this afternoon while court was still in session. That's why I didn't have a chance to warn him. As soon as Dirkson found out, he moved fast."

Steve waved it away. "It doesn't matter, Mark. I don't want your men duckin' service. If Dirkson hadn't served him, he'd have asked for a continuance until he could. So don't sweat it."

"Well, I hate to bring bad news."

"It's the only kind I get. So what else have you got?"

"Nothing good. Negatives all around. I got men out scouring Teaneck, New Jersey, looking for someone who saw Jeremy Dawson there that night. So far, no one did."

"He was there."

"So you say. According to Dirkson, he was in Manhattan, blowin' his uncle's brains out."

"You believe that?"

Taylor shrugged. "Hell, everybody in the courtroom believes that. I mean, I'm on your side and all that, but I don't want to give you any false hopes. Frankly, things don't look good."

Steve smiled. "Confidentially, I don't think you're shattering any illusions, Mark. But thanks just the same. You got anything else?"

Taylor shook his head. "Just negatives. California checked in. They're still trying to serve the subpoena, but Julie Creston's still a no-show. Presumably she's in Rio."

"Figures," Steve said.

"If she shows up, you still want her served?"

"Sure do."

Taylor shrugged. "O.K. I sure wish I knew what you were doing."

"Frankly, I wish I did too," Steve said. "So what about the subway station?"

"Nothing there either. No witness, no one saw nothing. The only bright spot is the token booth clerk doesn't recall seeing Jeremy Dawson that night. But that doesn't do you any good, 'cause if he was coming from Jersey, he wouldn't have come through the turnstile, he'd have come uptown on the train."

"I know," Steve said.

"He doesn't recall anyone else in particular, and why should he? And no other witness has come forward, with the exception of Joseph Bissel. And he didn't see it happen, he showed up after the fact."

"How soon after the fact?"

Taylor shrugged. "There I'm not sure. We know it was before we got there, because when Tracy asked the cop he already knew something about a kid with green hair."

"Exactly. So it had to be that night."

"But after the murder."

"Yeah, but how soon after?"

"Don't look at me," Mark said. "Hell, you had the guy on the witness stand, you could have asked him then."

"Yeah. I know."

"Well, why didn't you?"

"Well, it wasn't proper cross-examination because the prosecution didn't bring it out on direct. Even so, I could have brought it in. He testified he'd seen Jack Walsh that day. I could have asked him if he'd seen Jack Walsh *any other* time that day. Specifically, if he'd seen him later that night. More specifically, if he'd seen the charred remains of the man on the subway platform, and if that was indeed Jack Walsh."

"So why didn't you?"

Steve sighed. "I blew it. I missed a bet. Frankly, I was too concerned with the Jeremy Dawson identification. Too concerned with handling the witness just right. Shaking the identification without coming off like a bad guy. I had to play it just right. And then getting the kick in the chops when the son of a bitch actually *did* pick out the picture of Jeremy Dawson. I have to admit, that threw me a little."

"So what can you do now? Can you recall him for cross-examination?"

"I doubt it," Steve said. "Dirkson would object, and I'd have to make a showing of what I expected to prove. And as I said, it's not really proper cross-examination anyway, and Judge Grimes isn't gonna buy it. No, if I want him on the stand, I'd have to call him as my own witness."

"Are you gonna do that?"

"I don't know. Depends how things go. I'm just saying I *could.*"

"You want me to subpoena him?"

"Not now, Mark. Not the way things stand."

"What would you try to prove by him, anyway?"

"I don't know. But where the hell was he when the crime took place? Probably in that other subway station he hangs out in. But maybe not. And if he showed up right after the crime and talked to the cops, I could always argue that *he* was the one fired the bullet into Jack Walsh."

"With Jeremy Dawson's gun?" Mark said gently.

Steve considered. "There is that tiny flaw," he deadpanned.

They looked at each other and burst out laughing.

Tracy Garvin came in the door. "What's so funny?"

"Absolutely nothing," Steve said. "We've reached the stage of the case where you start getting punchy."

"I'll say. Look, would you mind coming down to earth for a minute?"

"What's up?"

Tracy jerked her thumb. "Got a reporter on the line. Wants to ask you a question."

"A question?"

"Yeah, and you're not going to like it."

"You mean you know what it is?"

"Yeah. The guy didn't want to tell me, but I told him he didn't have a prayer of getting through unless I knew what it was all about."

"What's the question?"

"Is it true you're considering pleading Jeremy Dawson guilty to a lesser charge?"

"Shit."

"Yeah. What do you want me to do?"

"Dammit to fucking hell, the goddam press."

"Can't you just deny it?"

"Sure, but any way it makes news. Then they'll just print my denial."

"How about 'No comment?' "

"They'll run the same story and say I declined to comment." Steve waved it away. "Anyway, I'm glad you're here. You and Mark can start making out subpoenas."

"Oh yeah?"

"Yeah. Dirkson's getting ready to rest his case. When he does, I gotta be ready."

"Who you gonna subpoena?"

Steve thought a moment. "Let's try Rose Tindel, Jason Tindel, and Fred and Pat Grayson."

"Fine," Tracy said. She pointed to the blinking line on Steve's phone. "But what about our friend here?"

"Oh yes," Steve said. He pressed the button, lifted the receiver a half-inch and put it down again. The light went out. "Damn," he said. "Must have disconnected."

"Now why didn't I think of that?" Tracy said.

"It doesn't matter," Steve said. "They'll run it anyway." He held up his hand, ran it over an imaginary headline. " 'DAWSON RUMORED TO COP PLEA: Jeremy Dawson's lawyer could not be reached for comment.' "

"So what's with the subpoenas?" Mark said.

"As soon as Tracy gets 'em made out, have your men serve 'em."

"Yeah, but on them?" Taylor made a face. "I mean what the hell are they going to testify to?"

Steve shrugged. "I have no idea."

"Then what's the point?"

"Well, I gotta subpoena someone."

Taylor rubbed his head. "Steve, pardon me, but isn't that abuse of process?"

Steve grinned. "No. That's the beauty of it. They're his relatives. I can say they're character witnesses."

The phone rang.

"Probably our friend again," Steve said.

"You want me to get it?" Tracy said. "Or just pretend we're not here?"

"Can't do that," Steve said. He pointed to the phone.

Tracy picked it up. "Mr. Winslow's office." She listened a moment, said, "It's for you," and passed the phone over to Mark Taylor.

Taylor said, "Taylor here," listened a moment, said, "Are you sure?" then said, "Shit," and hung up.

Taylor shook his head. "Doesn't matter what you tell that reporter now."

"Oh yeah?" Steve said.

"Yeah. His story just got knocked off the front page."

"How come?"

"I been busting' my chops tryin' to find someone who saw Jeremy Dawson in Teaneck that night."

"You found one?"

"No, but the cops did."

"And?"

Taylor shook his head. "And it's the worst. This comes straight from headquarters. The cops got a witness saw Jeremy Dawson seven o'clock that night breaking into the high school to get the gun."

# 39

JEREMY DAWSON LOOKED WOR-
ried when the court officers led him in. As soon as he sat down,
he leaned over to Steve Winslow. "What's goin' on?"

"What do you mean?"

"I hear talk. The cops got a witness."

"Yeah, they do."

"Who is it?"

"Some guy saw you breaking into the high school that
night."

"Oh shit."

"Hey, it's not the end of the world. Sit tight and remember
our deal."

"But—"

"No buts, you do it. Sit back, relax, and above all, no matter
what happens you don't grab my arm."

Judge Grimes entered, called the court to order.

When the jurors had been brought in and seated, Harry
Dirkson rose with the confidence of a man who has every ace
in the deck.

First he called Mark Taylor's photographer and established
the fact that Defense Exhibit A–2 was indeed a picture of Jeremy Dawson.

Then he called Claire Chesterton, who testified to the fact
that Jeremy Dawson had not returned home until after midnight on the night of the murder.

After that, Dirkson moved in for the kill. He called one of
the officers who had taken Jeremy Dawson's statement the day
he'd been arrested. Dirkson first established that the officer
had indeed read Jeremy Dawson his rights, and that Jeremy
Dawson had been cautioned that anything he said could be
used against him. The officer then testified that he had asked
Jeremy Dawson where he was on the night of February 26th,
and Jeremy had told him he went to an eight-o'clock showing
of the movie, 'Heathers' in Teaneck.

Steve Winslow did not cross-examine.

For his next witness, Dirkson called Tom Randell, a pimply-faced high school student, who testified to having gone to the movie, 'Heathers,' the previous Saturday night.

"And did you see anyone there you knew?" Dirkson asked.

"Yes, sir. I saw Jeremy Dawson."

"You know Jeremy Dawson?"

"Sure. I know him from school."

"Are you sure he was there that night?"

"Absolutely. I was in back of him in the popcorn line."

"Are you sure it was Jeremy Dawson?"

"Absolutely."

"There must have been other kids from your high school at the movie. How is it you happened to recognize him?"

The witness smiled. "Couldn't miss him. He had green hair."

Dirkson smiled back. "That's all."

"No questions," Steve Winslow said.

That drew a murmur from the spectators in the courtroom, who were surprised to see such damaging testimony go unchallenged.

Harry Dirkson was somewhat surprised too. He shot Steve Winslow a look before saying, "Call Martin Steers."

Martin Steers turned out to be a frail, elderly man with a cane. He made his way slowly to the witness stand, raised his hand and took the oath.

"Your name is Martin Steers?" Dirkson said.

"That's right."

"Would you speak up a little, Mr. Steers, so the jurors can hear you?"

"Sorry," Steers said. He raised his voice. "Yes, my name is Martin Steers."

"Where do you live, Mr. Steers?"

"In Teaneck, New Jersey."

"Can you tell me where you were on the night of February 26th?"

"I was walking home from the store."

"What time was that?"

"Around seven o'clock."

"Did you see anything out of the ordinary at that time?"

"Yes, I did."

"And what was that?"

Steers took a breath. "I was walking past the high school. The store is a block past the high school. It's on one side. My house is on the other. I always have to walk past the high school to get to the store."

"Yes?" Dirkson prompted.

"So I'd been to the store, and I was walking back with my groceries when I saw him."

"Saw who?"

"A boy."

"A boy?"

"Yes. A young boy. You know, a teenager."

"And what was the boy doing?"

"He was going into the high school."

"You mean through the front door?"

Martin Steers shook his head. "No, no. Not the front door. Through the other door on the side."

"The service door?"

"I don't know what it's used for. But it's not the front door."

"How did the boy open the door?"

"I don't know. He was some distance away. I saw him fiddling with the lock, then I saw him pull the door open and go inside."

"Did he have a key?"

"He might have. I couldn't tell. It was too far away."

"I see. Are you sure of this?"

"Yes, I am."

"Why are you so sure of it? Why did you notice it in particular at the time?"

"Because it was strange. Seven o'clock at night. For someone to be going into the high school then. The high school's closed at night."

"I see. Tell me, Mr. Steers. Did you report this to the police?"

"No, I did not."

"Why not?"

"Because I didn't know if I should." He shrugged. "I'm an old man. What do I know? I mean, maybe the boy's an equipment manager for one of the teams. Or maybe he has a job at night, he cleans the blackboards and sweeps the floors. I mean, how should I know?"

Dirkson nodded. "I see, Mr. Steers. But you did notice particularly the boy going into the school at that time?"

"Yes, I did."

"And would you know this boy if you saw him again?"

"As I told you, I would not. He was too far away, and his back was to me."

"I see," Dirkson said. "But tell me this. Was there anything about the boy you noticed, anything that would help you recognize him if you saw him again?"

The witness nodded. "One thing."

"And what was that?" Dirkson said.

"He had green hair."

There was a murmur in the courtroom.

Dirkson smiled and nodded. "Thank you, Mr. Steers." He turned to Steve Winslow. "Your witness."

As Steve Winslow rose, he could feel the focus in the courtroom shift to him, could tell that the spectators sensed that this was going to be good. The witness had not identified Jeremy Dawson. The witness was an elderly man with glasses, whose eyesight was probably not good, and who had admittedly only seen the boy from the back and at a distance. Plus, the witness had not seen fit to report the incident to the police, but was now attempting to portray it as something significant and suspicious. The presumption in the courtroom, Steve knew, was that he would tear the witness apart.

Steve didn't. He smiled and bowed. "No questions," he said, and sat down.

That produced a big reaction in the courtroom. Heads turning, people talking. Judge Grimes had to bang the gavel twice.

"Order in the court," Judge Grimes said. "The witness is excused."

There was a brief delay while Martin Steers made his way from the courtroom. Then Judge Grimes said, "Call your next witness, Mr. Dirkson."

Dirkson stood up. He bowed, smiled. "The People rest, Your Honor."

That produced an excited murmur in the court. Reporters scribbled furiously.

Judge Grimes banged the gavel again. "Very well. Ladies and

gentlemen of the jury, we have now completed the first phase of the testimony. The prosecution has rested its case. We will now be hearing from the defense." Judge Grimes turned to Steve Winslow. "Mr. Winslow, the trial has progressed rapidly, and I am aware that the prosecution resting at this point may have taken you somewhat by surprise. Under the circumstances, I am prepared to grant you a continuance until tomorrow morning, if that is satisfactory to you."

"I don't want it, Your Honor," Steve said.

Judge Grimes frowned. "You don't want a continuance?"

"No, Your Honor," Steve said. "I am not requesting a continuance at this time. If the court please, I would like to state my position with regard to a continuance. I would like to point out that the defendant in this case, Jeremy Dawson, has not been released on bail. He is incarcerated for the duration of the trial. Under the circumstances, I feel that the interests of justice demand that the trial proceed with all due speed. Therefore, I am not asking for a continuance just because the prosecution has rested its case.

"But out of fairness to the defendant, at this time I would ask Harry Dirkson if he would stipulate that the prosecution will not ask for a continuance after I have rested *my* case. I feel it only fair to the defendant to do so."

Judge Grimes frowned. He turned to Dirkson. "Mr. Dirkson, are you willing to make that stipulation?"

Harry Dirkson rose. He hesitated for a moment, glanced suspiciously at Steve Winslow. It was such a simple request, Dirkson didn't want to seem hesitant about granting it.

But Dirkson had dealt with Steve Winslow before. And he was well aware of Winslow's flair for the unorthodox.

Dirkson took a breath. "I would certainly like to agree, Your Honor. But I represent the people of New York, and their interests must be served. Opposing counsel, Your Honor, has a flair for the dramatic. In the event that Mr. Winslow should introduce some new evidence in this case which I had not anticipated and for which I was not prepared, I would naturally need time to deal with it. Therefore I cannot make that stipulation."

"That seems fair and reasonable, Your Honor," Steve said.

"And quite understandable. Therefore, I'm prepared to stipulate that if I bring out anything in my part of the case for which the District Attorney is unprepared, I will release him from the stipulation and consent to a continuance. And as I believe him to be fair, I will take him at his word. If he can point to any fact at all that I have brought out, no matter how trivial, that he is unprepared for and would like to research, I will not challenge it, and I will consent to any reasonable continuance the court should care to grant."

Judge Grimes nodded. "Mr. Dirkson," he said. "With that provision, would you care to stipulate?"

Dirkson ran his hand over his head. "Yes, Your Honor. With that provision, yes. I have several rebuttal witnesses ready, and I am quite prepared to proceed. I am merely reluctant to do anything that would bind me in the event of the unexpected."

"But in the light of Mr. Winslow's stipulation, you are also willing to stipulate?"

"Yes, Your Honor."

"Very well. Those matters are considered so stipulated. Now, Mr. Winslow. I take it, you are prepared to proceed?"

"I am, Your Honor."

"Very well. Now then. You reserved your opening argument at the beginning of the trial. Do you wish to make it now?"

"I do not, Your Honor," Steve said. "I think the facts are self-evident, and I'm willing to let them speak for themselves. I waive my opening argument."

Judge Grimes frowned. "Very well. You may proceed with your case. Call your first witness."

Steve Winslow smiled and bowed. "I have no witnesses, Your Honor. The defense rests."

# 40

THERE WAS A MOMENT OF STUN-
ned silence in the courtroom. No one could quite believe what
they'd just heard. Judge Grimes blinked twice, and his jaw actually dropped open.

Harry Dirkson lunged to his feet. "What?!" he roared incredulously.

That opened the floodgates. Suddenly the court was in an
uproar as everyone began talking at once.

Judge Grimes recovered, banged the gavel furiously. Even
so, it took several minutes to get the courtroom quieted down.

When order was restored, Judge Grimes said, "Mr. Winslow,
did I hear you correctly? You are resting your case?"

"That's right, Your Honor. The defense rests. Let's proceed
with the closing arguments."

Harry Dirkson could hardly contain himself. He was puffing
furiously and his face was bright red. "Your Honor, Your
Honor," he cried. "This is why I didn't want to stipulate. This is
exactly what I was talking about. This comes as a complete
surprise. I demand a continuance."

Steve Winslow raised his voice. "Now, Your Honor," he said,
"this is the very thing I sought to avoid. The prosecutor stipulated he wouldn't ask for a continuance, and here he is asking
for one."

"Mr. Dirkson," Judge Grimes said. "I thought you agreed to
stipulate."

"I was *tricked* into stipulating, Your Honor," Dirkson said.
"It was a trick on the part of Counsel. It has taken me completely by surprise, and the interests of the People demand a
continuance. Mr. Winslow himself stated that I could have one
if I was taken by surprise."

"Not so, Your Honor," Steve said. "My stipulation was if Mr.
Dirkson could point to one fact that I have brought out for
which he was unprepared I would not object to a continuance.
Since I have brought out no facts at all, he obviously cannot do
that. The interests of my client demand that the trial proceed. I
ask that Mr. Dirkson be bound by his stipulation."

"Mr. Dirkson," Judge Grimes said. "I must consider the stipulation binding. Are you prepared to proceed?"

"As I said, I have several rebuttal witnesses, Your Honor."

Judge Grimes smiled slightly. "But as the defense has put on no case, there is nothing to rebut."

"But, Your Honor—"

Judge Grimes held up his hand. "That is a moot point, Mr. Dirkson. The evidentiary part of the case is over. We have come to the closing arguments. Are you prepared to proceed with yours?"

Dirkson paused, took a breath. It had finally occurred to him that he was losing on all fronts, and all he was accomplishing was making himself look bad.

"I had not expected to argue the case so soon, Your Honor, but I am certainly prepared to do so."

"I will of course grant you a brief recess to prepare your summation. In fact, since that will run us close to the lunch hour, I am going to break now, and we will come back after lunch. Court is adjourned until two o'clock."

Judge Grimes's gavel had barely sounded when newspaper reporters were already tripping over each other in their haste to get out the door.

# 41

MARK TAYLOR AND TRACY GAR-
vin pushed their way through the crowd.

"What the hell are you doing?" Taylor said.

"Relax," Steve said. "Just act like everything was going according to plan. Try not to look like you think I'm a moron until we get out the door."

Steve took Mark and Tracy by the shoulders and turned and piloted them out of the courtroom. On the way he kept smiling and mouthing 'No comment,' to the few reporters foolish enough to think they might actually get a quote. Outside, they broke away from the crowd and headed for the coffee shop for lunch.

"All right," Taylor said. "We're out of earshot. What the hell is going on?"

"There's nothing going on," Steve said. "I rested my case."

"Damnit," Tracy said, grabbing him by the arm. "Now stop right there. I know you get some perverse pleasure out of being mysterious and enigmatic, but I'm on an emotional roller coaster here. *Why* did you rest your case? Why aren't you putting on a defense?"

Steve shrugged and shook his head. "Because frankly I don't have one."

Tracy stared at him. "I thought you were going to try every trick in the book to get Jeremy Dawson off."

"I am." Steve put his hands on their shoulders. "Come on, guys, let's have lunch."

Tracy shrugged his hand off. "I couldn't eat a thing. I'm still waiting for your explanation. Why didn't you put on a defense?"

"O.K.," Steve said. "Try to understand. Dirkson has put on his case. Nothing I could do is gonna weaken that case. I got no witness to call, no trick to play. And the way I see it, it hurts me more to do something ineffective than to do nothing at all."

"Hurts you? What about your client?"

"When I say me, I mean my client. And what's with you? I thought you didn't like him."

"I don't like him. But he's still entitled to a defense."

Steve smiled. "Good. I'm glad to hear you say it. I may quote you on that after I get him off."

Tracy frowned. "How the hell are you gonna get him off now?"

"I'm taking my best shot. It happens I got nothin', so my best shot is to do nothin' and proceed with the argument. So that's what I'm gonna do."

Taylor looked at him. "You knew this last night?"

Steve nodded. "Yeah."

"Then why did you have me subpoena all those witnesses?"

"Because I didn't want Dirkson to know what I was planning."

"My men wouldn't talk."

"I know that, Mark. But the people they subpoenaed would. That's why I had you subpoena the relatives. It's a sure thing at least one and maybe all of them went straight to Dirkson.

"Which is what I wanted. So he'd have no idea what I was doing."

"That's for sure," Taylor said. "*I've* got no idea what you're doing."

"I'm gambling, Mark. I'm taking my best shot at getting the kid off."

Taylor shook his head. "Well, maybe you know what you're doing, but I sure as hell don't. All I know is Dirkson's put on a convincing case. Hell, he's put on a damn near perfect case. He's got motive, method, opportunity. He's got the murder weapon and the will. I mean, Christ, Steve. At this point, there isn't a thing you could do that would get Jeremy Dawson off."

Steve sighed, and shook his head. "You could be right."

# 42

HARRY DIRKSON WAS IN TOP form for his closing argument. The anger and frustration he'd felt at being outmaneuvered by Steve Winslow had evaporated over the lunch hour, as it gradually dawned on him that though Steve had tricked him on procedure, by doing so Steve had virtually conceded the case. The evidence was uncontested, it was enough to convict, and Dirkson was sitting pretty. So he was confident and assured as he rose to argue the case.

"Ladies and gentlemen of the jury," he began. "I'm not going to make any lengthy argument here, because frankly I don't have to. You've heard the evidence in this case, and it is straightforward and convincing. And that evidence leads to one inescapable conclusion. And that is, that Jeremy Dawson killed Jack Walsh.

"I will review the evidence for you briefly. I don't think I really need to, but I will do so because I am the prosecutor and that's my job."

Dirkson smiled as he said that, and several of the jurors smiled back. He struck a pose and began lining out his points.

"You've heard evidence that on the afternoon of February 26th, a man answering the description of Jack Walsh was spotted in the corridors of Jeremy Dawson's high school. There is evidence that Jeremy Dawson left with this man. There is further evidence that Jeremy Dawson cut the rest of his afternoon classes. You have heard the evidence of the witness, Joseph Bissel, that Jack Walsh was seen with Jeremy Dawson in the very subway station in which he was found murdered. You have also the evidence from Joseph Bissel that Jack Walsh was writing something at the time.

"And what was he writing?" Dirkson strode to the court reporter's table and picked up the will. "I have in evidence People's Exhibit Seven, a handwritten will entirely in the handwriting of the decedent, Jack Walsh, leaving his entire fortune to Jeremy Dawson. And where was this will recovered? It was found in Jeremy Dawson's possession on the day after the murder."

Dirkson held up the will. "The significance of this document is twofold. It is significant that Jeremy had it the day after the murder, showing conclusively that he had been in contact with Jack Walsh. And it is significant in that it furnishes the motive for the murder. For having this document in his possession clearly shows that Jeremy Dawson had every reason to believe that by the death of Jack Walsh he stood to gain several million dollars."

Dirkson paused and let that sink in. "Several million dollars. Was there ever a more convincing motive for murder?"

Dirkson smiled and set the will back down on the table. "But that's the least of the evidence. We have the testimony of Carl Jenson, who saw the defendant on the very afternoon of the murder at approximately five-thirty. We know that that was after Jack Walsh had written the will. How do we know that? We know that by the will itself, which Jack Walsh not only dated, but also put in the time of execution. And what was that time? Two-thirty in the afternoon. Before Carl Jenson saw the defendant, Jeremy Dawson.

"And what words did Jeremy Dawson say to Carl Jenson at that time? You recall the testimony. Jeremy Dawson smiled and said, 'You be nice to me, Carl, 'cause I'm gonna be rich.'"

Dirkson paused a moment to let that sink in, then picked up the pace. "When is the next time we spot Jeremy Dawson? Well, we have the testimony of Martin Steers that at approximately seven o'clock a young man with green hair was seen breaking into Teaneck High School. Admittedly, the witness does not identify Jeremy Dawson as being that boy. He is an honest, credible witness and he tells us only what he saw. And what he saw is for you to judge. Was that boy Jeremy Dawson? You can draw your own conclusions.

"And to help you draw them, you should consider what happened next. At approximately ten-thirty that evening in Manhattan, Jack Walsh was shot and killed in the very subway station in the very spot where earlier that afternoon he had taken Jeremy Dawson and written out the will. And what gun shot and killed Jack Walsh? We have the testimony of the ballistics expert that the gun that fired the fatal bullet was the gun discovered by detectives the following day in the high school locker of Jeremy Dawson."

Dirkson smiled and spread his hands. "Does that help you draw your conclusions any? The murder gun was kept in Jeremy Dawson's locker. At seven o'clock on the evening of the murder, a boy with green hair was seen breaking into the high school, the high school where the murder weapon was kept. The high school where the murder weapon was found. Jeremy Dawson's high school. Jeremy Dawson's locker. Jeremy Dawson's gun.

"Now," Dirkson said, "you may ask, as I myself did, why did Jeremy Dawson hang onto the gun? It was the murder weapon, it could convict him, why would he keep it?" Dirkson held up his hand. "It is not sufficient to say that the defendant is not very bright. The explanation is that he wanted it, that he felt he might need it. Why? Well, there is evidence in this case that in Jeremy Dawson's locker along with the gun there was drug paraphernalia and several vials of crack. I leave it to you to figure out why the defendant might have wanted a gun.

"At any rate, he wanted to keep it. And because he wanted to keep it, he attempted to disguise his crime. And how did he do that? The testimony of the witnesses who were on the subway platform that night, as well as the lab analysis of the material left over from the clothes of the decedent, gives us the answer. And what is the answer?" Dirkson shook his head. "He set the body on fire. He poured gasoline on Jack Walsh's body and set the body on fire. A wholly despicable act, and hard to comprehend, and yet there was a motivation. In fact there were two. One, he wanted to disguise the crime by making it look like a random act of violence, a wilding incident. And two, he wanted the body burned so the bullet wound would go undiscovered. Which would have happened, had it not been for the thoroughness and skill of the medical examiner.

"But the bullet wound *was* discovered. The bullet *was* retrieved. And the bullet matches absolutely with test bullets fired from the gun found in Jeremy Dawson's locker.

"And what does all this evidence show? I will summarize it briefly for you. On the afternoon of February 26th, Jack Walsh sought out Jeremy Dawson at his high school. He took him to New York, took him down in the subway, and wrote him out a will, leaving all of his money to him.

"Jeremy Dawson left Jack Walsh and went home with the will in his pocket. He had the afternoon to think it over. To mull on it. To come to the one conclusion to which he eventually came. That if Jack Walsh were to die, he would be rich.

"Jeremy Dawson went home. He encountered Carl Jenson, had an argument with him. He went upstairs, showered and changed. By the time he came back downstairs it was clear the plan had already formed in his mind. We know that from those telling parting words: 'You be nice to me, Carl, 'cause I'm gonna be rich.'

"Jeremy Dawson left home and went to his high school. He broke in the side door and got the gun. He took the gun, went to Manhattan, hunted up Jack Walsh in the subway station, and fired a bullet into his brain.

"He then set the body on fire, and returned to Teaneck, arriving home around twelve-thirty in the morning.

"The only thing I don't know, ladies and gentlemen," Dirkson said, "is whether he broke into the high school that night to return the gun to his locker, or whether he brought it to school when he went to class the following morning." Dirkson held up his finger and smiled. "But that, ladies and gentlemen, is the *only* thing we don't know. Everything else is abundantly clear. Jeremy Dawson killed Jack Walsh. A cold-blooded, premeditated murder for profit.

"Your duty is clear, and I will leave you to it. And that duty is to bring back a verdict of guilty as charged."

With that, Dirkson bowed to the jury, and with a triumphant smile, walked back to his table and sat down.

# 43

STEVE WINSLOW LOOKED small. Maybe it was just after the bulk of Dirkson that made him look that way. But maybe not. Maybe it was the fact that nobody was really giving him their full attention. Maybe it was the fact that Dirkson's argument had been so persuasive that the verdict was a foregone conclusion, and nothing he could say could possibly make any difference, so why should anyone listen to him?

Steve Winslow stood in the front of the courtroom, a strange-looking figure in his corduroy jacket, blue jeans, and long hair. He stood and waited patiently for the buzz among the spectators to subside, for the reporters to stop scribbling, for the jurors to stop looking at one another and turn their heads to him.

Suddenly he clapped his hands together and spread them wide. He struck a pose, became an actor, a showman, smiling, raising his voice and commanding their attention rather than requesting it.

"Ladies and gentlemen of the jury," he said. "I just heard District Attorney Harry Dirkson's closing argument, and I thought it was great. And I'm sure you did too. And I have a feeling that a number of you find that argument convincing and think the defendant is guilty."

Steve smiled and held up his finger. "Which is why I'd like to remind you that you can't think that yet. Because you haven't heard *my* closing argument. After you've heard it, if you still think Jeremy Dawson is guilty, then it is both your right and your duty to do so. But I ask you to fulfill your duty as jurors and please bear with me, even though right now you may personally feel it's not going to do any good."

Steve smiled slightly. "I take it you all noticed that I did not put on a defense." Steve held up his hand, turned, pointed to the judge. "Now, Judge Grimes is going to instruct you that in a murder trial the burden of proof is on the prosecution, and the defendant is under no obligation to put on any defense, nor is he under any obligation to take the stand to deny his participation in the crime. Judge Grimes will further instruct you that his failure to do so must in no way be considered by you to be an indication of guilt, that you should put it from your minds, give it no weight and not let it affect your deliberations in the least."

Steve smiled and shook his head. "Well, ladies and gentlemen, if you can do that, I think you're all destined for sainthood. Personally, I don't think there's a person in this courtroom who isn't thinking right now, 'Gee, why didn't he put on any defense?'

"Well, rather than strike it from your minds, ladies and gentlemen—which frankly I don't think is possible—I'd like to tell you why. The reason I didn't put on a case is because the prosecution has made my case for me.

"I know you don't think that now, but that's because you've only heard the evidence, and you haven't had time to deliberate on it and consider what it means. I've already done that, because frankly, to quote Mr. Dirkson, 'That's my job.'"

Steve was watching the jurors when he said that. None smiled, but he certainly had their attention. He pushed on.

"Harry Dirkson has already interpreted the evidence for you and told you what he thinks it means. Now I'm going to tell you what I think it means.

"Before I do so, I must digress a moment to explain something about the law. This is a case involving circumstantial evidence. By that I mean there is no eyewitness to the crime. There is no one who saw the assailant fire the bullet into the brain of the decedent. You are asked to conclude that happened from the circumstances which the prosecution has laid out."

Once again, Steve indicated the judge. "Judge Grimes will instruct you that in any crime involving circumstantial evidence, if the circumstances of the crime as laid out by the prosecution can be explained by any reasonable hypothesis other than that of the guilt of the defendant, then you must find the defendant not guilty. That is the doctrine of reasonable doubt. The prosecution must prove the defendant guilty beyond all reasonable doubt. He is presumed innocent—you're all familiar with the book, whether you've read it or not—he's presumed innocent until proven guilty. And he is *not* considered proven guilty if there is a reasonable explanation for the circumstances that tend to show his guilt. If such a reasonable explanation exists, you must find the defendant not guilty.

"Well, ladies and gentlemen, I'm going to give you a reasonable hypothesis. But I'm going to go a little further than that.

"As I said, I didn't put on my case because the prosecution proves my case for me. I'm going to show you how that is by building a reasonable hypothesis. Then I'm going to go beyond that by showing you that it is not only a reasonable hypothesis, but it is the *only* hypothesis which can be drawn from the facts. In short, I will show you that what the prosecution just told you, could not and did not happen.

"Now, let's look at the evidence. I have no quarrel with the evidence Harry Dirkson just laid out for you. It's only his interpretation of it. I think we can all concede the following things happened: on the afternoon of February 26th, Jack Walsh showed up at Jeremy Dawson's school, found Jeremy and asked him to go with him. Jack Walsh took him to Manhattan to the 66th Street subway station, where he was seen by Joseph Bissel. He proceeded to write out a will leaving everything to Jeremy Dawson. That will is here in evidence, and you will have a chance to look at it during your deliberations.

"Now, as Mr. Dirkson said, we know the time that that happened because Jack Walsh put it in the will. It was two-thirty in the afternoon. Jack Walsh wrote out the will and gave it to Jeremy Dawson to keep.

"What happened then? Jeremy Dawson left Jack Walsh and eventually returned home. How do we know that? We know that by the testimony of the witness, Carl Jenson, who stated that Jeremy Dawson returned home at approximately five-thirty.

"What happened between two-thirty and five-thirty? I don't think there's much question as to that. Jeremy Dawson made his way back to New Jersey—probably read the will to himself several times on the bus going back—and in the course of the afternoon he gradually became imbued with the thought, 'By god, I'm going to be rich.' Not an illogical hypothesis. And we have the statement of Carl Jenson that Jeremy said almost exactly those words.

"Now, Jeremy Dawson arrived home at five-thirty, encountered Carl Jenson. Carl berated him for skipping school, demanded to know where he'd been. Jeremy replied in a flippant, hostile manner, went upstairs to take a shower. He showered, changed and went out, after saying the now immortal words, 'You be nice to me, Carl, 'cause I'm gonna be rich.'

"And where did Jeremy Dawson go? Well, we have the testimony of Martin Steers, who saw a young boy with green hair attempting to break into Teaneck High School around seven o'clock. Can we conclude that that boy was Jeremy Dawson?"

Steve held up his hands, paused, looked around questioningly. Then he nodded. "Absolutely. I don't think there's a shadow of a doubt that that boy was Jeremy Dawson. I think there's no question what Martin Steers observed was Jeremy Dawson breaking into Teaneck High School."

Steve smiled. "Now, I see by your faces that some of you are puzzled. I would assume that you, like Harry Dirkson, expected me to argue that point. But it's not a point I care to argue. I think the boy was Jeremy Dawson. So far, the prosecution's and my interpretation of the case is the same."

Steve held up his hand. "Here's where we differ. The prosecution would have you believe Jeremy Dawson broke into the high school to get the gun. The gun kept in his locker. I think there's a much simpler explanation. You will recall the testimony of the officer who served the search warrant on Jeremy Dawson's locker. When he searched it, he found in the locker drug paraphernalia and several vials of crack. I think a much more likely explanation is that Jeremy Dawson broke into the high school to get the drugs. We know from Carl Jenson that Jeremy didn't keep drugs at home, because Jenson searched his room. We know Jeremy kept drugs in his locker, because that's where they were found. And Jeremy Dawson was a crack dealer and a crack addict."

Steve held up his hand. "Now I'm not condoning or excusing that behavior. Frankly, I think it stinks. But that's neither here nor there. The fact is, I think what happened on the night of February 26th was that Jeremy Dawson got so excited by the prospect of inheriting Uncle Jack's money, so keyed up by the thought that he was going to be rich, that he decided, what the heck, he'd use up some of his merchandise and spend the evening getting high smoking crack. I think that's a perfectly reasonable hypothesis."

Steve broke off, looked up to find the jury staring at him incredulously. He smiled. "Yeah, I know. In the first place, you can't believe I'm admitting he did that. And in the second place, you're saying, 'Yeah, but that leaves a few small questions unanswered. Like, for instance, who killed Jack Walsh.'

"Well, the reason that leaves that question unanswered is because I'm explaining to you what Jeremy Dawson did, and the simple fact is Jeremy Dawson had absolutely nothing to do with the murder."

Steve smiled again. "Yeah, I know. That's a sort of unsatisfactory explanation. So let's answer the question. Who killed Jack Walsh?"

"I refer you once again to the testimony of Carl Jenson. Jeremy Dawson returned around five-thirty, Jenson questioned him, Jeremy Dawson made rude replies and went upstairs to take a shower and change.

"If you will recall my cross-examination of Carl Jenson, at this point I asked him if Jeremy Dawson had ever cut school before, and then I asked him if Jeremy had ever been suspended. He said, yes, for drugs. I asked him if he had ever searched Jeremy Dawson's room and he admitted that he had, but he had found no drugs. He said that that didn't prove anything because Jeremy was selling them out of his locker.

"Now," Steve said, "during your deliberation you have the right to ask to have any portions of the testimony read back to you." Steve picked up a paper from the defense table. "I call your attention to the following exchange:

"Question: 'I see. So you searched his room?' Answer: 'Yes, I did.' Question: 'And did you find any drugs?' Answer: 'No, I didn't.' Question: 'And did that make you think maybe the school was wrong?' Answer: 'No, because he didn't have them at home, he had them at school. He was selling drugs out of his locker.' Question: 'You know that now because of what the police found in his locker. But you didn't know it then.' Answer: 'Yes, I did.' Question: 'How?' "

Steve Winslow looked up from his reading. "At this point the court reporter has written the word 'pause.' You will recall, that was because the witness did not answer. Then the question is repeated: Question: 'How, Mr. Jenson?' Answer: 'I don't know. I just know.' Question: 'How did you know?' Answer: 'Well, it stood to reason.' "

Steve set the transcript down on the table. "It stood to reason," he said. "And certain things stand to reason here. Carl Jenson admits having searched Jeremy Dawson's room. Jenson states that at the time he knew Jeremy Dawson was selling drugs out of his locker. When asked how he knows, he becomes evasive and does not answer, finally saying 'it stood to reason.' Now, you don't have to take this from me, you can look at the transcripts yourselves. It's part of the evidence in this case, and part of what you must consider.

"And from this, what reasonable hypothesis can I draw? From this I draw the reasonable hypothesis that Carl Jenson knew that Jeremy Dawson was selling drugs from his locker, because after he searched his room and found nothing, he contrived to search Jeremy Dawson's locker. At which point he would have discovered the drugs.

"And the gun.

"If so, why would he keep silent? Why wouldn't he tell someone? Well, you've seen Carl Jenson on the witness stand. You've seen his demeanor, you know what kind of person he is. I think we can safely say that Carl Jenson didn't tell anyone because he was the type of person who felt that information was power. The drugs and the gun were facts he filed away for future reference. He could blow the whistle on Jeremy Dawson, get him in trouble, but it wouldn't do anything for *him*.

"Now, how would Carl Jenson have gotten into Jeremy Dawson's locker? I put it to you that Jeremy Dawson as the prosecution has sketched him, a flaky crack head, was the type of person who couldn't trust himself to remember his locker number. He would have it written down someplace. And if he had it written down someplace, it could be discovered by someone who searched his room.

"Which brings us to the day of the murder. Jeremy Dawson returns home, exchanges heated words with Carl Jenson, goes upstairs, takes off his clothes and takes a shower. Carl Jenson is terribly suspicious. He thinks that Jeremy Dawson has been with Jack Walsh. He wonders what went on between them. Jack Walsh is an eccentric man. He could have done anything. He might have given Jeremy money. Jenson wants to know.

"While Jeremy Dawson is in the shower, Carl Jenson steals upstairs and searches his clothes. What does he find?"

Steve strode over and picked it up from the clerk's table. "He finds this. A handwritten will, executed that very day, leaving the bulk of Jack Walsh's fortune to Jeremy Dawson.

"Well, imagine how Carl Jenson must have felt. All of his worst fears had just been confirmed. He had every reason to hate Jack Walsh. He had every reason to hate Jeremy Dawson.

"I don't know if he had a plan then. It must have been pretty jumbled in his mind. But one thing he knew for sure. Jeremy Dawson was *not* going to get away with it.

"So what did he do? He waited and planned. He put the will back in Jeremy Dawson's pocket and went downstairs as if nothing had happened. When Jeremy came downstairs, once again he tried to engage him in conversation, tried to get a rise out of him. Well, he got one all right. The immortal words. 'You be nice to me, Carl, 'cause I'm gonna be rich.' "

Steve paused and held up his finger. "The last straw. You can imagine the response: 'Not if I can help it.'

"Jeremy Dawson leaves. Does Carl Jenson follow him? You bet he does. He's not letting Jeremy Dawson out of his sight.

"And what happens? Jeremy Dawson goes and breaks into the high school. Jenson knows why—he's going to his locker to get drugs. Why doesn't Jenson think Jeremy's going there to get the gun?" Steve smiled and spread his hands. "Because no one's been murdered. So these's no reason to think Jeremy would be going there for any reason *other* than the drugs.

"So Carl's there and he sees him go in. And he sees something else. He sees Martin Steers *see* Jeremy Dawson go in.

"And I would think it was about then that the plan began to form. It was then that Carl Jenson put it all together. The gun in the locker. The witness who saw Jeremy breaking into the

high school. The will in Jeremy's pocket. He put that all together, and suddenly Carl Jenson realized if the gun in Jeremy
Dawson's locker killed Jack Walsh, he would have a perfect
frame.

"And one that solved all his problems. Particularly his problem about the will. Because Carl Jenson was always a schemer.
He'd already consulted lawyers about Uncle Jack's estate, so
we can assume he knew all the legal angles. In particular, he
would have known that no person convicted of murder can
inherit anything from the person he killed. So murdering Jack
Walsh and framing Jeremy Dawson would knock out Jeremy's
will and leave Carl free to inherit.

"So he does it. As soon as Jeremy Dawson comes out of the
high school, Carl Jenson goes in the same door. He already has
the locker combination from when he searched it before. He
opens the locker. The gun is there. He takes it, goes to Manhattan, kills Jack Walsh.

"How did he know where to find him?" Again, Steve picked
up the handwritten will from the court reporter's table. "From
this. From the will Carl Jenson read. It's right here, and you
can look at it yourselves. In it, Jack Walsh not only put the date
and the time of the will, but he also wrote down the location
where it was written—the 66th Street subway station. Jenson
has read the will, so he knows Jack Walsh is hanging out there.

"But what if he wasn't there? Well, if he wasn't, the plan
wouldn't have worked, and Carl Jenson would have had to
return the gun to the locker and then think of something else.

"But he *was* there. Just where the will said he'd be. He was
there, and Carl Jenson found him and walked up to him and
he shot him.

"And what did he do then? Well, at that point he had a problem. He had to put the gun back in Jeremy Dawson's locker so
it would convict him of the crime."

Steve stopped and shook his head. "But that was a little
much. Even for Jeremy Dawson. Even for Carl Jenson's *opinion* of Jeremy Dawson. He found that hard to swallow. Just as
the prosecution found it hard to swallow. Just as you're probably finding it hard to swallow now. I mean, come on, the guy's
so stupid he puts the murder weapon back in his own locker?

"But that was the premise under which Carl Jenson had to operate. The gun had to be found in Jeremy Dawson's locker to link Jeremy Dawson to the crime. How could he do that without making it seem such a clumsy, obvious frame?

"And what is the answer? He set the body on fire. He set the body on fire so it would appear Jeremy Dawson set the body on fire in an attempt to disguise the crime. So the prosecution would have reason to argue, as it is arguing now, that Jeremy Dawson could logically have kept the gun, because he expected the crime would be written off as a wilding incident, and the fatal bullet never discovered."

Steve shook his head. "Well, that's mighty thin. But the prosecution's arguing it. I'm sure they're not happy about it, but they're arguing it. They're arguing it because they have to. Because it's the only grounds on which they can support their theory that Jeremy Dawson killed Jack Walsh. Because if that doesn't hold water, neither does their whole theory. Which shows you what a weak case they actually have."

Steve paused and looked at the jury. "I want you to think about that for a moment. I want you to think about the prosecution's case. I want you to think about the fact that they've been forced to argue that Jeremy Dawson burned the body so he could keep the gun. I want you to realize that that is the weakest part of their case, the part they would be most eager to build up and support. And I want you to consider that they have not done so. That they have, in my opinion, sluffed the matter off."

Steve paused, shrugged. "Now, you can say the matter is debatable. The prosecution says one thing, I say another thing, so we have a dispute."

Steve paused again and raised his finger. "But there is *one* fact in this case on which there is *no* dispute. One fact on which *all* the witnesses agree. And that fact is this: whatever else may have happened, on February 26th and February 27th, *the defendant, Jeremy Dawson, had green hair.*"

Steve waved his finger. "Green hair. A green mohawk. That fact is indisputable. On that, all the witnesses agree.

"And now, I ask you to consider this. We know the prosecution was attempting to shore up the one weak point in its case, the point that Jeremy Dawson burned the body. The prosecution and the police, with their extensive manpower, have been conducting an exhaustive search to uncover evidence connecting Jeremy Dawson to the crime. You've seen for yourself the results of their work in locating Martin Steers, who saw Jeremy breaking into the high school.

"But there is one thing you haven't seen. Which is why I ask you this: with all the publicity surrounding this case, with all the efforts of the police department to uncover information pinning the crime on Jeremy Dawson, and with the prosecution so desperate to prove that Jeremy Dawson burned the body—" Steve raised his voice, "—is it conceivable, is it remotely possible, is there any chance whatsoever—" Steve paused, and then hammered it in: "—that on February 26th *a service station attendant sold a can of gasoline to a boy with green hair,* and the police haven't found him?"

Steve paused. Some of the jurors blinked. Some looked at each other.

Steve nodded. "Yeah. Pretty incredible. If a service station attendant had sold a can of gasoline to a boy with green hair, he'd remember it. And with all the publicity surrounding this case, he'd hear about it, and he'd come forward. And even if, by some far stretch of the imagination, he didn't hear about it, the police would still find him.

"But they haven't found him, have they?" Steve said. "We know that because if they had, he'd have been the star witness for the prosecution, the most damning witness of all, the one who clinched the case. But they haven't found him. And they can't find him, and they won't find him, because he doesn't exist. Because Jeremy Dawson didn't buy a gallon can of gasoline on February 26th. And Jeremy Dawson didn't set the body on fire.

"And if he didn't do that, he didn't fire the fatal shot, because by the prosecution's own argument, *if, and only if,* he set the body on fire, would he have fired the fatal shot and then kept the gun."

Steve shook his head. "Not possible. Couldn't have happened.

"And now consider this: if a straight businessman in a suit

and tie, a man like Carl Jenson whom you have just seen on the witness stand, were to walk into a filling station looking somewhat hassled and say, 'My car just ran out of gas on the highway, can you sell me a gallon can?' would the filling station attendant think anything of it and even remember it? You know and I know he would not."

Steve looked around and shrugged. "You see why I put on no case. The evidence as it is is overwhelming. Jeremy Dawson could not have committed the crime. Carl Jenson could.

"As you review the evidence in this case, I want you to remember what I told you at the start. It is a case of circumstantial evidence. In such a case, for the prosecution to get a conviction, it is necessary that the circumstances point only to the guilt of the defendant, and are not open to any other reasonable interpretation. I ask you to look carefully at the evidence, examine it, consider what it means.

"And then weigh it.

"And when you do, remember this: it is not necessary for the defense to tip the scale. We don't have to make the stronger case. I personally believe there is more evidence in this case that Carl Jenson committed the murder than that my client did. But you don't have to agree with that to bring in a verdict of not guilty. It is not necessary that you consider it more likely that Carl Jenson committed the crime. It is only necessary that you consider it *possible*. Any reasonable hypothesis other than that of guilt. If you believe it *possible* that Carl Jenson committed the crime, you must give the defendant the benefit of that reasonable doubt, and return a verdict of not guilty.

"Ladies and gentlemen of the jury, your task is clear. I leave you to you sworn duty."

Steve smiled at the somewhat dazed looking jurors, bowed and sat down.

It took the jury two and a half days to bring back a verdict of not guilty.

# 44

MARK TAYLOR CAME IN GRIN-
ning like a Cheshire cat, flopped into the overstuffed chair and
said, "Heard the news?"

Steve Winslow looked up from the stack of law books on his
desk. In the two weeks since the verdict he had been boning up
for the will contest, a task for which he was admittedly not
well suited, and one which he did not particularly enjoy. Thus
he was not in the best of moods, and he frowned at the inter-
ruption. "No," he said. "What?"

"The grand jury just indicted Carl Jenson for the murder of
Jack Walsh."

Steve set down the book. "You're kidding me."

"No. Got it straight from the horse's mouth."

Steve chuckled, shook his head. "Son of a gun."

"I thought that might interest you."

"I'll say. So what's the case against him?"

"I don't know all the details, but apparently they got a fingerprint from Jeremy Dawson's locker."

Steve grinned. "You're kidding."

"No. And the damaging thing about it is it's from the *inside*
of the locker."

"Holy shit."

"Yeah," Taylor said. "Only thing is, when you think about it
it's kind of like the argument you made for Jeremy Dawson. I
mean, Jenson's got to be the stupidest murderer ever lived, not
thinking about fingerprints when he swiped the gun."

Steve considered that. "Maybe not."

"What do you mean?"

"Well, if that's true, it's like I said in court. If Jenson knew
the gun was there, it's cause he searched the locker back when
Jeremy was suspended from school. The irony is, he probably
left the fingerprint back then."

"Yeah, well either way, it fries his ass."

Steve chuckled, shook his head. "Son of a bitch." He jerked
his thumb. "You tell Tracy?"

"Yeah."

"How'd she take it?"

"What do you think? She was pretty surprised. Why?"

"She's been giving me a hard time the past two weeks, ever since the verdict. She thinks I pulled a fast one getting Jeremy Dawson off. She thought I sold the jury a bill of goods."

"Yeah, well frankly so did I," Taylor said. He shrugged. "Only thing is, it don't bother me none. Personally, I thought it was damn fine work. You're telling me she's bent out of shape?"

"Pissed as hell," Steve said. "So this has got to be a bit of a jolt. I'm surprised she didn't follow you in."

"Mail came," Taylor said. "I left her dealing with that."

"Yeah," Steve said. He indicated the law books. "Life goes on."

"How's it going?"

"The will contest? Not good. Frankly, I expect to lose."

"Oh yeah?"

"Yeah. I'm going through the motions, but I think it's a lost hope. Not that I'm losing any sleep over it. It's not like Jeremy's losing everything. Even if the will doesn't stand up, he still gets a fifth."

"Yeah, but do you get a fee?"

Steve shook his head. "Not on the will contest. I can't see taking a percentage for losing. But I'll sure as hell take a fee for the murder rap."

"Glad to hear it," Taylor said. "I'm running a tab for you, but I hate to charge you when you haven't been paid."

"Don't sweat it, Mark. Turn in your bills. The money will be there.

"So tell me about Jenson. Is the fingerprint all they got?"

"It's all I *know* they got. They probably got something else."

Steve pursed his lips. "It's interesting, when you think about it. Dirkson may have a bit of a problem."

"What's that?"

"On the question of identity. If you'll recall, the only way they identified the body was on the testimony of Carl Jenson."

"Say. That's right."

"But that may not matter."

"Why not?"

Steve grinned. "Because when the relatives think it over and realize they can get a larger slice of the pie if Jenson's convicted, plus they can't inherit at all unless the body is Jack Walsh, whaddya want to bet at least one of them also happens to remember that old whiffleball accident when Uncle Jack hurt his leg?"

Taylor laughed. "No takers. I'm sure they will."

"Still, Dirkson can't be all that happy about it."

"Yeah, well there's one thing that's gotta make him ecstatic."

"What's that?"

"You're not Jenson's lawyer." Taylor chuckled. "Jesus Christ, I still can't get over that summation. I mean, it was like you were tellin' the jurors black was white and making it sound logical. I never seen a jury quite so dazed.

"And Dirkson. Hell, you see the look on Dirkson's face when you sat down?"

"I did sneak a peek."

"It was great. It was like a cartoon, you know, where the guy walks off the edge of the cliff, stands there and looks around, and suddenly realizes he's standing in midair." Taylor nodded. "Yeah, Dirkson's gotta be glad."

The door opened and Tracy Garvin came in holding a letter.

"Tracy," Steve said. "I understand you heard?"

Tracy waved it away. "Yeah, yeah, they indicted Jenson. That's nothing. Take a look at this."

She held out the letter.

"What's that?" Steve said.

Tracy opened her mouth as if to say something, then laughed and shook her head. She looked slightly overwhelmed. "I think you better read it."

Steve took the envelope, pulled out the pages. He unfolded them and started reading. His eyes widened. "Holy shit."

"What is it?" Taylor said.

"Jesus Christ," Steve said. "Listen to this. This is a letter dated February 26th.

" 'Dear Mr. Winslow:

" 'I regret that I did not have a chance to adequately express my appreciation for all the work that you have done in my behalf. I apologize if I have seemed ungrateful. What you did was of great help to me, and I hope that I, in turn, may be of some help to you.

" 'By now you are probably wrestling with the problem of a holographic will purportedly leaving all of my fortune to Jeremy Dawson. With regard to that, I hope the enclosed document may be of some help. I am entrusting that document and this letter to a close friend with instructions to mail them to you at the proper time. Since you are reading this letter, that proper time is now.

" 'I hope this document will clear up any confusion that may have arisen concerning my estate. I also hope my relatives will not be too disappointed when my estate is finally divided among them, and they realize just how much of my assets I was able to convert to cash in the past year. Still, there is plenty left to go around. And, what the hey, you can't take it with you.

" 'Please excuse me if I am in a somewhat whimsical mood, but I must say I am extremely happy with the way everything has turned out.' "

Steve looked up from the letter. " 'Sincerely, Jack Walsh.' Son of a bitch."

"That's nothing," Tracy said. "Wait till you read the will."

Steve set the letter aside, and looked at the other document. "O.K., here goes. This will is dated February 26th, 4:30 P.M."

" 'I, Jack Walsh, being of sound mind and body, do hereby revoke all prior wills and make this my last will and testament. In revoking all prior wills, I specifically and especially revoke the unfinished and unsigned handwritten will begun by me on this same day, purportedly leaving my entire fortune to Jeremy Dawson. I revoke that will, and any and all other prior wills, and do make this my last will and testament.

" 'I hereby appoint the Chase Manhattan Bank to serve as executor of my estate, and to dispose of my property as follows:

" 'To Steve Winslow, who furnished me with such valuable legal advice, and fought so valiantly in my behalf, I leave the sum of one hundred thousand dollars.' "

Taylor whistled. "Jesus Christ."

"You can stop sweating your fees now," Steve said.

"I'll say. Go on. What else?"

" 'To Carl Jenson I leave nothing because he's a schmuck.' "
Steve looked up. "That's the very phrase I gave him."

Tracy nodded. Her eyes were bright. "The man did have a
sense of humor, didn't he?"

"Go on," Taylor said, impatiently. "What about the money?"

" 'All the rest, remainder, and residue of my property I leave
to my relatives, Rose Tindel, Pat Grayson, Claire Chesterton,
and Jeremy Dawson, in equal amounts, share and share alike.

" 'In the cases of Rose Tindel, Pat Grayson and Claire Chesterton I leave the money outright with no restrictions, though
knowing them and the men they married, I would expect them
to run through the money inside of a year.

" 'In the case of Jeremy Dawson, who is a minor, I leave the
money in trust, and appoint the Chase Manhattan Bank sole
trustee. It is my instructions that they manage the money for
him and furnish him with living expenses, if and only if, he is
attending school, in which case they shall pay for his education, and all the expenses attendant therewith. Said trust shall
remain in effect and terminate only in the event Jeremy Dawson should receive a college degree from a four-year, accred-
ited college, at which time the Chase Manhattan Bank shall
turn over the entire amount of the trust to Jeremy Dawson
absolutely and without restriction.' "

Steve looked up. "And that's it. Dated, signed, sealed, all legally binding. Absolutely remarkable."

"Isn't it?" Tracy said.

"Yeah," Steve said. "And what a coincidence."

"What do you mean, coincidence?" Taylor said.

Steve leaned back in his chair and grinned. "Well, aside from
the hundred thousand to me, all this will really accomplishes
is negating Jeremy Dawson's will. That and setting up the trust
to try to make the boy fly right. But having this will, it's the
same thing as if I lost the will contest. Jeremy Dawson's will is
knocked out, and the prior will applies. And this will, in effect,
is just like the prior will."

"Except for disinheriting Carl Jenson," Taylor said.

"Right," Tracy said. "But if Carl Jenson is convicted of killing

Jack Walsh, he couldn't inherit anyway. That's it, isn't it, Steve?"

"Exactly," Steve said. "If Jenson's convicted, aside from paying me, this will and that will do exactly the same thing."

"The point," Tracy said, "is how could Jack Walsh have known to do that? How could he have known Carl Jenson couldn't inherit because he was gonna be convicted of his murder?"

Taylor blinked. "Run that by me again."

"What Tracy's saying," Steve said, "is that Jack Walsh wrote this will as if he knew Carl Jenson had killed him."

Taylor frowned. "You'll pardon me if that doesn't clarify things."

"What I mean, Mark, is whatever date there might be on this will and this letter, it's obvious they were both written after the trial."

Mark Taylor's eyes widened. "You mean?"

"That's right, Mark," Steve said. "Today's bullshit theory day. We just hit the daily double on bullshit theories. First, the bullshit theory that Carl Jenson committed the crime. Second, the bullshit theory that the body wasn't Jack Walsh."

"You're kidding."

"Not at all."

"Then who the hell was he?"

"Like I said in court, just some derelict who had the misfortune of happening to have no teeth."

"Wait a minute. Wait a minute," Taylor said. "This is getting out of hand. Now you're saying Jack Walsh killed him?"

Steve shook his head. "No. Carl Jenson did. But I think it's safe to say Jack Walsh *meant* to kill him."

Taylor shook his head. "This is coming a little fast. You and Tracy seem to know what's going on. But would you mind putting it in plain English?"

"I can't speak for Tracy," Steve said. "But I'll tell you what I think happened. Basically, the situation is this. Jack Walsh wanted to disappear. And more than that, he wanted to twist his relatives' tails doing it.

"So he came to me. Partly to get advice on writing the will, and partly because Carl Jenson was following him, and he knew his going to a lawyer would drive his relatives bananas.

"Anyway, he got the information, and he's planning to act on it. But the relatives lock him up in Bellevue. I get him out, and when I do he learns it was with Jeremy Dawson's help.

"Now, Jack Walsh was shrewd in a lot of ways. And I don't think he bought for a minute that Jeremy Dawson helped him out of the goodness of his own heart. I don't think he had any illusions about Jeremy Dawson, I think he saw him for what he was, and realized Jeremy helped spring him in the hope he'd be grateful. But that didn't matter, because he knew if he wrote Jeremy Dawson a will, the relatives would think he was taking Jeremy at face value and was actually leaving all the money to him.

"So he sought out Jeremy, and wrote out the bogus will. And to make sure Jeremy couldn't really inherit, he took the precaution of leaving the will incomplete and unsigned. He also wrote out his other will right away.

"With that done, he was all set. He'd already lined up his scapegoat, the toothless man who was going to take his place. He got him down in the subway station, and on some pretext or other he gave him his coat, the coat with the wallet in the pocket. Then he probably sat around drinking cheap wine with the guy until he passed out.

"Then he hung out and waited.

"Now, I have no doubt in my mind the crime he was planning was for much later in the evening, say two or three in the morning. Much less chance of being observed, of anyone being around.

"Anyway, he's hanging out down there, probably out of sight in the tunnel, because he doesn't want to be seen, and he knows those tunnels like the back of his hand. And while he's waiting there, who should come along but Carl Jenson."

"Well, this has to be a rude shock to him. Jenson arriving there can blow the whole show. All Jenson has to do is see some other guy is wearing Uncle Jack's coat, and the pitch is queered forever.

"But, irony of ironies, Carl Jenson doesn't notice. He sees the guy lying there, face down with Uncle Jack's coat on, right where the will said Uncle Jack would be. So he takes the guy for Uncle Jack, produces a pistol and shoots him in the head.

"The platform's deserted at the time, probably an express is going by to muffle the shot. At any rate, nobody notices and Jenson beats it out of there.

"All well and good. Except now Jack Walsh can't wait until two or three in the morning, he has to act now. He sneaks out of the tunnel, douses the body with gasoline, sets it on fire, and gets the hell out of there."

Steve spread his arms wide. "After that, a shave and a haircut, some clean clothes, if he hasn't done that already, and off he goes free as air. Ever since he's been sitting back, watching the show, and probably laughing his ass off."

"Jesus Christ," Taylor said. "You really think that happened?"

"Sure do," Steve said. He pointed to the will. "This will and that letter make it a damn near certainty that happened."

"Then when you produce 'em people will know?"

Steve shook his head. "Hell, no. To me they confirm theories I've had for some time. But there's nothing specific in 'em. By anyone else they'll be taken at face value."

"If you know all that," Taylor said, "how can you keep quiet? You're letting him get away with murder."

"Murder? What murder? He didn't commit any murder."

"Well, attempted murder."

"It isn't even attempted," Steve said. "He's guilty of *intent* to commit murder, that's for sure. But he didn't do it. Lots of people wanna kill people. It's no crime unless you actually do it."

"According to you he burned the body."

"That's right. But that's not attempted murder. You can't kill a dead person. It's certainly a crime—I'm not sure exactly what—but it isn't murder."

Taylor shook his head. "Christ, I don't know. To hear you talking, it all sounds logical. But still. I mean, why would he go through that elaborate charade? He had the money. It was his. If he wanted to take off, why didn't he just do it?"

"For one thing, he wanted to get back at his relatives. For

another, he wanted to disappear in a way that no one would ever find him.

"There's something else too, that I don't really feel so good about."

"What's that?"

Steve sighed. "That is, however stupid I may have made that Bellevue psychiatrist look, I think what the guy was saying was basically true. That, though he may have been shrewd and cunning in many ways, Jack Walsh was not actually a sane man."

Steve rubbed his head. "Even so," he said, "I can't help liking him, somehow. Even though he intended to commit a murder. Even though he burned the body. I can't help feeling a certain satisfaction that he's out of it now. That he got away with it. That, even if someone put two and two together and wanted to make a case against him, by now there isn't a prayer that Dirkson or I could ever find him."

"Oh yeah," Tracy said. Her eyes were gleaming. "Well now, I think you're being a little naive."

Steve looked at her. "Now what the hell does that mean?"

"I don't know about you, but I don't think finding him would be all that hard."

Steve frowned. "What the hell are you saying?"

Tracy smiled. "You'll forgive me if I take a little bit of satisfaction out of this. It feels good to be a step ahead of you for once." Tracy pushed the hair out of her eyes. "You really can't figure out where Jack Walsh is? After all the work you had Mark Taylor do?"

"Me?" Taylor said.

"What are you talking about?" Steve said.

"I'm talking about Julie Creston. With the boyfriend in the shower. The boyfriend she was so anxious to get the detective out of her apartment so they wouldn't have a chance to meet. The rich boyfriend who was taking her to Rio."

Steve stared at her. "Are you telling me—"

Tracy held up her hands. "Hey," she said. "I can't take any credit for this. After all, I'm no big hand at deductions. I just happen to be young, and I happen to be romantic, and that's why I think what I think."

Tracy smiled. "That and the fact that I'm not the big lawyer who reads the contracts, I'm just the secretary who opens the mail."

Steve frowned. "The mail? What are you talking about?"

Tracy jerked her thumb at the envelope on Steve's desk. "The mail."

Steve looked. The envelope was lying face down next to the letter and the will.

Steve gave Tracy a look. Then he picked up the envelope and turned it over.

It was postmarked Rio.